Kinzua State:
Virga

By
Dennis Geiger

Amy,
Thanks for your
interest.

Dennis

Kinzua State: Virga is a work of fiction. Names, characters, dialogue, places, and incidents are the products of the author's imagination or are used fictitiously. Characters and incidents are not to be construed as real. Any resemblance to actual events or persons, living or dead, is entirely coincidental.

∾

To all persons with mental health concerns who
struggle to recover their lives, and to those individuals
and families who support and provide services
throughout the recovery process.

∾

꩜

Acknowledgments

I would like to thank Joe Ulrich, author and friend, for his cogent suggestions and support during the process of writing this book. I also would like to thank my wife, Diamond, for her encouragement, patience, and love.

꩜

The Arrival

We crowd the small loading dock of the forensic unit: the charge nurse, four security aides, and me. Like the rusted window bars behind us, we stand narrowly apart silently awaiting the county sheriff's security van that will be delivering the most depraved patient Kinzua State Hospital has had in several years.

Garner Overton is reported to be a highly volatile and unpredictable predator with a long history of persecutory criminal behavior against women. Court transcripts referencing his recent abduction of a college co-ed and the mental anguish he inflicted upon her read like a depraved film script.

...June 15, 2004: Mr. Overton kept the victim barely fed and clothed during her imprisonment in the confines of his insect and vermin infested basement. According to the victim, she was allowed to use the toilet but only in a chamber vessel and under the scrutiny of Mr. Overton. Additionally, Mr. Overton would sponge bathe the victim while she was chained to the basement wall, all the while singing children's songs.

The victim attested that although Mr. Overton slept near her, he never sexually or physically assaulted her. He would mostly stare at her and sketch her from various angles. Apparently, he was satisfied in subduing and controlling the victim...

The July morning air is heavily laden with humidity, and rain clouds are beginning to form. As I stretch my neck, I spy a red-tail hawk catching an updraft in an apparent attempt to escape a trio of crows tormenting it for being in their territory. One on one, the hawk could easily hold its own, but being outnumbered it seeks shelter in the higher altitude of the troubling sky, soaring upward, leaving earthly woes behind.

"Here they come," Ron Peters, chief of security, says, pointing in the direction of a marked van with lights flashing.

Regaining my focus, I take a deep breath and exhale slowly. I am not here to provide any hands-on assistance, only to gather information about Overton's behavior as he enters the unit. Several court-appointed psychiatrists and psychologists have disagreed on how mentally ill Overton actually is. Some argue that he is psychopathic, while others believe he has a sadistic personality disorder. Consequently, Dr. Agnes Daltry, superintendent of Kinzua State, wants to start gathering clinical information about Overton immediately upon his arrival at the hospital. Aggie, as she wishes to be addressed by friends, directed me, a clinical psychologist, to be present when Overton is physically transferred from the sheriff's department to our care.

"Observe and note every nuance of the man, Jerome. I don't want us to miss anything about this case. Overton's stay at KSH will be drawing the attention of news agencies throughout the Commonwealth. I want to be prepared for anything that arises. I expect you to personally take responsibility for his case," she instructed.

The beeping sound of the van backing up to the loading dock is harsh and piercing, increasing the tension I already am experiencing. I wonder if the others are as tightly wound as I am. Glancing at Cameron Frankl, the forensic unit's day shift charge nurse, I see very little emotional expression. Tall and stout, she is stone-faced and riveted to the task at hand. All of the security aides are somber as well. We all appear to be in the zone, ready for the unexpected.

The grating back-up alarm ceases, and two deputies emerge from the van. Both are very large men, with equally large heads, dressed in dark, navy-tinted uniforms and hats, giving them the appearance of blue Minotaurs. One deputy has a well-manicured mustache, while other is clean-shaven. Scowling, they appear to be all business.

"Morning folks," the clean-shaven deputy says. "I'm Deputy Norell, and this here is Deputy Muller."

"Gentlemen," Cameron says in her foghorn voice. "Have either of you brought a patient to Kinzua's forensic unit before?"

"That's an affirmative," Deputy Norell replies.

"Well then you know that we need you to escort the patient upstairs to our sally port for screening, and if there aren't any problems he will be allowed to enter the unit, at which time you then will be free to go," Cameron explains.

"Shouldn't be a problem, ma'am. He's behaved himself during the entire trip, hardly made a peep. Plus he's chained up. He can't do much except shuffle and wet his pants," Deputy Muller replies with a smile.

"All right then, let's get him unloaded and upstairs," Cameron says sharply, turning to unlock the security door.

Ron Peters and the other three security staff members move closer to the van, while I back up out of the way.

As Deputy Norell opens the side door to the van, Deputy Muller climbs in to unlock the manacle that secures Overton's leg chains to the floorboard. From my angle I can see that Overton is smirking as he watches the deputy work. My imagination envisions Overton lurching up and delivering a swift kick to the deputy's head, then throwing himself at the other deputy, overpowering him before turning his attention on me.

"Okay, you're free to get up and walk out," Deputy Muller says.

"I was hoping you would say that. Thanks for the lift, boys; see you around," Overton quips.

"Get your butt out here, wise guy," Deputy Norell says, grabbing Overton by the arm and yanking him out of the van.

"They do have medications to soothe that temper of yours, Deputy," Overton says.

"All I want to hear from you is 'yes sir' and 'no sir.'"

Overton continues to smirk and seems to be amused by the reaction he's getting. Stretching himself against the confines of his shackles, Overton appears to be of medium height, but with a disproportionate massive chest. His thinning brown hair is overshadowed by bushy eyebrows, layered on top of protruding eye ridges. His dark eyes are deeply sunk in thick facial folds giving him the appearance of an aged boxer who lost one too many matches. According to his pre-admission data sheet, Overton is forty-five years old. He appears much older.

Overton looks around, taking in the setting, and locks his eyes on mine. Appearing to be sizing me up, his grin morphs into a sinister sneer.

"Who's this pixie?" he asks, looking at me.

"Shut up, Overton! Just keep shuffling along," Deputy Norell says. "Sorry there, Doctor, he has little respect for anyone, including himself." The deputy grabs the collar of Overton's jumpsuit and jerks him toward the entryway door.

"Doctor? Hell, he's no doctor. He's a lower-class mama's boy who couldn't cut the mustard at the factory where the rest of his family probably worked. First one to go to college in your family, *Doctor*?" Overton yells my way, as both deputies drag him along.

First notation, Overton is highly perceptive and analytical. He quickly assessed visual cues about me, and extrapolated inferences with improbable accuracy. I wonder how he honed his skills of perception.

"Shut up, you pervert, and keep moving," Deputy Norell says, yanking harder on Overton's jumpsuit.

Ron and the aides move in to assist. Then suddenly, to everyone's surprise, Overton collapses to the cement floor. "You state parasites will have to earn your bloated wages; I'm not walking," Overton announces.

"If you want to be dragged, Overton, we can accommodate you," Deputy Norell says, grabbing hold of the collar of the jumpsuit. "Give me a hand, fellas, and we'll see how well he likes brush burns."

"Gentlemen, let's not go through that struggle," Cameron interjects. "I'll get a gurney, and we can wheel him up much faster." Cameron opens a side door and takes her leave. Her cleated heels can be heard echoing down the hallway.

Overton remains in a prone position while we all uncomfortably kneel next to him. Hovering above him, I am reminded of how some birds of prey trap snakes with their talons, then scan the horizon awaiting some invisible sign to fly aloft with their bounty.

I study Garner's face and notice that his complexion has remnant scars of adolescent acne. Sizable pockmarks descend into the folds on his neck. His crumpled mug is interesting, but as a teen he probably was seen as homely, if not repulsive. The approaching sound of metal wheels clattering draws me back. Cameron comes in sight with a psychiatric aide pushing a rusting stretcher toward the door's threshold.

"All right, gentlemen, let's lift him up on the gurney," Cameron instructs.

The men gather around Overton, turn him over and grab an arm, a leg, or a fistful of clothing. Straining together they manage to lift him no more than a few inches before letting his weight thud against the concrete slab.

"Again, boys," Ron orders. But again they fail to reach the top of the gurney.

"He's exerting his force against us," Ron declares. "It's like trying to separate magnets."

Cameron quietly moves in and kneels next to Overton. She extends out her arm and places her splayed fingers across his chest. She musters a perfunctory smile while locking her eyes on Overton. "Mr. Overton, we recognize your superior will to resist. Now, can we proceed with the inevitable?" she asks, coldly gazing into his eyes.

Overton stares momentarily at Cameron's jutting jaw that nearly touches his face. He smiles, deflates his torso, and seemingly goes limp.

"Okay, gentlemen, try again," she directs the men.

With much less effort than before, they succeed in getting Overton on the gurney. Quickly strapping him down, two of the aides give each other high fives. Overton lets out a derisive laugh, while Cameron casts a reproachful eye on the men.

၌

Building For The Future

Over a century ago, Dr. Franklin Manchester, Kinzua State Hospital's superintendent, insisted that the center section of the fourth floor of Dix Building be gaily painted since he intended it to be used for patient recreational activities. Accordingly, the hospital's painters selected the brightest whites, yellows, and blues available to them to create a carnival ambience where dances, plays, and cinemas could lift the spirits of the chronically disturbed. However, because of an ever-expanding patient population, a larger recreational building was constructed in 1950, relegating the fourth-floor amusement area to a mundane status. In the spring of 1964, that was about to change.

The whirl of their masonry drills sprayed plaster on both Rakey Shine and his new co-worker, Gunner Albaum, powdering their faces with white dust. Putting down his drill, Rakey asked Gunner, "Did you see the president on the evening news last night, lad?"

Wiping his face with his sleeve, Gunner replied, "No, I don't much watch the news since Murrow retired. He's the only one my father trusted, and I trust my father."

Rakey made a humphing sound before speaking. "Well, Johnson was on last night, and he said that by '65, the conflict in Vietnam should be over with. You turn nineteen next year, don't you, Gunner?"

"Yeah, so?"

"Well, you'll miss out on catching some of that action over there if the war ends next year."

"No sweat off my nose if it does."

"Can't catch a girl without ribbons on your chest, Gunner."

Gunner grunted and wiped his face.

Rakey noticed that Gunner's face was streaked and smeared with wet plaster. "What the hell, Gunner, are you crying?"

Gunner turned his head and again wiped his face.

"Hell, you are crying. What's wrong, boy? What's going through that head of yours?"

"Just getting a bit choked up about destroying this ceiling, I guess."

"What? What are you talking about?"

"Well, my Grampy Sven worked hard putting up this ceiling, and now I'm helping tear it down. He'd be mad as all get-out if he saw what I was doing."

"We ain't going to destroy it, boy. We're only going to cover it up, that's all. Look, this here is going to be a dropped ceiling, and over there in that corner we got to put up a catwalk to access that old trap door, case there's a fire and the fire brigade needs to get up to the roof's beams. See what I'm talking about, over there?" Rakey pointed toward the existing opening in the ceiling, which leads to the fifth floor beneath Dix Building's roof. "Your granddaddy wouldn't be that upset. We're only covering up his work, not tearing it down."

Gunner spied what Rakey was pointing out, and seemed to take some solace in knowing that the ceiling gilded with ornate flowered frescos would remain intact, that he wouldn't be dishonoring his grampy or the other craftsmen who toiled to add some aesthetics to the fourth floor of Dix Building.

"And another thing..." Rakey stopped short. Below the scaffolding he saw two men entering the room. Dr. Abraham Knappenberger, superintendent of Kinzua State, and a younger man wearing a thick Harris tweed had stopped at the newly installed circulation desk. Dr. Knappenberger was showing the stranger the layout for the future medical library. "As you can see, Karl, this isn't a huge room, but one of sufficient size to hold the journals and books we need to keep our psychiatric residents engrossed and hopefully educated," Dr. Knappenberger said.

"Yes, Abraham, I see can see where it will work out very nicely, indeed," The man replied in a Gaelic accent.

Dr. Knappenberger looked up and spied the workers above. "Is that you, Mr. Rakey?"

"Yes, it is, Dr. Knappenberger. How are you today, sir?"

"Very well, thank you. Who is that working with you today? I don't seem to recognize him," Dr. Knappenberger said, squinting at the young man next to Rakey.

"This here is Gunner Albaum, Dr. Knappenberger. He just started working with us a few weeks ago."

"Albaum? By any chance, are you related to Axel Albaum, Mr. Gunner?"

"Yes, sir, I am. He's my father."

"Well then. Mr. Gunner. you will have quite a challenge ahead you. Your father was working here before I came and I haven't met anyone yet—no offense Mr. Rakey—who could put in a day's work like he did. I was disheartened when he retired last year. How many years did your father work at Kinzua State, Mr. Gunner?"

"Forty-two years, sir,"

"Forty-two years, my oh my, that is a large part of one's life, isn't it son?"

"Yes, sir, it is. And God willing, I hope to best it, sir," Gunner said boastfully.

"Well, that's the spirit, lad," Dr. Knappenberger replied. "Incidentally, gentlemen, this distinguished doctor standing next to me is Dr. Karl St. Regor. He will be the new director of our psychiatric residency program."

"How do you do, sir?" Rakey responded, tipping his cap.

"Hello, sir," Gunner said, raising his hand as a greeting.

"Gentlemen, top of the morning to you," Dr. St. Regor said, briskly snapping his heels together.

"Well, carry on, men, and be careful up there. Don't want anything happening to you or that art work above your heads," Dr. Knappenberger said. "We will never see the Commonwealth investing in a fresco ceiling like that one during any of our tenures." Turning to escort St. Regor back toward the elevator that services the Dix Building, Dr. Knappenberger added, "And gentlemen, never forget that all that you do is appreciated by both patient and staff alike."

"Thank you, sir. It's most kind of you to say so," said Rakey.

After the two men exited, Rakey said to Gunner, "I guess you heard about that St. Regor fellow?"

"Nope, don't know anything about him," Gunner replied.

"Well, word is that he was a teacher in Wales, before coming to America. Only came here because Dr. Knappenberger went to one of his lectures over there and was so taken by St. Regor that he offered him a job at KSH," Rakey explained. "I heard that the man is a genius or something close to that."

"My father says a man is as smart as his common sense is long."

"That I understand, Gunner. But this St. Regor fellow is said to have the touch for healing people who are hurting—in the head, I mean," Rakey said, tapping his head with his drill. "Anyway, that is why we are working up here, to make this room into a library for St. Regor to train other doctors. So, let's get to it, Gunner. The day will be done before you know it, and we won't have anything to show for it."

The men resumed drilling, silencing any further talk.

⟳

Inspired

It was back in October 30, 1977, one week after being hired as a psychologist at Kinzua State, when I found myself outside Karl St. Regor's office door, hesitating to knock, not sure if I was really deserving of his time. After all, it was only four weeks since I'd graduated from my doctoral program at the University of Virginia, and I had hardly any clinical experience worth mentioning. I couldn't believe that this renowned teacher was willing to consider me as a co-leader of one of his therapy groups. Of course, my supervisor, psychology department director Phyllis Bergist, put in a good word for me and even the hospital's superintendent, Dr. Salvadore Domio, had casually endorsed me as a possible acolyte for Karl's mentoring. Nevertheless, I was hesitant. I had worked with esteemed professors, both tenured and nationally recognized at the University of Virginia, but Karl was known for his clinical acumen both in America and internationally. His expert status was one of the reasons that Kinzua State had attracted so many bright and ambitious psychiatric residents and had won the support of community advocates. Karl's reputation served Kinzua State well, but put the fear of God in me.

I recall that with some positive self-talk, I finally had worked up the courage to knock.

"Come in," Karl said, his voice maintaining a lilting quality.

"Good morning, Dr. St. Regor."

"Karl, please. Come in, Jerome, and make yourself comfortable. I was about to have a cup of tea. Would you care to join me?"

"Thank you, sir...ah, Karl."

I continued to stand, waiting to see where Karl would sit. His office was large by most standards but sparingly decorated with both private art and pastoral photos, apparently of Wales. Most psychiatrists had their offices in Dix Building, but Karl had chosen to locate his in a stone cottage situated on the southern lawn next to Dix. The cottage previously was a treatment center, which included a recreation hall and crafts center. At the time Karl moved into the cottage, it served primarily as a storage area for artifacts accumulated over the hospital's eighty-year existence.

"Cream or sugar?" Karl asked, pouring the steaming black tea into ornate china cups.

"Black, please."

"Oh, are you a traditionalist, Jerome?"

"Pardon?"

"Unadulterated tastes are correlated with purist beliefs...traditionalism."

"I fear I am more of an idealist, Karl."

"Idealists usually take several lumps of sugar, seeking the most pleasant of experiences, I assume."

"Well, I've always seemed to be outside of the rule. And what about you? Are you a traditionalist?"

"At my age I take a little cream and one lump. At your age I wanted it black and robust, pure and strong." Karl picked up his cup and moved slowly across the room, settling in a cushioned rocking chair. He was a tall man of lean proportions, clean-shaven with a full head of silver hair that lightly touched the collar of his tweed jacket. He beckoned for me to sit in a rocker next to him.

"So, you want to be in the poetry group, Jerome. Why?" Karl seemed to be studying me as he peered over the rim of his cup.

"Well, to tell the truth, I'm not sure if I really belong in the poetry group. I know I want to be a co-leader in a group with someone who is experienced, so that I can learn how to effectively conduct a group. That is why Phyllis—Dr. Bergist—recommended I ask you to mentor me."

"I see. So, you don't have any special interest in the type of group?"

"Well, I would prefer one that is more process-oriented. I conducted skill acquisition groups at Virginia's counseling center: assertiveness training, stress management, and the like. But I don't have much experience with more dynamic groups. And Phyllis said that is what you specialize in."

"Not specialize in. Conduct out of necessity. You see, Jerome, mental hospitals have evolved into treating patients as if they were soulless, like hapless animals. We medicate them, house them, condition them to respond in prescribed ways, so they don't cause any problems to anyone, and then pat them on the head when they behave as expected. We have completely ignored their soul, their spirit, their inner Eros. Tell me, Jerome, what makes a human being uniquely human?"

Taken aback, I lift my cup and pretend to drink, buying time to formulate a cogent response. "I suppose a human being means behaving in an intelligent and intentional manner."

"Jerome, those qualities would not separate us from the majority of primates or other animals. Most creatures are intelligent and behave with purpose, albeit instinctually. No, no, my boy, what makes us human is that we desire to understand and transcend our human condition. To be more than creatures of habit. To discover and manifest our unique potentials. To create ways of responding to God. These are the traits that makes us more than animals, more than caged prisoners dominated by fear and the powers that be."

Karl leaned back into his chair, flushed with passion and conviction. Breathing deeply, he leaned forward again.

"The desire to be human is with us all, Jerome. You, me, and those unfortunates living in that building." He pointed in the direction of Dix Building. "They need us not only to combat their illness but to restore their humanity. To enable them to escape from the constraints of their psychoses and society's prejudices, but also to help them express their desire to transcend their fate.

And that is why I conduct a poetry group. To give them an opportunity to find their voice. To express what is in their soul. To be inspired to move beyond their present situation. That is what I want for them. Now, are you interested in joining me in this quest?" Karl sank back into his chair and looked at me intently.

"I do. More than I realized. If you will have me, I would very much like to be part of the group."

"Do you write or read poems?"

"I'm afraid I have only dabbled in writing, but I truly enjoy reading poems."

"More than satisfactory. Come tomorrow and join us. Nine o'clock. We are in the group room across from the barbershop, or is it the hairdresser? Whichever is the politically correct term, do you know where I mean?'

"Yes, I remember seeing it during my orientation class."

Karl rose and shook my hand. "Good, we will see you then."

That was twenty-seven years ago, when Karl was very much alive and a force in the lives of patients as well as my own.

ᕼᓂ

An Old Habit

The summer of 2004 has been exceptionally wet and dreary. It is taking its toll on the mood of both staff and patients. Some patients stay holed up in their rooms, sleeping or trying to sleep. Ophelia Helms lies on her bed mulling over her plight.

Three days of rain, no sunshine. Not the type of summer to lift one's spirits. As if sunshine would be enough to burn away these layers of shame and bitterness that cover me. And even if it could, how would the sun find me? I keep giving them reasons to restrict me to this ward, to the third floor of this stone fortress, closed to the sun's rays, to rays of hope.

At tomorrow's team meeting, I'll ask for ground privileges. Getting some fresh air should help. Until then, one more opening. Expose some flesh. Let it bleed. A quick way to gain some relief. And thankfully, sleep always follows. At least something to be grateful for.

Ophelia removes a false painted fingernail and lifts away the shard of CD taped to the underside of the nail. Only half an inch of a sharp edge, but enough to make a cut on the inner part of her thigh. She has decided to no longer use her inner forearms and bring attention to herself. Staff members might inspect her arms but they won't think of checking her legs.

Being small, the shard is difficult to grip. But eventually, with enough pressure, Ophelia succeeds, penetrating the light resistance that her delicate skin offers. A thin ribbon of blood slowly surfaces accompanied by a pain that shivers up her spine. The sensation is exhilarating, fulfilling, soothing.

Ophelia covers her wound with a washcloth, pulls down her nightshirt, and crawls into bed. She puts the shard under her pillow, covers herself. She easily drifts asleep as a pink glow slowly spreads across her cheeks. A temporary respite from her memories.

∽

Lepers And Spirits

After parking my pickup truck, I head to a side entrance on the northern wing of Dix Building. A light rain coats the building's massive sandstone exterior, making it appear dark and foreboding. Nearly 125 years old, Dix has endured a lot of weather and change. Entering the hallway leading to my office, I reflect on how at one time this building was bursting with patients. Nearly 4,000 during the early '50s. Then with the advent of powerful psychotropic medications such as Thorazine, and a political movement to discharge patients to community facilities, the population of afflicted souls at the hospital dwindled to several hundred, freeing bedrooms to be converted into office space.

At one time my office was a patient's room, actually two patient's rooms, before the wall was removed. With some beige paint and cheap pastel drapery, few visual reminders remain to attest that scores of tormented souls, trapped firmly in their delusions and hallucinatory fixations, at one time slept and passed time where

I now have my desk, filing cabinets, piles of journals, and a hospital-issued computer.

It was only four years ago, in the year 2000, that holes were bored through the office's terrazzo-covered concrete floor enabling electrical computer cables to connect me with the hospital's server and an e-mail information highway. Or at times, more accurately a traffic jam. As some of the hospital's curmudgeons like to point out, staff members seem to spend more time e-mailing each other than making contact with patients. Gauging by my computer screen, patients might not see too many staff members on the wards this morning.

I dutifully start the process of reading, responding, and deleting...*staff must complete the mandated course on fire safety... the Procurement Office requires you to submit a statement of your financial contracts with the Commonwealth... parking in any designated administrative parking spot will result in both a citation and disciplinary counseling...*

The next e-mail is from Phyllis directing me to substitute at the stimulation track for another psychologist who called in sick. I will need some preparation time, so this morning's poetry group will be a short one. I stretch and glance at the wall clock. It is 8:55 a.m. Time to make some patient contact.

Locking my office door, I head down the hallway to the first-floor group room. I arrive in time to greet the group. "Morning everyone!" I begin watching folks take their seats around the table. Autumn Scheller, reserved and fragile, is sitting, as customary, next to Lincoln Crowfoot, who inscrutably stares straight ahead. Harvey Louser is off in a corner by himself busying himself with slips of scribbled paper that only he can decipher.

Kendra Desam has her head on the table appearing to be asleep for the moment, while Ophelia Helms has her chair turned to the opened window, apparently coolly detached from the rest of humanity.

"I have an announcement," I say. "Because I need to fill in for another psychologist, we will be leaving fifteen minutes early today. I hope you can stand having some free time."

Harvey's hand shoots up. "Since you are running out on us, can I go first?"

"I guess you could go first, Harvey, as long as you agree to be on the timer." I have learned that in order to limit Harvey's run-on inconsequential expressions it is best to allow him only a specific amount of blathering time. Grabbing an egg timer off the corner table, I set it for two minutes. I place it in front of him and say, "Okay, Harvey. Get ready, get set, go."

Harvey stands abruptly. His dark-brown hair is disheveled and flows wildly against his red striped shirt that clashes against his green-checkered trousers. He lurches into his narration.

"The United Nations under God, to whom I do not give my allegiance, is a conspiracy wish by the Russian people in order to divide the righteous with their minds from their thoughts and sexual urges that were taken away during pubescence..."

As Harvey sallies forth with his word salad, everyone appears to be frozen, lost in some space warp where their minds can drift to endure the pummeling of nonsense. Apparently, our common gift to Harvey is to find a way to tolerate his circumlocutions, the most blatant manifestation of his intractable schizophrenia.

Over the last twenty-seven years, I have come to understand that schizophrenia takes many shapes and comes in different varieties. Some folks are soundly smothered by the disease, hardly able to give attention to anyone or anything outside themselves. Some are only disturbed in circumscribed areas of daily living and can communicate rather clearly with others. Only when stressed do their thought processes become distorted and find expression in delusional or bizarre ideation. Harvey, unfortunately, is governed most of the day by psychotic perceptions. Incredulously, he somehow can comprehend his surroundings well enough to adhere to hospital rules and expectations, yet all the while he mentally mills about with paranoid, paleologic thinking.

Eventually, the timer sounds off and, dutifully, Harvey ceases his rant, grabs his crumbled pieces of paper, and plops down.

"Well, that was a very unique series of statements, Harvey. Would anyone like to comment on Harvey's prose?" I ask.

Kendra speaks up. "If I stay here as long as Harvey, will my brain go as bad as his?"

Harvey doesn't seem to register Kendra's mocking comment. He remains focused on scribbling down more of his loose associations.

"Hopefully, you will be able to express yourself in a clear and satisfying manner, Kendra, no matter how long you are at the hospital. Do you have anything you want to express right now?" I ask.

"I'm not too good at poems, Doctor M. But I like hearing others recite theirs." Kendra replies.

"Well, as you know, no one is forced to speak in group, Kendra. I merely thought you might have something to share, and that is why you spoke up."

"I only spoke up because I don't understand Harvey."

"Who does?" Ophelia chimes in, still staring out the window.

"Do you have a poem to share, Opie?" I ask.

When a person interrupts, it may be a sign that they have something they no longer can suppress. That is what Karl would advise me when I was under his tutelage.

"A poem, a poem, well, maybe I do, Jerome," Ophelia says, smiling impishly.

"Let's see, how about this one." Ophelia turns in her chair and faces me, her soft facial features belie the hard defensive tone of her voice. Although not a stereotypically attractive twenty-something, Ophelia has a supple, captivating carriage and an intriguing boyish face. She combs her fingers slowly through her mousy brown hair, looks at the ceiling, and begins her recitation. "This is called 'Back Alley Teardrops.'"

> All around you
> The evolving truth of life
> And here you
> A leper of living
> Shaking and hiding
> Hoping to be hugged

Ophelia returns her gaze to the window. Sitting more erect in her chair, a tinge of pink appears across her pearlescent complexion.

"Thank you, Opie. I appreciate you sharing that poem. You knew it by heart. Have you repeated it often to yourself?"

"I suppose I have," Ophelia says, turning toward me, staring warily, perhaps wondering if I am implying something is clinically wrong with her.

"I'm simply curious if over time you have found comfort in your poem."

"I never thought about it bringing me any comfort, but now that you mention it, maybe it did," Ophelia says, sounding less guarded.

"I found your poem to be comforting," Autumn says, looking toward Ophelia.

Ophelia stares quizzically at Autumn before speaking. "That's good to hear, I guess."

"Thank you, Autumn, for your words of appreciation. Does anyone else have anything to say about Ophelia's poem?" I ask, looking around the room. No one responds.

"Can anyone identify with the phrase *leper of living*?"

"The only person in this room who couldn't would be you," Ophelia asserts.

"So you think everyone but me knows what it is like to be an outcast?"

"Well, you don't look like you have been living on the outside like the rest of us, Jerome."

"I guess it does look like I haven't been skipping any meals, and I do receive a regular paycheck and some respect now and then, but I haven't always been on top, and like you I have my share of psychological scars."

"You do, Doctor Masonheimer?" Autumn responds.

"Yes, like everyone else, I have had to struggle now and then, Autumn."

"My people believe a worthy struggle can strengthen the spirit," Lincoln says.

"I think Nietzsche said something like that as well," I respond. "And Buddha, too."

"Nietzsche was a communist, and Buddha was the anti-Christ," Harvey shouts.

"Okay, okay," I say, holding up my hands as a signal for Harvey to stay calm. "We still have a few minutes before we need to end. Does anyone have another poem to share?"

"What about you, Jerome? Why don't you share a poem? Maybe one from the days of your struggles," Ophelia says in a mocking tone.

"Yes, Doctor Masonheimer, share one of your poems," Autumn pleads.

"As you know, the rule is that poems should originate from group members. However, I think maybe I could recite one I wrote that would be appropriate to bring some closure to this morning's group. Now, let's see if I can remember it," I say, scratching my head, looking out the window. "I believe it goes like this..."

With ears to the sky
The rabbit listens for the fox
With nose to the ground
The fox searches for the rabbit
Locked in a struggle to survive
They fail to see the farmer
Who with two shots

Now sits wearing his fox hat
Eating rabbit stew

Harvey's hand shoots up.
"Yes, Harvey?"

Standing quickly, Harvey gazes at the ceiling and says, "My mother made good rabbit and squirrel stew, but we never shot any fox. Did shoot a bear once. It looked like a Russian, and it may have started a war, I don't know." With that Harvey sits down.

"Thank you for those personal remarks, Harvey."

"Are you saying, Doctor Masonheimer, that sometimes we get so caught up in our worries that we lose sight of what is around us?" Autumn asks.

"That is a pretty fair interpretation of that poem, Autumn. I would only add that for me becoming lost in my uncertainties created a dangerous situation, which I failed to pay attention to."

"Somebody was going to shoot you?" Kendra asks.

"I doubt it, but I wasn't sure."

"How's that?" Ophelia asks.

"I really don't want to say," I reply.

"Oh, so it's okay for us to bare our souls but yours is off limits," Ophelia shoots back.

"Well, technically, yes, it is. This is a group for patients, not for staff. However, I think it might be important right now for me to disclose a bit more to clear up any misunderstanding."

Self-disclose only if it helps move the focus back to patient issues.

"Many years ago, when I was starting out as a psychologist at this hospital, I befriended another staff member who was having marital problems. One day he asked me to go with him to his family to help him explain why he wanted to leave his wife. I agreed, and we started driving to his family's home down south. But before heading out of town, he stopped by his house supposedly to pick up some money. While we were there, his wife came home. They began to argue, and I was accused by the staff member of influencing him to leave his wife. This infuriated the wife, and she threatened me. To make a long story short, she begged him to stay, and eventually they reconciled, leaving me feeling used and exploited."

"So then what did you do?" Ophelia asks.

"I wrote those verses that I read to you. And swore that I would be more careful befriending anyone I really didn't know very well."

"I used to stay locked up in my room because I was afraid that others might hurt me," Autumn says.

"Not a bad idea," Ophelia says. "There are plenty of creatures feasting on the night."

"You mean Russian Bears?" Harvey asks.

"Not any of your imaginary bears, dippity-do. I'm talking about demented and twisted men who will exploit you, and more," Ophelia replies, returning her gaze to the rain-streaked window. She obviously knows firsthand about being exploited, which would account for her cynical attitude and defensive posture. I note this and will come back to it when the opportunity presents itself.

I glance at the time on the wall clock. "I need to go to my next assignment. I appreciate everyone's involvement in today's group. Please keep jotting down your poems and thoughts, and feel free to bring in a poem you read that others might like to hear," I say.

Slowly, everyone leaves, except Lincoln. He sits board-erect staring mysteriously at something distant and outside the room. "Is there something wrong, Lincoln?" I ask, approaching him where he sits.

"My spirit is wandering again," Lincoln says in a monotone voice. His long black hair frames his chiseled Native American facial features - stoic and grave.

"You mean like it did last year?"

"Yes."

"I see. How much time do you think we have before a problem occurs?"

"It is approaching."

"Do you think we need to tell your doctor?"

"I already have. He said there is no spirit, only my brain that needs more medication."

Spoken like a true pharmaceutical fanatic.

"We both know, Lincoln, that spirits are part of your life and culture. Dr. Chankra may need to learn more about you. What do you think we should do about your spirit?"

"Watch the sky; the wind will lead the way for the spirit gods to speak to us."

"I see. Well, then we wait. Will you be okay to go back to the ward?"

"Yes."

"Okay, I'll check in with you tomorrow."

Lincoln rises and walks out, leaving me alone to recall the last time his spirit wandered.

∾

A Question Without An Answer

After finishing my substitution at the stimulation track, I head down to my office. As I approach the office door, I hear my phone ringing. I manage to get to it before the answering machine kicks in. "Hello," I fumble with the receiver. "Hello."

"Dr. Masonheimer?"

I don't recognize the man's thick Asian accent. "Yes, this is he."

"Dr. Masonheimer, this is Dr. Yusuf."

Dr. Yusuf is the recently hired forensic psychiatrist. I have yet to meet him, but others have told me that he appears to be a decent fellow, although a bit dark and mysterious. "Yes, Dr. Yusuf. How may I help you?"

"Dr. Masonheimer, I have just finished my evaluation of Mr. Garner Overton."

I wait for him to continue, but he doesn't. "I see, Dr. Yusuf. And what did you conclude?"

"I conclude that he needs to be psychologically assessed, Doctor."

"I see. So, you would like me to evaluate him?"

"That is correct, Doctor. When could you do this?"

Procedurally, requests for psychological services are forwarded to Phyllis. Typically, she dispenses our assignments at a weekly department meeting. But with Overton's case being managed directly by the superintendent, and she having assigned his case to me, I am responsible for any psychological services provided to him.

"Normally, Dr. Yusuf, I would refer your request for psychological services to Dr. Bergist. However, since Dr. Daltry has ordered priority status to Mr. Overton, I will clear my schedule and start testing him tomorrow."

"Very good. Very good. Is there anything else, Doctor?

"Ah, I guess not," I respond, a bit confused. "Oh, wait. Ah, what exactly are you hoping psychological assessment procedures will provide you with?"

"The pathological state of Mr. Overton's mind."

"You mean the type or nature of pathological symptoms he is exhibiting?"

"No. Those are quite evident, Dr. Masonheimer. What is not so obvious are the abnormal forces in his mind. Those need to be identified. Can you do that, Doctor?"

An interesting question. If this were 1944 instead of 2004 and I were an unlicensed psychologist inculcated in psychodynamic doctrines, I would gladly boast that I could identify the intrapsychic worms boring their way through Overton's mind. But because the practice of psychology currently is tethered, or some say imprisoned, by science and brain-based research even using the word "mind" is considered by behavioral specialists to be blasphemous, let alone believing that psychic forces drive behavior, abnormal or not.

"I will do my best, Dr. Yusuf."

"Very good, Doctor. I will await your findings. Good day to you."

I let the buzzing of the receiver reverberate in my ear for some time before hanging up.

Well, Dr. Freud, what are you going to do now?

I decide that a consult is needed. So I head down to Phyllis's office. With her door ajar, I stick my head in and discover that Eliot LaFleur is seated across from Phyllis. "Oh, sorry. I didn't realize you two were having a meeting."

Before I can back up, Phyllis waves me in. "Come in, Jerome. Eliot and I are finishing up. Come in."

I glance at Eliot. He's beaming, clasping a messy ream of computer printouts spread across his lap. Short and obese with oversized tortoise-shell glasses dwarfing his elfish face, Eliot has the appearance of a cartoon character. Nearly sixty years old, with wiry strands of gray hair surrounding a generous pate, Eliot remains an enigma to me and everyone who encounters him. Although he is an accomplished researcher and a geropsychologist, Eliot is more renowned for his peculiarities, particularly his olfactory perceptions. Eliot unapologetically believes that by systematically sniffing the air, he can assess the emotional climate of a room. Supposedly by sensing and identifying pheromones mysteriously emitted by the room's occupants, Eliot believes he can tap into the looming sentiments that, according to him, dominate any ambience. He has been known to make announcements like "There is an impending rupture of compassion," or "Smothering resentment is clogging the air," or "Blithe yearnings are saturating the room," all merely by flaring his nostrils and inhaling deeply. However farfetched his pronouncements may be, to my dismay Eliot is uncannily more often right than wrong. How he performs these olfactory feats is beyond scientific explanation.

My gaze shifts to Phyllis. "I was wondering if I could run a clinical dilemma by you?"

"Of course. Are you all right with Eliot joining in?"

Although instantly annoyed at the suggestion, I acquiesce. "Sure, the more minds the better."

Eliot smiles broadly. I position a chair in between both Phyllis and him. They look attentive, patiently waiting for me to begin. "A few minutes ago, I received a call from Dr. Yusuf requesting that I test Garner Overton, which is something I was planning to do anyway. However, Yusuf is interested in knowing what mental operations are responsible for Overton's aberrant behaviors."

"Cause and effect answers," Eliot says.

"Yes, and perhaps even more. I got the impression he wants to have a clinical narrative to explain Overton's unique psychopathological acts."

"You mean a psychodynamic explanation?" Phyllis asks.

"That's the impression he gave me."

"Sounds old school," she replies.

"Yusuf? Is that Turkish?" Eliot asks.

"I don't know. Could be. Why?"

"Well, many Eastern European and Southwestern Asian areas still have enclaves of Freudian loyalty. Of course several South American countries do as well."

"As do several North American psychoanalytic training centers," Phyllis adds.

"Well, none of the assessment instruments I had intended to use provide a dynamic explanation of aberrant behaviors," I say.

"What tests were you planning to use?" Phyllis asks.

"Since an MMPI was done prior to Overton arriving at the hospital, I was going to give a Millon or a Hare Psychopathy. A neuropsychological screening might be a good idea as well, to rule out any organic component."

"What about a Rorschach?" Phyllis asks.

"I no longer have much confidence in that procedure," I say.

"There isn't much credible research to support it, either," Eliot adds.

"Well, Yusuf might expect it," Phyllis replies.

"You're probably right. I guess I could throw it in to satisfy his dynamic tastes."

"I would suggest that you wait until you complete and score all the testing before you worry too much about what the report will look like," says Phyllis. Will you be personally administering the tests?"

"Probably. Unless I use our intern for some of the administration."

"I think that would be a good experience for her," Phyllis replies, nodding in agreement.

"That's strange. I just caught a slight waft of brewing terror," Eliot interjects with his nose elevated and sniffing the air.

Phyllis and I glance at each other, raising our eyebrows in unison.

Reluctant Roles

This summer the psychology department has one university intern, Elsa Heinzelman. As is typical with interns, Elsa is in her mid-twenties, inexperienced, and eager to sink her teeth into pathology. Tired of spending time in the classroom listening to dowdy professors provide textbook accounts of psychopaths, Elsa wants to encounter one firsthand and triumph in curing his exploitative habits.

Blue-eyed, petite, with a flawless cream complexion, Elsa is arrestingly attractive. She pins her sienna hair in a tight bun, wears heavy rimmed glasses and dresses in dark designer pantsuits, which give her a strict, professional appearance. Highly intelligent with a forceful personality, Elsa requires a firm rein and assertive reminders in order for her to adhere to her apprentice role. She is idealism with an attitude, and I'm showing more gray each day.

"Good morning, Dr. Masonheimer," Elsa says brightly.

Without turning away from my computer screen and recent batch of e-mails, I reply flatly, "Morning, Elsa."

"Are we going to the forensic unit this morning, Dr. Masonheimer?"

"Indeed, we are, Elsa, as soon as I finish responding to some of these posts."

"Is there anything that I need to know before we visit the unit?"

"Many things, just give me a second and I'll go over them with you."

Elsa turns her attention to my bookshelf and scans the titles. I'm hoping there are enough interesting tomes to keep her occupied.

"I see you have some of Rollo May's and Irving Yalom's books, Dr. Masonheimer. Does this mean you are an existentialist?" Elsa queries, her head cocked and eyes affixed on book jackets.

"Painfully existential, Elsa."

"Too much angst isn't healthy. I recently read that Scandinavians are prone to depression, perhaps because of their existentialistic philosophies," Elsa says, without turning her head.

"Kierkegaard was Danish."

"Denmark is part of Scandinavia."

"Well, that's depressing." I turn to face Elsa. "Perhaps we should switch to a topic that I know something about—the forensic unit. Have a seat."

She takes a chair opposite me, looking disinterested.

"Let's begin with a brief history of the forensic unit. First, it is relatively new to the hospital. The forensic unit began operating in 1974. Initially providing inpatient services to only a few nearby counties, it now provides services to over twenty counties, which means it has an important function to play in both the mental health sector and criminal justice sector. Currently the emphasis is on completing evaluations to see if patients are competent to stand trial; however, there is still quite a bit of treatment being provided to stabilize acute symptomatology. Besides psychiatric medications, some psychotherapy interventions can be very helpful. Unfortunately, at the present time we don't have a full time psychologist assigned to the forensic unit. Instead, we have several psychologists rotating through. This month, I have the lucky rotation." I see Elsa appears more interested.

"What about security measures?"

"I'm glad you brought that up. Security is a critical piece of forensic work. It is imperative that the patient be protected from himself, from harming others, and from escaping. As you may know, patients on the civil side of the hospital, which includes all non-forensic patients, are also legally committed to the hospital to receive treatment. However, unlike forensic patients, civil patients are expected to be provided rights and freedoms. Thus, we strive to make sure they are in the least restrictive setting possible, in accordance with their clinical readiness, while forensic patients always are confined to a maximum-security environment. And this means locked doors, locked windows, and having security staff accompany patients throughout the building or buildings as the case may be."

"Buildings? I thought there was only one forensic building at the hospital."

"Indeed, there is only one Forensic Unit; however, at times patients are escorted to Dix Building for dental services. They also are transported to the local general hospital for medical procedures. During these times maintaining security is essential."

"How can a patient be secured if they're not in a locked building?"

"Generally, forensic patients are manacled onto a wheelchair or gurney and accompanied by several security staff members, which has worked rather successfully to date."

"Sounds draconian to me," Elsa says, looking rather grim. "Doesn't the hospital try to preserve the dignity of forensic patients?"

"Judicial edict trumps many of the civil rights of patients, especially forensic patients. Our hospital is expected to provide the same level of security that a jail would, which means restricting movement and other freedoms."

"Well, it doesn't seem right that a mentally ill person who is in jail should be treated like a hardened criminal."

"Most aren't career criminals, Elsa. However, some are indifferent to the rights of others, and if given the opportunity would exploit or even harm others. Besides, mental illness is only assumed until proven; that is why many are sent here."

For the moment, Elsa keeps her thoughts to herself.

"Since it is raining outside, perhaps we could use the tunnel to walk to the Forensic Building. That is, if you are willing," I say.

"The last time I used the tunnel, I got almost as wet as if I had been walking outside," Elsa replies.

"Dr. LaFleur told me that last week workmen were patching the ceiling of the tunnel leading to the Forensic Unit. Maybe it's as dry as his humor. Care to find out?"

"Why not? I'm always ready for something new and exciting."

"Okay, I'll grab what I need and we can be off. There is more that I need to tell you before we get there, but we can talk as we walk." I pick up the test kit off my desk as well as a legal notepad, and with Elsa in the lead, I lock the door.

"Let's take the tunnel entrance down by the reimbursement office. It always seems cleaner for some reason," I suggest.

"You're the boss," Elsa responds.

As we walk the hallways of Dix Building, I inform Elsa of the orientation requirement for all new staff, particularly interns.

"We can set that up this morning after we see our patient, Garner Overton, who, incidentally, will require some extra precautions on our part."

"Why is that?"

"Garner Overton has a long history of exploitation. He apparently is a master of reading others and taking advantage of their vulnerabilities. He will be alert to any weaknesses that we may unwittingly express. So we will need to present ourselves as professionally as we can."

"No friendly smiles allowed?"

"Respectful attention? Yes. Acts of friendliness? Not during our clinical time."

"You're saying that it's not all right to be a friend to a patient?"

"Treating patients in a friendly manner is fine. However, being friendly is not the same as being a 'friend,' which I don't believe staff should be to patients. There is a difference between being friendly and being a friend. Our role is to provide a service to patients. No reciprocity is expected, as might be the case with friends. Plus, with friends there is an equal exchange of personal information. But back to the point. With Overton, we need to stay strictly within our role as a professional psychologist. We can't provide him with any opportunity to access our personal lives."

Staring straight ahead, Elsa suppresses a sneer.

We reach the door leading to the underground passageway. Immediately upon unlocking it, a dank, musty odor greets us.

"You first," I say, waving my arm in the basement's direction.

"Sure, sacrifice the intern to the spiders," Elsa jokes.

"Mentoring has its privileges," I reply.

The heavy steel door slowly closes behind us, then loudly clicks shut, darkening our descent. The staircase's stone steps are smooth and well-worn from years of foot traffic. For nearly a century, the underground tunnel system had served as a passageway between buildings for both staff and patients until an administrative decision was made banning patients from using it without staff supervision. There were just too many nooks and crannies in the tunnel for patients to sneak off into and engage in forbidden acts or to hide from staff. Even though it was rare to lose someone down here, it was possible. Very possible. It happened earlier this year, when the patient Ester von Michaels eluded staff for weeks in the tunnel.

How long has it been? At least four, five months since my search for Ester brought me down here with Duffy and several other patients. Seems like four or five days ago. Duffy has been dead that long...poor Duffy...still miss you, my man...

"Dr. Masonheimer, aren't we taking this direction to the Forensic Unit?" She receives no answer. "Dr. Masonheimer?"

Elsa's voice brings me around, and I turn to face her, shaking off my disorientation. "Yes, of course. You're absolutely correct. Go ahead and lead the way," I reply. "Merely got lost in a memory."

"So, in addition to being filled with angst, you also are prone to dissociation? Careful, Dr. Masonheimer, someone might take your keys away from you," Elsa chides.

"Sometimes, we are only one step away from that. Only one step away."

෬

Biding One's Time

Garner Overton has been on the Forensic Unit for nearly a week, and so far he hasn't found any easy avenues of escape. The security staff is extremely cautious and mostly work in pairs. Even if one could be overpowered, the other member would be right on top of the situation, signaling other staff members in the process. And every locked door seems to lead to another locked room equipped with security cameras. Although it isn't a county jail, the unit still isn't an easy place to break out of. And being on the third floor discourages any idea of jumping out a window. Besides, the thick steel bars surrounding the windows are bolted sturdily to the exterior brickwork. So for the moment, the only option is to sit and wait for an opportunity to present itself. And something will come up. It always does.

∾

Pushing Boundaries

Arriving at the electronic mesh door separating us from the elevator, which leads to the Forensic Unit, Elsa and I stop and identify ourselves using the speakerphone system attached to the wall. I press the buzzer on the black box, and wait.

"This is Mr. Bleu. Please identify yourselves while looking toward the camera," a male voice bellows.

Elsa and I look up at the small video camera focused on us. "This is Dr. Masonheimer from the psychology department, and with me is Elsa Heinzelman, a psychology intern."

"And what is the purpose of your visit, Dr. Masonheimer?"

"We are here to test Mr. Overton."

"Okay, I'll buzz you in. You do know that I will still need to scan you when you exit the elevator, don't you, Doctor?"

"Yes, I do."

Momentarily, the mesh door unlocks and we enter the vestibule leading to the elevator. The door closes with a loud metallic click, reverberating throughout the tunnel behind us.

"Feels like we're in a David Lynch movie," Elsa says.

"It is somewhat surrealistic, isn't it?"

"How will they be scanning us when we get upstairs?"

"With an electronic wand. Painless and non-intrusive."

"No pat downs?"

"Only if the wand starts beeping. You're not concealing anything metal, are you?"

"Just my Glock."

"Very Funny! But don't even utter that word when we get upstairs. These folks are humorless when it comes to security, and rightfully so. Their jobs are on the line, and that is something they take seriously."

We remain uncomfortably silent as the elevator slowly ascends. Coming to an abrupt stop, the elevator door opens, and we face the security guard.

"Come on out and stand over here," the guard orders, waving his wand like a sword.

After being scanned, Elsa and I are escorted to a private cubicle to meet with Overton. It's a small rectangular room painted institutional lime green, containing a single window protected by exterior iron bars, and a heavy metal screen locked from the inside. The window is in need of cleaning, and what little light does sneak through is diffuse and gray. A large plastic table crowds three faded orange vinyl chairs surrounding it. I position one of the chairs against the wall nearest the door, and place the other two on opposite sides of the table.

"Where should I sit?" Elsa asks.

"You take the chair nearest the door, and I'll sit at the table. We'll have Overton sit across from me."

"You aren't going to sacrifice the intern?"

"You already earned your badge of courage blazing a trail in the tunnel."

"You don't think I'm strong enough to handle Mr. Overton?"

"I don't think the both of us together are strong enough to handle him. That's why we won't be meeting him alone. Not today and not at any time in the future. There will always be two staff members when Overton is in the room."

"It's a good thing I know karate," Elsa says, mimicking a chop with her hand.

"If it ever comes down to a fight, Elsa, do what deer do when attacked."

"You mean run?"

"Exactly."

"It's not my nature to run, Doctor Masonheimer."

"Whenever we find ourselves in a dangerous situation at this hospital, our aim is to get out of it as safely as we can. Our goal is not to prove we are strong and courageous. That is for Hollywood heroes or heroines. So, if we ever find ourselves in danger, we're getting away as fast as we can. Understood?"

Elsa merely looks at me with an expression of resignation.

Before either of us utters another word, the door opens, and the security guard enters. "Here's Overton," he says, shouldering the wall to let the burly patient through.

Overton walks by the guard and points to the chair near the window. "Reserved for me, I assume," he says.

"Would you mind?" I study him carefully as he enters.

"For the over-achieving doctor, I would be glad to oblige." Overton squeezes his bulk between the table and wall and sits down, quickly casting an eye on Elsa. "Well, Doctor, we meet again, and once more you aren't alone. Of course, this time the company you are with is much more attractive. Introductions are in order, Doctor."

"Mr. Overton this is Elsa Heinzelman, an intern in the psychology department. And I am Jerome Masonheimer, a licensed psychologist. We are here to follow through with the psychological testing that Dr. Yusuf ordered."

"Ms. Heinzelman, I'm Garner Overton. I am very happy to meet you and look forward to working closely with you." Overton lowers his head in Elsa's direction. "Doctor, will we be needing the presence of Mr. Bleu here?"

"It ain't up to the psychologist, Overton. I'm staying as close as stink on you. Dr. Yusuf's orders."

"Does a psychiatrist trump a psychologist, Doctor?" Overton asks, grinning.

"Dr. Yusuf is in charge of this unit, and if he wants a security person with us then that is what we will have," I reply.

"You know your place all so well, Doctor." His grin widens.

"How long is this going to take?" the guard asks.

"This morning we shouldn't be more than thirty or forty minutes."

"I'll get another chair." And with that he leaves us.

Unexpectedly, Overton abruptly rises. I flinch back in my chair. He sits down slowly. The vertical creases on his face form a set of parentheses framing the smirk stretching ear to ear. "Got a tic, Doc?"

I notice Elsa stifling a giggle as I try to regain composure. Shortly, the security guard reenters, nosily maneuvering his chair through the doorway. "Ready when you are, Doc," he says.

"Okay, let's get started," I say, opening my folder and removing a test booklet and scoring sheet. Normally, patients would be given these materials with a number two pencil and instructed how to proceed. Given Overton's potential for possibly using the pencil as a weapon, I decide to both read the questions aloud and write down his answers. Privacy will take a back seat in this situation, and besides, Elsa and the security guard are ethically charged to maintain confidentiality. To reduce a favorable bias response, I give Overton a second scoring sheet and instruct him to point to his response choice instead of speaking it aloud. To my surprise he cooperates, and within thirty minutes we are finished.

"That is all we will do today," I say as I gather my papers.

"I was just warming up. Why stop now?" Overton asks.

"I appreciate your interest, Mr. Overton, but we want to score this procedure before we select the next assessment instrument."

"Instrument? Still trying to pretend you're a real doctor, Doctor?"

"You have been very cooperative, Mr. Overton. We will be back either tomorrow or the following day." I rise and Overton offers me a handshake. I extend my hand and he grips it forcefully. He resists releasing my hand, then suddenly does. His eyes shift from mine toward Elsa's.

I move between Overton and Elsa and gesture for her to leave. Instead, she leans in front of me and extends her hand to Overton. He smiles and reciprocates with what appears to be a gentle clasp. I move slightly forward touching their hands with my folder. Overton reluctantly lets go of Elsa's hand, letting his fingers slide slowly across hers.

"Are you finished here, Doc?" the guard asks.

"Yes, we are," I reply, nudging Elsa out the door.

"Until we meet again," Overton says.

I wait until we are in the elevator before letting Elsa know how upset I am. "What happened back there wasn't smart on your part, Elsa. It was poor judgment for you to offer your hand to Overton. He wanted some way to make contact with you, and you provided him with that by extending your hand."

"I don't think it was unnatural to offer a handshake. It is something I do all the time, and I've seen you do it as well."

"I told you before we entered the Forensic Unit that we needed to be especially careful with Overton. He's a pro and will take advantage of any sign of weakness."

"A handshake is a sign of weakness?"

"An unnecessary handshake can be seen as a sign of wanting to be close."

"I don't understand."

"Other than being a professional observer, you didn't interact or have any shared activity with Overton that would warrant a handshake. In fact, I chose not to initiate any physical contact with him. But when he took the lead, I didn't want to give him the impression that I was afraid of him. So, I shook his hand."

"You're splitting hairs."

"No, I'm not. I'm talking about why and how we need to be objective and careful with Overton. We cannot underestimate his manipulative nature or be caught up in it."

The elevator abruptly stops at the bottom floor, jarring us.

"Look, Elsa, you may disagree with me about how cautious we need to be with Overton, but I need you follow my advice. I'm responsible for your safety and for conducting a thorough evaluation of Overton. We need to be highly objective and professional with him. If you don't believe you can do that, then say so."

Elsa hesitates and bites her bottom lip. After a few seconds she says, "I still want to be part of this testing assignment, so I will be more careful around him."

"Okay. Let's switch subjects then. At our department meeting this afternoon, Paula Cotton will be conducting a case conference that will highlight the typical clinical features of psychopathy, somewhat like Overton presents but probably without the bizarreness that he exhibits. Both of us might learn something from Paula's presentation that we could apply to our work with him. So, please ask questions and take notes."

Elsa nods politely, but I get the feeling that she's shining me on. Then again I might be getting too sensitive in my advancing years. I break away from Elsa and the confines of the building and head outside for some fresh air and a walk. The rain has stopped, and the overcast skies are parting, letting some rays of sunshine peek through. Before long all I'm thinking about is how lucky I am to be living in an area surrounded by rolling hills and birds singing. Life is good.

~

Vigilant Of The Past

"Where did you get it?" Ophelia asks Kendra. "Never mind where I got it, just light it," Kendra responds.

"I want to know what I'm smoking. So tell me where you got it, or the lighter stays with me."

"Oh, for Buddha's sake! I got if off that new patient. The Chinese girl."

"You mean Kim Huong? She's Vietnamese."

"And that changes what?"

"How did she get it past nursing?"

"Same way you get your sharps past nursing. She hid it in her bra. Come on, light this fatty."

"Why did she give it to you?"

"Why are you so paranoid? I got it, and I'm sharing it. Isn't that good enough?"

Ophelia stares at Kendra trying to read the lanky, dark-skinned girl. Ophelia has known Kendra for about six months. Enough time to have a fondness for her. Long enough to have stolen away for trysts and escapes to off-campus stores. Long enough to trust her, but Ophelia has had her share of bad trips from laced weed before, and she isn't anxious to have another, especially since she has been on an emotional rollercoaster for the past few weeks. She wishes she could blame PMS, but she stopped menstruating months ago, after her last anorexic episode. No, Ophelia wishes it were something other than what she knows the problem to be: the past.

"Okay, let me have it," Ophelia says reaching into her jean pocket for her contraband lighter.

"About time, Opie," Kendra says, handing the short, fat blunt to Ophelia.

They huddle closer together, receding deeper into the thick base branches of an ancient and enormous rhododendron bush, commonly referred to by patients as the Love Nest.

∾

What Is Beneath
The Soil

After her presentation yesterday, Paula Cotton spoke with me about a newly admitted patient who she interviewed that might be a good fit for the poetry group. Paula described Cora Ruth Wiesendagen as a quiet, old-fashioned woman who is reserved and tentative about expressing herself, except through poems. She is a seventy-two-year-old widow suffering from intractable depression. She recently lost her husband of fifty-four years, which apparently was the tipping point for her.

Although I should be scoring Overton's test results, I decide to head up to the women's closed ward to find Ms. Wiesendagen. I skip the elevator in favor of hiking up three flights of stairs where I encounter Gunner Albaum kneeling on the bottom step of the stone staircase apparently repairing a broken tread.

"Hey there, Gunner."

"Doc, how are you?" Gunner labors to stand, then extends his hand. Although he is of medium height, his bent posture makes him look smaller and older. His blonde hair is thinning and fading to gray. His weathered face is dry and ashen. His watery blue eyes, sad. With his bib denim overalls, Gunner looks the part of a maintenance man.

We shake and pat each other's arm. "Good to see you, Gunner. How have you been?"

"Each day's a struggle, Doc. But at my age, what can I expect?"

I don't have the heart to tell him he probably is only a couple years older than I am. "Given the hard work you do every day, it takes its toll."

"So, Doc, you searching for another missing patient?" Gunner asks, referring to my search for Ester.

"No, no missing patient today, Gunner. Just on my way up to the third floor to see someone. How did that step break?"

"Old, that's all. We all break apart eventually," Gunner says, looking wistfully at the jagged edge of the thick slate tread, his shoulders hunched over.

A pretty morbid response, but it fits with what I know of the man. "How many more years do you have, Gunner?" I ask, referring to his work time at KSH.

"Got forty now. Oh, I could go any day if I wanted. But, I don't know what I would do with myself if I didn't have this place to fix up."

"You should consider going into the repair business. With the population aging as it is, there would be plenty of demand for someone with your skills to do odd household repairs."

"Did give that some thought, Doc. But then I would have to deal with the public, and I ain't accustom to that. For the past forty years, I only had one customer, and she never once complained about my work," he says, reaching out to pat the stairwell's wall.

"Yeah, I guess you have a point there."

We both grow silent.

"Well, I best be off. Got a patient to see."

"You're a good man, Doc"

"So are you, Gunner. See you around."

"Not unless I see you first," he says with a strained smile.

Like some aging men who have limited interests outside of work, Gunner probably will have a hard time creating a new life for himself once he retires. I wonder if I will as well when my time comes.

I reach the third-floor landing and insert my key in the Women's Closed Ward door, unbolting it easily. Peering around, I quickly relock the door and head down the corridor to the ward's nursing station. The hallway is fairly quiet, and few women are to be seen. It's peculiar how some days one can walk on the wards and find them eerily empty, as if everyone suddenly disappeared. Then at other times be overwhelmed by swarming souls, raucous and demanding of attention to the point of driving one mad, searching for an escape hatch.

As I pass by rows of single bedrooms, I glance around, curious to see who's cloistered inside. A few rooms are unkempt with possessions strewn about and their owners under covers. But most of the rooms are unoccupied, beds made, and clothing put away—a sign that their occupants are at an activity or a scheduled appointment. I pause at Wilma Sour's room and see that she is gesticulating in front of her window, apparently engaged in a personally meaningful conversation with herself. She doesn't notice me, and I move on.

Approaching the last room on the right, I note the name tag taped to the door, which is ajar: Cora Ruth W. Knocking lightly, I peek inside. The room is exceptionally tidy, but Cora Ruth isn't there. So, I head to the nursing station to find out where she might be. Sitting at a small wooden desk, Paige Schantz is filling the cigarette tray for this morning's patient smoke break. Paige momentarily glances in my direction before returning her attention back to the tobacco tray.

"Hey, Paige, do you know where I can find Cora Ruth?" I ask the spunky psychiatric aide.

"How much is it worth to you?" Paige asks, leaning back in her chair, thumbing the suspenders on her denim overalls.

"Five minutes of free counseling."

"We couldn't even get through introductions in five minutes, Jerome. Cora Ruth is in the bathroom, should be out soon. So, how have you been?"

"Not bad, what about you?"

"Excellent, got rid of my husband and bought a rottweiler, a much smarter companion, eats less to boot."

"Sounds like you are faring pretty well, Paige. What do you know about Cora Ruth?"

"Not much. She's a pretty quiet lady, keeps to herself and never complains. Now if the rest of the ward could be that way, my job would be pretty easy."

"Does she appear depressed to you?"

"She appears unhappy. Then again, who wouldn't be living in a place like this? I know I would be."

"Unhappiness can be a symptom of depression."

As we are talking, the bathroom door slams shut, and a small, gray-haired woman walks by wearing a faded gray knitted sweater over an apron dress. Walking with a slight stoop, she appears crumpled, worn down.

"Cora Ruth, come here dear," Paige says softly, motioning for the woman to approach the nursing station.

Slowly, Cora Ruth turns toward the voice beckoning her. I can see that she is pale with finely creased skin, appearing much older than seventy-two, until I see her eyes. They are grayish-blue, clear and bright, gleaming with intelligence.

"Cora Ruth, this is Jer...Dr. Masonheimer. He is here to talk with you."

"Hello, Ms. Wiesendagen."

"Doctor," Cora Ruth extends her hand.

We shake, and I am surprised how firmly her small-boned hand grips mine. "I was hoping we could talk somewhere in private."

"We could for a short time. I have to go to the green-house in twenty minutes," Cora Ruth says, looking at the ward's clock hanging above us.

"All I need is a few minutes. We could go to the inter-view room and have some privacy."

Cora Ruth nods in agreement and waits for me to lead the way. I unlock the door and wait for her to have a chair before sitting down across from her. "How would you prefer I address you?" I ask.

"My given name is Cora Ruth. That is what I have been called all my life. So, I imagine that is what you should do as well."

"You could call me Jerome if you wish."

"I would rather not, if you don't mind. I was brought up to address doctors as Doctor."

"I'm a psychologist, not a physician."

"Did you go to college to be a psychologist?"

"Of course."

"Then you earned a professional title, and that is how I will address you."

"Very well, Cora Ruth. I appreciate your respect. The reason that I am here is that Paula Cotton, the psychologist who spoke to you when you first arrived at the hospital, told me that you like to write poems."

"I don't really write poems, Doctor, just ditties. Poems are written by people who are educated in poetry. I only went to high school, Doctor Masonheimer.

"Ditties count as far as I am concerned. I conduct a group where people bring in their ditties to share. Would you be interested in attending that type of group?"

"I'm a bit backward, Doctor. Speaking in front of a group wouldn't be easy for me."

"Most of the people in group are somewhat reserved as well, and you wouldn't need to speak up if you didn't feel like it."

"I see. All right then, I'm willing to try it," she replies, again glancing at the clock.

"I can tell you don't want to be late for your greenhouse assignment."

"It's the only thing that seems to keep me going right now—dirt and flowers."

"Sounds like it means a lot to you."

"Being able to make something grow has always given me purpose."

"That I can understand. I'm into gardening as well—vegetables mostly."

"Do you can?"

"No, I'm afraid I don't. I did when my mother was alive but let it go ever since. A lot of work, as you know."

"There's meaning in doing hard work, Doctor."

Sounds just like Mom.

"No argument there. Well, speaking of work I'll let you get to yours, and I'll go back to mine. The poetry group is on Tuesday and Thursday from eleven until noon. I assume you will be back from the greenhouse by that time. Won't you?

"I'm there from nine to ten-thirty. So, yes, I should be back by then."

"Great, I'll wait for you to return to the ward around ten forty-five and then escort you to group."

"Very well, Doctor."

"Thank you for your time, Cora Ruth. See you on Tuesday at ten forty-five."

I watch her saunter slowly down the corridor. Cora Ruth appears to be moving out of habit, without direction. I hope we can change that.

ᕬᕲ

The Costs Are Passed On

The next morning, I arrive at work ten minutes early hoping to analyze Overton's test results before going up to the wards. Taped to my door is an envelope. Opening it I discover a handwritten note from Phyllis informing me that she will be at a medical appointment until eleven, which means I need to represent her this morning at the superintendent's daily communication meeting. Even with Dr. Salvatore Domio gone and Aggie now in the role of superintendent, there still is an edginess that pervades these meetings, making me appreciate the fact that I spend most of my working day with patients.

Since the meeting won't start until eight-thirty, I start the test analysis. Not more than five minutes into my work, I stop to see who is knocking on my door.

"Morning, Rome," Hobart (Woody) Tickle says, grabbing for my garbage can. Woody is KSH's resident curmudgeon. Tall, gray, and out of shape, Woody was once the director of therapeutic activities before opting out to work as a custodian. Instead of a coat and tie, he now wears jeans and a dirty old baseball cap. A bright and loquacious man who at times can become insufferable with his elocutionary rants, Woody is forever engaging in scathing attacks of the hospital's administration.

"Morning, Woody," I reply, hoping that if I head back to my desk he will collect the trash and leave.

"I guess you heard about the latest bone-head decision our administration is making," Woody says, the bags around his eyes sagging like his oversized trousers.

I really need to take the sign off my door that says, "Malcontents welcomed."

"Not really sure what decision you're talking about, Woody."

"Good point, Rome, there's too many to keep track of. I'm referring to the latest asinine decision to close the greenhouse. A Capitol City pronouncement to which our front office bootlickers have rolled over and acquiesced to. Can you imagine what the consequences of closing the greenhouse will have on our patients' welfare? As you know, Rome, for many, the greenhouse is therapeutic, not to mention a source of personal income. Work fosters self-esteem, but our administration wouldn't fathom that, given that they don't gainfully work. They merely put on their expensive attire, drive to their assigned parking spaces, and keep each other busy for hours by exchanging meaningless e-mails, all the while collecting exorbitant salaries. Reprehensible leeches."

I wonder how Woody found out about the greenhouse closing. I hadn't heard anything. Then again I'm not obsessed with finding out what the latest administrative issue is, like he is.

"I have to agree with you there, Woody. If the greenhouse closes, many patients will lose out, and so will the public. The prices at our greenhouse are quite low, comparably speaking."

"Ah, good point, Rome. I hadn't considered the mercantile angle. You may be right; perhaps some calls were made to our unscrupulous state representatives by local businessmen to eradicate a competitor."

"I wasn't implying that other greenhouse owners had conspired to get ours closed, Woody."

"Don't be so humble. I can tell you have a nose like mine to ferret out the corruption that runs rampant in our government, including this hospital."

I glance at the clock and realize I'll be late if I don't get a move on. "Woody, I've got to go."

"Off to resolve a patient problem? You're a good man, Rome."

I don't have the nerve to tell him that I am about to meet up with his sworn enemies. "Woody, chill out with the administration for a while. Give yourself a chance to relax."

"Guardians of the truth never rest, Rome." And with that, he rolls his cleaning cart down the hallway.

If Woody is right about the greenhouse closing, it will hit Cora Ruth particularly hard. Maybe I will be able to find out more at this morning's meeting.

Hurrying, I make it to the superintendent's office just as the door is being closed. I quickly give a cursory greeting to the secretary and find a chair in the corner, near the window next to Hunter Marshall, the therapeutic recreation director. Looking around the room, I notice that Myrna Blass, the director of nursing, isn't here, which is unusual given that she typically presents the patient status report. Aggie starts the meeting by announcing that Myrna will not be attending, as she is involved in a patient crisis in Manchester Building. Instead, Reed Boyer, the newly promoted assistant director of nursing, will be substituting for Myrna.

Aggie gestures to Reed to begin, and dutifully he starts reading the report he has been provided. "Good morning, everyone," Reed says assertively. "Today's census is two hundred and twenty one, which includes four patients on leave. Last night, there was a medical crisis on the Men's Closed Ward. Jimmy Lee Olum barged into the staff's break room and swallowed the entire contents of an open coffee can. He had to be restrained and escorted to a treatment room, where he managed to break free and ingest several packets of alcohol wipes, before being restrained again. Nursing successfully extracted the packets from his mouth and throat; however, the charge nurse, Jake Worman, was bitten during the procedure and required medical attention. The doctor on call ordered Jimmy Lee to be taken to the emergency room at Cornplanter General, and while there he had his stomach pumped out. As of this morning, Jimmy Lee is still at the hospital, in stable condition and receiving sedation."

"Let's hope he doesn't break into their medical supplies and start a crisis down there," says Dr. Winston (Winnie) Pierce, chief of psychiatry. "We barely eked out a contract with their hospital this year to treat our patients. Jimmy Lee could test the limits of their good will. Do we have staff sitting with him?"

"Yes, sir, we do. We have two aides by his bedside, and we have agreed to wrist and leg straps for security purposes," Reed says.

"Good thing he is at Cornplanter General; we could never get away with using those restraining techniques here," Winny says, referring to our hospital being prohibited by Capitol City from using any type of physical or mechanical restraints.

"Nevertheless, we should monitor how they are restraining him," Aggie says. "We need to systematically observe how Jimmy Lee is fairing while being restrained. Reed, please tell Myrna that I want to meet with her in my office as soon as she returns from this morning's crisis. Olga, I want you to attend the meeting as well," Aggie says to the director of quality assurance and compliance. "Please, go on with your report, Reed."

"Thank you, Dr. Daltry," Reed replies. "In Manchester Building, at ten-thirty in the evening, Riley Smidt assaulted an aide while being escorted to the bathroom. No injuries were reported. Riley was counseled and returned to his room."

"In what manner did the assault occur?" Olga asks.

"He... ah...touched...that is...grabbed the aide's... ah...breast," Reed stammers.

"I thought Riley's arms were paralyzed," Winnie says.

"One is, sir."

"I see. So, he touched...grabbed the aide with his good arm?"

"Apparently he did, sir," Says Reed.

"Wasn't he told to keep a one-arm's length distance from staff?"

"Well, sir, I believe he prefers using his bad arm to measure distance, at least with this aide, sir."

"I see," says Winnie, chuckling. "And why was a female staff member taking Riley to the bathroom?"

"Last night we were short male aides, so we used one of the female staff to escort Riley to the bathroom. In a tight spot, we do that. However, we still disallow male staff to escort female patients to the bathroom," Reed quickly adds.

"I would hope so," Aggie speaks up. "Was this female aide hurt by Riley?"

"No, ma'am. She wasn't physically hurt, only offended."

"No harm, no foul," Reudi Sanchio, the business director, says.

Glaring, Aggie snaps, "Spoken like a male, Reudi."

"Sorry. I didn't mean any harm."

"No harm, no foul," Aggie chides. "Is there anything else, Reed?"

"No ma'am."

"Well, then. Let's move on to the latest news from Capitol City," Aggie says. "This morning I received a phone call from the General Accounting Office. Apparently, it will cost the Commonwealth nearly fifty thousand dollars to upgrade our greenhouse to the latest fire and safety codes. This amount is considered to be too expensive, and as a result we are being ordered to cease all greenhouse operations by the end of this month."

Woody's source was right.

"What about the patients currently assigned to the greenhouse? What happens to them?" asks Marsh.

"Unfortunately, Marsh, they will need to be assigned to a different program," Aggie replies.

"Many of them will be more than disappointed, Dr. Daltry. A lot of them will be crushed," Marsh adds.

I jump in. "I agree with Marsh. Several patients have their identity tied up in the greenhouse. I know that Cora Ruth Wiesendagen looks forward to her greenhouse assignment. She says it keeps her from becoming more depressed. For her it will be a huge loss."

"I can appreciate that for some it will be a loss. However, unless we can figure out a way to come up with fifty thousand dollars, the greenhouse will be deemed unsafe and it will need to be closed," Aggie responds.

"Maybe we could have a bake sale," Reudi quips.

No one laughs or bails him out.

"I'm sorry for this latest piece of bad news, but with the state budget in the red, the governor is looking to make cuts across all state agencies, including mental health. We can expect further cost-saving measures in the future as well," Aggie says, somberly.

Both Marsh and I shake our heads. Once again I leave a meeting feeling worse than when I came in.

◦‿◦

Pathology Abounds

Ihead back to my office after the superintendent's meeting determined to make progress on the test analysis. Turning the corner, I see someone sitting on the wooden bench next to my door. As I get closer, I recognize that it is Dr. Gobind, one of our senior psychiatrists. A naturalized citizen from New Delhi, she still dresses in traditional Indian attire and speaks with a distinct Indian accent. Around sixty, squat, double-chinned, with long braided white hair, she can be insufferable with her demands.

"Hello, Dr. Gobind. Have you been waiting long?" I ask.

"He's back," she says with exasperation.

"Who's back?"

"That bipolar who reminds me of a wild stallion, Killer. He's back, and I want you to work with him." She steps into the office, her yellow sari floating around her like a mist. "Last time you managed to keep his intrusive behaviors limited to your department. He found enjoyment in pestering you and thankfully left me alone. I want you to see him as soon as possible."

"I don't know if I have room to see him, Dr. Gobind, and maybe he doesn't want to see me."

"Oh, he'll want to see you. I told him to see you, and he went into a manic episode just hearing your name. I assure you he will see you."

"We haven't even had a treatment plan meeting for him. Maybe he doesn't need therapy."

"Jerome, he is a nuisance. He needs therapy. I already wrote the order."

"And what do you think the goal of therapy should be?"

"To get his id under control, and to stop being an irritant to others."

"Dr. Gobind, he has bipolar symptoms. He is loaded with energy. Therapy isn't going to change that."

"Leave that to me. There is plenty of room for his medications to be raised. We will squash his mania. You just get him to be more mindful of his place," Gobind says. "I must be off. Call me when you have made some progress." And having said that, she collects the folds of her sari, awkwardly turns, and shuffles down the hallway.

I don't know how seriously to take her, but given that I have worked with this patient during previous admissions, I probably will see him one more time, for continuity sake.

Daniel Killebrew, who prides himself with the nickname of Killer is definitely a memorable character. A hulking black man with unruly curly locks and a ubiquitous toothy grin, Daniel recognizes no boundaries between him and anyone else. His will has a straight connection to his motor track. Highly animated, with fluttering hands, bulging eyes, and a booming voice, Daniel is chaos personified. The last time he was at the hospital, he became so engulfed with glee when he saw me that he scooped me up in his arms and excitedly pranced around while singing, for all to behold. Unfortunately, to my chagrin, some visitors witnessed this shenanigan, and I was reprimanded for behaving unprofessionally. Like I had any control over the situation.

Daniel adopted the moniker Killer from the renowned baseball slugger, Harmon Killebrew, who was known affectionately as Killer. Daniel tried playing baseball as a youngster, but with his gangly coordination never could master swinging a bat or fielding a ball. So instead, he went out for track and field only to find that smoking and sprinting weren't compatible. Subsequently, he gave up running on the track and drifted toward running for drug dealers instead. With his effusive but harmless personality, Daniel was well received by pushers, especially since all he wanted for his troubles was a dime bag now and then.

I resign myself to seeing Daniel—I refuse to call him by his nickname—but not before scoring Overton's test. After about fifteen minutes, I finally have a profile. It isn't good. Elevations on almost all pathological dimensions, and the validity indices are in the normal range. So, Overton is willingly admitting he has abnormal features, particularly in the areas of masochism and sadism. The next step is to check out how he ranks on a pure psychopathy assessment. A neuropsychological screening is needed as well. I decide to set up the next testing session after I interview Daniel on Men's Closed Ward.

I take the elevator to the third floor and upon opening the ward's locked door, I nearly bump heads with Luther Slaughter, a psychiatric aide, who is leaning against the doorjamb. Luther's face will never grace a cover of *Gentleman's Quarterly*. Beginning with his swollen lower lip, which veers downward exposing an uneven row of discolored and misshapen teeth, his nose droops like an overripe pear, and his bloodhound eyes beg for buckets of eyewash. With slouching shoulders and a ballooning abdomen, he is the antithesis of what one would expect a battle-ready soldier to look like. But a soldier is exactly what Luther fashions himself to be.

Unlike many flag-waving patriots, most of whom were against conscription and putting themselves in harm's way, Luther didn't try to avoid being drafted in the army during the Vietnam conflict. When his number was drawn, Luther answered his country's call. However, he endured only four weeks of military indoctrination before receiving a section eight discharge for being mentally unstable. This may explain why he is transfixed upon potential threats, both real and imaginary, against America, Cornplanter County, and more specifically, within the hospital itself.

Constantly clad in camouflage fatigues, which includes bloused pants cupping a pair of Vietnam-era jungle boots, Luther struts the hallways on alert, awaiting an impending terroristic invasion. Unlike other psychiatric aides, Luther is rarely found sitting in the nursing station. Instead he marches dutifully up and down the ward's hallways, stopping to peer out windows, as if on perpetual guard duty. He only breaks this pattern when directed to perform a service for a patient, which surprisingly he does in a fairly competent manner. He takes his orders and executes them with precision and without question as any good soldier would. It also keeps him from being fired.

Since the hospital doesn't have any doctrinal or dress code standards, employee quirks and eccentricities are tolerated along with fringe beliefs and paranoid leanings. Coupled with the patients' oddities, staff members like Luther make for a colorful work environment, to say the least.

"Whoa, Luther. Didn't see you lurking there," I say.

"Jerome," Luther replies.

"Seems pretty quiet up here today."

"Always quiet before a storm breaks."

"Expecting something to go wrong?"

"I'm always ready for the unexpected, Jerome, as you should be."

"I try to pay attention."

"It's not just watching what is in front of you. You've got to watch your back, too. Nobody else will."

"You make it sound like someone is out to get us, Luther."

"Aren't you watching the news? Immigration is unchecked. Drug lords are invading our schoolyards. Homosexuals are carrying guns. Terrorists want to destroy America."

"What TV are you watching. Station KKK?"

"This is no damn joke, Jerome." He glares at me. "Our nation is being invaded by foreigners and drug cartels. The courts are taking prayer and the flag out of our classrooms. When did you last see anyone pledge allegiance to the flag? You haven't, have you? When did *you* last pledge allegiance? Probably not since elementary school. Am I right?"

"Well, I...I don't remember the last time, Luther. Maybe it was back in elementary school."

"That's what I'm saying. We're straying from the flag. We can change that, Jerome. Right here, right now."

"What do you mean?"

"You and me Jerome, we can take that pledge," he says, reaching into his back pants pocket.

To my amazement, Luther pulls out a polyester American flag the size of a welcome mat, which he unfurls, and with one hand drapes against the wall. Taking off his cap and placing in between his knees, Luther puts his free right hand across his heart. "Right now, Jerome. Right here. Let's hear you say it."

I nervously look around to see if anyone is watching this farce. Several patients have stepped out of their rooms and are approaching us.

"Right now, Jerome. Let's hear you say it," Luther says more loudly than before.

Moving beside me, Harvey Louser, starts the pledge. "I pledge allegiance to the flag of the United States of North America..."

"Right now, Jerome," Luther almost shouts, not seeming to care that Harvey is fracturing the pledge.

"...and to the public for which I don't stand..."

I feel like running down the hallway, but relent to the pressure and join in with Harvey. "...one nation, indivisible..."

"Under God, Jerome. Under God," Luther insists.

"Under Jesus Christ," Harvey interjects.

"It's under God, but I won't argue with the son of God," Luther says.

I quickly sputter, "With liberty and justice for all."

"Amen!" says Harvey.

"One more time, and with feeling," Luther demands.

"Got to go, Luther, got to go," I say, walking backwards and offering a salute.

"Who's with me?" Luther asks.

Harvey and several other patients surround Luther and the flag. Their voices struggle to be in unison.

Entering the nursing station, I encounter Jake Worman, the charge nurse, who, although busily copying information from a chart glances up in my direction. "I see you have Luther fired up, Rome," the brawny nurse quips. Jake must be in a good mood. Generally, he is grave; some would say humorless. Given that he has been working for nearly thirty years on a closed ward with chronically psychotic patients, being short on humor is understandable, but not advisable. Moreover, wrestling with out-of-control men for that many years has knocked the lightheartedness out of Jake, not to mention giving him a sore back, dark sunken eyes, and thin graying hair.

"The man's a tinderbox waiting to go off no matter who comes through the door," I reply. "I've never seen him pull out the flag before. Is that new?"

"Yeah. So far he has taken it out of his pocket only a few times. Only when he thinks someone isn't a patriot."

"Meaning what? That I'm a commie or, God forbid, a socialist?"

"Well, Rome, you are collecting a check from the Commonwealth's taxpayers."

"And you two are working for free? I served in the army just like you. What did Luther do?"

"He got drummed out."

"That's what I understand. And then he has the audacity to question the loyalty of others?"

"Take a breath, Rome. The way you're carrying on, you may need to be referred to the stress management group."

"Maybe you're right. I'm making this out to be more than what it is. Listen, I came up here to find Daniel. Is he on the ward?"

"Killer? Yeah, he should be here. His room is in the back wing across from the Medication Room. Since he got here, he's has been sleeping a lot and staying out of trouble. We like it that way. So don't stir him up like you did Luther," Jake says, his smile fading.

"Just for you, I'll try my best."

I head down the hallway to the back wing. As I approach Daniel's room, I notice a foul body odor. With his door ajar, I gently knock and peer inside. Daniel is lying in bed, apparently asleep. Should I wake him is the question. Snorting, he rolls over, flopping a smelly fungus-infected foot in my direction. Gasping, I back out of the room. In friendlier air, I decide to catch him later.

~

Coveting More Than Beauty

"**W**ake up, Overton, you got another testing session this morning, so there's no sleeping in for you," Ernie Allison, the security guard, orders. "We're all hoping that psychology intern comes again to sweeten our eyes. So get up. Don't want her turning around and hightailing it out of here just because you're not ready. Although watching her walk away would be a booty-full sight, indeed."

Overton doesn't need Ernie to tell him about Elsa's beauty, back or front. A blind man could see that. What staff members don't seem to notice is that Elsa exudes something much more attractive than her physicality. Something more appealing and valuable, particularly to Overton. Confidence. Actually, overconfidence in her ability to handle men, even dangerous men. And that is precisely what Overton finds alluring about Elsa.

Self-assured women have always captivated him. He is attracted to their belief that they can control men either with physical charms or their intellect, especially men weakened by sexual drives, which Overton believes he no longer is victim to. For most of his youth, Overton observed women from a distance. Typically, they didn't want anything to do with him because of his craggy, acne-scarred face. Hence, in order to examine women closely, Overton discovered it was necessary to capture and confine them to his lair. It was hellish for them but wickedly wonderful for him.

To scrutinize Elsa close up, just the two of them— now that's a thrilling thought.

How It Starts

"See you tonight around five-thirty," I say giving Despina a long kiss.

"Don't be late, hon. It'll take almost an hour to drive to Apotsos's, and if we don't arrive in time for our reservations, they'll give them to someone else," my wife says.

"I won't be late. I promise." Stealing another quick smooch, I pick up my keys and attaché case. I didn't really want to drive an hour to eat out, but it's our anniversary, and Despina really likes the authentic Greek food served at Apotsos's. So I make a point to stay aware of time and not be late.

As the garage door opens with groans and creaks, I turn the key and...nothing. Just a metallic click, click, click. *No, not today. Give me a break.* I try again. Same results the second try and the third. Dead battery.

Fuming, I go back inside, and yell, "Despina, can you give me a ride to work? My battery's dead."

From upstairs she yells back, "I can't leave until nine-thirty or so. I need to shower and be at the beauty shop by ten. So you'll need to wait."

"Well, that means I need to call in and let Phyllis know I'll be late," I say, heading to the phone. I have scheduled my second testing session with Overton for this morning at 8:30. Phyllis can either cancel the session or direct someone else to do it. I advise against sending Elsa, at least by herself. No point in giving him an opportunity to be manipulative. Although Elsa thinks she handle Overton, she is underestimating his guile.

∽

Surrounded By Tension

After Despina dropped me off at the hospital, I went directly to Phyllis's office to find out what she had decided regarding Overton's testing. She told me that she had sent Eliot to do the neuropsychological screening that I had intended to do. Given that Eliot is our department's neuropsychological expert, it made good sense to choose him. Phyllis said Elsa went with Eliot, and as far as Phyllis knew everything went as expected.

I call Eliot to get a firsthand report, but only get his voice mail. Given that it's midmorning, he probably is in a therapy session. I leave a message inviting him to get together with me over lunch.

Although it's early, Cora Ruth will be coming back from her greenhouse assignment in a few minutes, so I head upstairs to wait for her. As I walk up the staircase, I encounter Olive Minot, a patient who likes to be called Pepper. I haven't seen her in many weeks and immediately notice that she has changed her hairstyle to a boyish cut, which is very becoming. She looks rather fit and moves more quickly than I remember.

"Hi, Pepper."

"Oh, hello Dr. Masonheimer. How are you?"

"Fine, thank you. You look well, Pepper. I like your haircut. Something new, huh?"

Pepper looks directly at me, but her eyes are not aligned. That hasn't changed from day one. She touches her hair. "I'm doing much better, especially since my medications have been changed. I'm not as tired and seem to be thinking more clearly. I have a boyfriend," she says, dropping her gaze.

"You do. Well, that's great. Anyone I know?"

"Hubie Hoosier." She still avoids looking at me.

"Hubie! No kidding. Wow. Hubie. Well, that's great. He's a nice guy. Of course, you probably already know that."

"He's kind to me. For now that is all I ask." She looks up and her eyes are more focused.

"Makes sense to me, Pepper. Well, my best to Hubie and you. I need to be off. Take care."

"You, too, Dr. Masonheimer. Bye," she says, awkwardly waving her hand

I'm always amazed at the boyfriend-girlfriend relationships that form at this hospital. I never can predict who will connect with whom. Unlike the real world, physical attributes seem to play very little part in drawing folks together; intangibles appear more important. I make a mental note to do a study on dating relationships someday when I have the time.

When I enter Women's Closed Ward, Cora Ruth is already waiting for me by the door. Ophelia is waiting as well. "Have both of you signed out?" I ask.

"Legibly?" Ophelia responds.

"I could read her name when I signed out," Cora Ruth adds.

Turning toward the nursing station, I wave my arms, hoping to catch someone's attention. Paige sees me and walks out of the office. I shout, "I have Opie and Cora Ruth. Be back by noon."

Paige gives me a thumbs-up.

"You really must learn how to trust people, Jerome," Ophelia says.

"I'll work on that. Let's go." I unlock the door, and as they pass I notice that Cora Ruth is carrying a notebook. After locking the door I ask, "How was your greenhouse assignment today, Cora Ruth?"

"Very busy. Gladiolas needed to be cut and arrangements made for a wedding. Time went by quickly," she responds.

Due to Cora Ruth's slow gait, we move slowly to the passenger elevator located midway between the north and south sides of Dix Building.

"Aren't you going to ask me how my assignment went, Jerome?" Ophelia asks.

"How was your assignment this morning, Opie?"

"Didn't have one. But I did find a poem to share in today's group."

"Really. One of your own?"

"Oh yes. One of my own."

"Good." I press the button for the elevator to take us down. The door opens abruptly, and inside the elevator are two recreation aides and a half dozen patients from Men's Closed Ward, including Delbert Schupp and Sherm Fiddler—men that I have known for some time and whom I have come to admire for their fortitude. Their psychiatric conditions have weighed heavily on them, but they continue to believe that something will happen to change their fate.

"Hey, Sherm. Del. How are you guys?" I say.

Delbert spreads his lips in a wide grin, while Sherm just stares at me.

"Looks like you guys have a full house. We can wait for the next one."

"No, no, come on in. We can make room for you," Ernst Wilco, one of the recreation aides, says. He starts nudging some of the men to make room. Given that the elevator's safety limit is eight passengers and Ernst and his colleague are large men, adding three more people seems risky. And perhaps too crowded for Ophelia, who is shaking her head and mouthing "No way" to me.

"Thanks, Ernst, but we really would feel more comfortable waiting for a less crowded elevator. Take care, Sherm, Del," I say.

"Up to you, Rome," Ernst replies. He lets the door close, and in the second or two it takes to close I see Sherm point a finger to his ear and then the ceiling. I think he is telling me that he is keeping an ear open for another signal from above. One of his delusions regarding Chinese satellites. I make a mental note to find time for him in my schedule.

Eventually, another elevator arrives and we make our way to the psychology department's group room. I unlock the door and take up my position in front of the table surrounded by multicolored plastic chairs. Ophelia takes up her usual position by the window, while Cora Ruth remains standing, unsure where to sit.

"Take a seat wherever you wish," I say.

"Don't sit in Harvey's chair," Ophelia says. "He'll freak out more than he usually does."

Cora Ruth remains standing.

"This would be a good spot," I say, pulling out a blue chair near the front of the room.

As she sits, other members start arriving. Within a few minutes, all are present. I introduce Cora Ruth to the group, and as usual Harvey wants to go first. After five minutes of fractured narration, Harvey plops back in his seat. Everyone appears numb except Cora Ruth, who looks baffled.

I offer her some clarification. "Harvey's recitations are quite unique. He typically doesn't expect that anyone will respond to his...expressions. So, at this point in our group, we look to see who else has something to recite."

Cora Ruth seems a little less confused but remains quiet. To my surprise, Kendra raises her hand. "I have a poem to read."

This is a first. Kendra has never shared a poem before. *I wonder, why now?* "Wonderful, Kendra. Is it a poem you wrote?" I ask.

"No, I didn't write it. I found it scribbled on the back of a book in the dayroom. If that doesn't count, somebody else can read."

"No problem with finding a poem to read. Any poem, any time, is okay for this group. Please, go ahead."

Standing, Kendra holds the paperback and starts to read. "This is called 'Gypsy Lady.' It doesn't say who wrote it."

Face of night
Taurus eyes and hair
Skin with foreign smells
Stained in oily hues of cinnamon and black
She sleeps dark and firm in a crimson room
Surrounded by plants, birds, placenta tones
Dreaming of a different world.

Smiling proudly, Kendra sits down. I am struck how the poem seems to fit her. Dark skin, Asian Indian, mysterious. If not for her recurring and unpredictable suicidal gestures, Kendra could be someone readily encountered on a college campus. Even though she consistently refuses any involvement in therapy outside of the poetry group, I like her and believe she can turn her life around.

"That's an interesting poem, Kendra. What do you like about it?"

"It reminds me of my sister. When she was alive, I mean." Kendra grows somber.

"Is it a good reminder?"

She shakes her head. "I guess not. Now that we are talking about. I would like to move on to someone else."

"Would it be okay if others comment on your poem?"

"No, I want to move on. Let's move on." A wish on many levels.

"Okay, we can honor that." I note to keep an eye on Kendra from this point forth. "Does anyone else have a poem to read?"

"I can read another one," Harvey volunteers.

A chorus of "No's" rings throughout the room.

"Perhaps we should give someone else a chance, Harvey," I suggest.

"I'll read one," Ophelia speaks up. She turns away from the window while remaining seated, and unfolds a paper drawn from her pocket. "This is something I wrote a few years ago. I call it 'Where forth art thou Venus.'" Mimicking a theatrical voice, Ophelia recites her lines.

Through my window
The dense snow
Reflects late sunlight
Stinging my eyes

Turning away
I briefly glimpse
A baby blue glint
Trapped within

Outside I stare
Into the receding blue
Scooping and clutching
My palm holds white

Again and again
Cold and white

The blue recedes
Evading my grasp

Vexed I slice
White to red
Red to blue
The setting sun bleeds

Atop a bloody
Streaked sky
Venus distantly shines
Through my window

Before returning her gaze out the group room's window, Ophelia flashes me a mischievous grin, as if to say, "See what you can do with that one." Like Kendra, Ophelia has rejected invitations to explore her problems. Her treatment team has recommended that she receive individual therapy, but Ophelia has ignored their suggestions, opting for superficial treatment approaches, and only then to keep from losing any privileges that she might have. I know she is using this group for ulterior motives, but I also know she can be drawn into revealing more than she intends.

"Hmmm. Seems to be quite a few messages in that poem, Opie. Would you care to elaborate on it?"

"That is what you get paid the big bucks to do, Jerome."

This brings a slow-forming smile to Kendra's face. It also brings a frown to Cora Ruth's brow. "To me, it contains many references to yearning and reaching out. What do others think?" I ask, looking around the room. No one speaks at first.

"I think it shows a lot of anger," Cora Ruth says, her voice unsteady.

"Do you think?" Ophelia says.

"I think Cora Ruth is right," Autumn says. "I think that it shows hurt and anger."

"Something you wouldn't know anything about, right Autumn?" Ophelia shoots back.

Autumn, surprised by Ophelia's reaction, pulls back into her chair.

"I have seen that sky," Lincoln says.

Except for Harvey, we all turn toward Lincoln. He is looking at Ophelia, and with a gentle voice, continues. "I painted that sky after I learned how our lands were taken away, and flooded for promised votes."

I'm not sure if others know what Lincoln is talking about. I suspect he is referring to the federal treaty that was broken by the Eisenhower administration in order to appease steel mill owners who wanted the government to build a dam to stop the Allegheny River from flooding their factories, and in the process flooded several Indian burial grounds.

"Your sky must have had different shades of red," I say.

"Earth blood red," Lincoln responds.

"Isn't it interesting how you were able to see the colors in Ophelia's words," I point out.

"Words that don't bring forth images are useless words," Lincoln replies.

Another silence ensues. "Would anyone like to say anything else about Ophelia's poem? Or recite a poem?"

No one responds.

Sometimes tension brews in silence, eventually finding a path to escape.

Cora Ruth slowly rises and says, "I guess I'm ready to try." She reaches inside a pocket and brings outs a small notepad. Flipping its cover, Cora Ruth selects the first entry. She reaches into her other pocket and retrieves a pair of wire-rim glasses that are in need of repair, one earpiece bonded to the frame with adhesive tape. Bent over, Cora Ruth looks drawn and weary. Looking in my direction, she clears her throat, and in a grainy voice begins reading.

"I call this 'Trapped.'"

Two collies had we
Both showed turns of spite
Loving and gentle with me
But towards my husband would snap and bite

With coats thick and long
A blanket I could weave
From the brushings they would prolong
By lying quiet, so naïve

Then a drunk driver
Careened into them both
Forcing me to become a survivor
To live this life that I loathe

Time creeps painfully by
I exist only on memories
Sweet recollections that fortify
My spirit trapped in this disease

Finished, Cora Ruth removes her glasses, then slips them in her dress pocket.

I can't tell if she is relieved or more tense after her reading. I know the poem is referring to her sons, and their tragic deaths. I don't want to reveal that information to the group, however. That is her choice. Not mine.

"Thank you, Cora Ruth, for sharing that personal poem. Does anyone want to say something about this poem?"

"I once had a beagle. It was run over by a truck. It was pretty old anyway," Harvey says.

"I find it to be a heart-aching poem," Autumn says. "Very sad."

"I have been sad and depressed for many years," Cora Ruth says. " I can't seem to shake it, and I don't know if it'll do any good talking about it."

"I'm glad you are talking and willing to share your poem," Autumn replies thoughtfully.

"Don't hold your breath that baring your soul will help you much," Ophelia pipes up. "It isn't going to bring back whatever you lost...collies, beagles or whoever."

"Speaking your truth can lift your heart, if not raise the dead," Lincoln says.

"I wish you would stop that," Ophelia nearly shouts.

"Stop what?"

"Your cutesy tribal talk. You think those arrows of wisdom that you let go are profound, don't you? Well they're not. They're annoying and not helpful to anyone but you."

I'm prepared to intercede, but Autumn speaks up, and rather forcefully for her.

"Speak for yourself, Opie. I find Lincoln's words to be not only helpful but sensitive. I think you have issues with receiving help, Opie."

"Aren't you a little spitfire today," Ophelia responds. "The defender of tribal rights."

"Trying to belittle someone to elevate yourself doesn't solve your problem, Opie," Autumn says.

"And what is my problem?"

"I don't know for sure, but you react in a hostile way. Maybe someone was hostile to you."

"Thank you, Miss Therapist, for that huge insight." After that, Ophelia completely turns her chair around, her back to the group.

I let a few seconds tick away before speaking. "It is not unusual for emotions to rise when we hear things that we don't like to hear."

"Maybe I shouldn't have read what I did," Cora Ruth says.

"No, reading your poem was the right thing to do," I say. "That is what this group is about. To put into words what we believe is meaningful to us. From what I have witnessed, each one of you did the right thing today. You all spoke from your heart. And even if it doesn't seem like we benefited from what was said aloud today, we need to let some time go by and see what emerges."

I look around inspecting everyone's face and non-verbals. They appear tight and disturbed.

I decide to try a tension-breaking exercise as a way of ending group. "I would like if we could reduce some of the stress that we are experiencing before we leave today. I invite you to join me in a one-minute stress busting exercise."

I walk over to where Ophelia is sitting and extend my hand to her. "Are you willing to take my hand?" I ask.

Ophelia turns and glares at me. She doesn't immediately make any movement, and my hand floats in front of her. I wait for her to accept or reject me. The tension is palpable. To my relief, Ophelia slowly places her left hand in mine. However, she remains seated facing the window.

"Kendra, would you stand next to Opie like I'm doing and take her other hand?" I ask. She obliges. "Now, Cora Ruth, if you would stand and take Kendra's hand, please. Autumn, would you take Cora Ruth's hand, and Lincoln, you take Autumn's. Harvey, would you take Lincoln's hand and my hand?"

Harvey shakes his head. "I don't like touching nobody."

"Okay, Harvey. Why don't you just watch and try to figure out what is happening," I reply.

I reach around Harvey and grab Lincoln's hand. Forming an amoebic shape, we are connected. "Now, I am going to squeeze Opie's hand and she is going to pass what she receives from me to Kendra, who will pass it to Autumn, and so forth. All right, here we go."

I begin by squeezing Ophelia's hand and dutifully she passes the squeeze on to Kendra, who passes it to Cora Ruth, who passes it along in turn to the others. It takes a few rounds before a pulse starts slowly emerging. But shortly it moves through us increasing in speed. Eventually, the electricity zooms along like an excited heartbeat. Entranced, we become less conscious of our individuality, less aware of our tension. Stress melts and is replaced with amusement as we lose ourselves in this simple activity. When I see even Lincoln flash the thinnest of smiles, I know we have lightened our load.

I lift both Ophelia's and Lincoln's hands high, squeeze them equally, and declare that we are "one and done."

"Thank you all for being willing to join in this exercise. Harvey, did you want to say anything as an observer?"

"Orgies are communist plots. Are we done?"

"For today, indeed we are. We will get back together on Tuesday. See you all then," I say.

I take Cora Ruth and Ophelia aside and ask if they can head up to the ward on their own. They assure me that they can. I remind them that I will be calling the ward in five minutes to make certain they arrive as expected. As I lock the door, Lincoln approaches me. His face is taut, and his eyes appear to express apprehension. In a soft voice he says, "The time is near."

"You mean regarding your spirit?"

"Yes."

"What should I do?"

"Come when you are called." And with that he leaves.

~~

Justifiable Concerns

Still reflecting on what Lincoln just said, I fail to notice Eliot approaching me. "Do I smell pensiveness?" he quips.

"Eliot, thanks for coming." I'm actually glad to see him, which is unusual for me. "Yeah, you caught me being absentminded, but I'm back on point and can't wait to hear how your testing went with Overton. Do you want to head over to the staff dining room? I'll buy lunch."

"Do I smell schmoozing?"

"You must have a head cold, because it smells like genuine curiosity to me."

Eliot manages a brief chuckle as we head to the dining room. After ordering subs, a black coffee for me, and a cherry Coke for Eliot, we find a table in the corner away from gossipy ears.

"So, tell me about it. What tests did you do, and how far did you get?" I ask.

Swallowing a mouthful of the hoagie, Eliot dabs his mouth before talking. "Phyllis suggested we do an executive functioning and a general visual motor screening. That was fine with me, but I estimated that it would take at least two hours to complete those tests. I wasn't certain Mr. Overton would cooperate for that amount of time. So, I did one and then waited thirty minutes before doing the other."

"I see. That would mean you were there from eight thirty to almost eleven thirty a.m. That's a long time for both him and you."

"Oh, I didn't stay for all the testing. I had other assignments."

"What do you mean? How did testing get done if you weren't...wait a minute, you didn't leave Elsa there to finish the testing, did you?"

"She gladly volunteered to do the visual motor test and assured me she had given many of them. So, I thought, why not? That is what interns are for anyway," Eliot says, getting ready to take another bite.

I stifle an urge to knock the sub out of his hands and twist his yellow bow tie off his neck. "Please tell me that someone was with Elsa when you left her, and I don't mean Overton."

"There was a security guard in the room, although when I was there he had fallen asleep from time to time."

"Damn it, Eliot. Didn't Phyllis tell you to make sure Elsa wasn't in a position to be exploited by Overton? I know I told Phyllis that over the phone. Didn't she tell you?"

Eliot's eyes widened. "Well, Phyllis said I was to make sure Elsa wasn't left alone with Mr. Overton. And with a security guard present, she wouldn't be. Anyhow, I saw Elsa just a few minutes ago, and she said everything went according to plan and that she finished the testing without any problems. You know, Jerome, you are emitting a large amount of hostile pheromones. Are you all right?"

"Where did you last see Elsa?"

"She was heading outside. I assume she was having lunch off campus because she had her car keys in her hands. Elsa appeared fine, Jerome. Really, she did."

I leave my food and Eliot without regret and head out to the front entrance parking lot. I look around for a black Honda Accord and spot one, except it's an older model and not the '04 that Elsa drives. I decide to wait outside and head to a recently refurbished gazebo where I will try to center myself with the help of some hatha yoga breathing exercises. Inhale, hold, exhale, relax. A hundred repetitions should put my head in a better place.

I'm on my twenty-fifth set when I spot Elsa parking her car. Feeling much more at ease, I regain my sense of urgency by jogging in her direction. She notices me approaching and waits by the staircase leading to the front doors of Dix.

"Didn't know you were a jogger, Dr. Masonheimer. And one who doesn't use sneakers."

"I'm not. Only wanted to catch up with you. I understand that Dr. LaFleur left you to finish the testing with Overton. Tell me what happened."

Taking off her sunglasses, Elsa's eyes flash annoyance with my question. "I gave the test, and within thirty minutes, it was done. Pretty straightforward. Nothing else to report about it."

"What about Overton?"

"What about him?"

"Was he cooperative? Did he do anything unusual?"

Sighing, Elsa is noticeably irked by my questions. "He behaved like a gentleman. Put forth a good effort to copy the designs, asked few questions, and didn't hit on me, if that was on your mind."

"Nothing more. No comments or insinuations?"

"Like what?"

"Like, he never was treated so respectfully by anyone like you before. Anything like that?"

"Not that I remember. You could ask the guard. He was there all the time."

"Was he awake?"

"Huh?"

"Never mind. Look Elsa, I don't like you being there with him without another psychologist. And from now on, you won't be. Is that understood?"

She nods her head. "Anything else, Dr. Masonheimer?"

"No, not right now."

Without saying another word, Elsa turns and enters Dix.

⤳

Ready To Be Helped

Elsa's impertinence has me seething. I decide to let off steam by walking around the campus. I start off jogging, but slow down to a brisk walk. It is a beautiful July day, sunny, around eighty degrees, with soft clouds lingering lazily above. A groundskeeper is mowing an expanse of field between Dix and the Forensic Unit, and the aroma of fresh cut grass takes me back to my childhood when I would rake into piles the clippings from my father's mowing of our yard. A bittersweet memory. The sweetness of the air surrounding my yearning to be playing baseball instead of helping my father. My father casting a scowl at me for being so sullen. Perhaps I react the same way with Elsa.

I know she is idealistically considering Overton as a person who sometimes misbehaves in an abnormal manner, and thus believes he should be treated sympathetically. And to a certain degree I agree with her, but Overton is not ready to consider himself merely a person who misbehaves badly. He knows himself, as much a person can truly know oneself. He isn't going to get off the crooked path he is on through kindness. It will take a yeoman's effort to therapeutically reach him. I don't know if I can, let alone Elsa. Hell, I'm not sure if my old mentor Karl could. It will take more than one person. It will take a team of therapists.

"Dr. Masonheimer," a distant voice calls out.

I look farther down the walking path and spot Cora Ruth hurrying in my direction, waving her hand to get my attention. I wave back and increase my pace. She is walking more rapidly than I imagined she ever could. She looks distressed.

"Dr. Masonheimer, I need to talk with you," she says breathlessly.

"What's the matter Cora Ruth?"

"Dr. Masonheimer, I have just heard the most troubling news. I have heard that the greenhouse will be closing. Do you know? Is this true?"

"Yes, I sadly found that out myself the other day. I wish it weren't true, for your sake."

"I don't know what I will do if I can't work with plants and dig in the soil. It is the one thing that has helped me deal with my losses. And if it is taken away, I don't know what I will do."

She truly looks distraught and I have very little to offer her in the way of consolation. "I imagine it will be hard to not work at the greenhouse," I say, adding, "I would be willing to meet with you and talk more about it, or any other issue, if you think it would help."

Cora Ruth breathes heavily and wrings her hand. "Do you mean right now?"

"Well, I could take some time right now if it would help. However, I was thinking about us meeting more often. If you would be willing, I could ask your treatment team for their permission."

She appears locked in thought. Perhaps too big of a risk to talk about what has been left unsaid, but not unknown. It isn't easy for us to put our pain into words, especially when we have to feel the pain all over again by exposing ourselves to hidden images and memories, longings, and realizations. Few of us relish such an invitation.

"I guess I should," she says, sighing heavily. "I guess I should."

"Okay, then. I will meet with your treatment team and let you know about when we can set up a time."

"All right, let me know. Are you sure you can't do anything about the greenhouse closing?"

"I'm afraid not. It is a decision made by people in charge of the purse strings. Sorry."

Cora Ruth nods absently, then moseys slowly down the walking path. The bean counters have no concept of the anguish they have wrought.

～

Taking No Chances

Cameron Frankl scans the forensic office's communication board, which lists the medical appointments scheduled for forensic patients. "We need to get Mr. Overton to the dental office for his ten a.m. appointment," she says aloud.

The security guard, Kirk Bleu, writing in a chart next to Cameron, looks up and asks, "You talking to me, Camie?"

"Just talking out loud, Kirk," Cameron replies.

"Careful, Camie, your keys could be taken away from you for doing that."

"Yes, I suppose you're right, Kirk. Have you seen Ernie or Gus this morning?"

"Nope. Haven't seen many dayshift staff since I signed in. Where is everyone?"

"I'm about to find out," Cameron says, picking up the office phone and dialing the nursing office.

Emma Worman a registered nurse who typically is assigned to the women's wards answers. "Hello, this is Mrs. Worman. How may I help you?"

"Emma? Why are you working at the command post?" Cameron asks.

"Short staffed down here as well as on the wards, Cameron. Got pulled from my ward just a few minutes ago to work the phones. What can I do for you?"

"Can't seem to find several of my staff members over here in forensic. Where is everyone?"

"Same place as my staff, either sick or at a mandated training program. Who are you looking for?"

"Meckley and Allison."

"Let me check the call-off sheet. Meckley called off sick. So did Allison. That leaves you with Bleu and Banks. Except that Banks is at mandated fire and safety training until ten a.m. Don't know why Bleu isn't over there."

"Oh, he's here. And all ears," Cameron says, glancing at Kirk leaning in her direction. "Look, I need you to send me at least two staff members with security clearances to work over here."

"Well, that's a tall order, Cameron. With this summer pneumonia going around, finding available staff is like finding compliments from the front office. I'll transfer you to the security office here in Dix. They have clearances, and maybe they could help you out."

Cameron cradles the phone and peers out the Plexiglas window separating the office and the dayroom, where all the patients have been sequestered. Some of the patients are playing cards, some are slumbering in chairs, and some are restlessly circling the room. Off in a corner, staring out a window, Garner Overton is alone with his thoughts. Since his arrival a week ago, he has been cooperative. Cameron wonders how long this honeymoon period will last. She hopes long enough for all the psychological and psychiatric evaluations to be completed and for Overton to be delivered back to the Bush County jail before anything goes awry.

"Hello, this is Ron Peters. How can I help you?"

"Mr. Peters, this is Cameron Frankl over in forensic. This morning I am short of staff and need some assistance in escorting a patient to Dix Building for a dental appointment. Are you in a position to spare some of your security people to help me out?"

"You need more than one staff person?"

"For this patient, yes, I need more than one."

"Okay, I'll send over two men."

"Thank you very much. Have a good day." Cameron hangs up the phone. She decides she will personally meet the security staff when they arrive and instruct them on how to secure Overton for his dental appointment. She doesn't want any slip-ups.

"Sounds like you won't need to take Overton over yourself, Camie," Kirk says.

"I'd probably feel better if I did, Kirk. Would feel a lot better."

∾

The Trance

I'm pulling into the east parking lot when my cell phone rings. Stuffed in my attaché case, I fail to answer it in time, but as I walk toward Dix I retrieve the telephone message. A crisis on Men's Open Ward involving Lincoln. I hurry to the ward and spot a mob of staff members standing at the entrance to Lincoln's room. As I approach, the stench of excrement is everywhere.

"Did a commode back up?" I ask Emil Worman, one of the many nursing aides crowding the hallway.

"Right church, wrong pew, Rome," Emil quips, pointing toward Lincoln's room.

I part my way through gawking staff members and see that Lincoln is spread eagle, naked on the floor, staring wide-eyed at the ceiling. Covering him are blotches of smeared feces. Jake is kneeling next to him attempting to get Lincoln to talk. Jake doesn't appear to be making any headway, as Lincoln continues to stare at the ceiling and utter incoherent words.

I force my way in. "Anything I can do to help, Jake?"

"Do you speak Seneca?" he replies.

"What do you mean?"

"Lincoln's been mumbling in his native tongue, and I can't make heads or tails of what he's saying."

I draw closer to Lincoln, kneeling next to him. Concentrating on the sounds that he is muttering, I am no longer aware of the fetid smell. Instead, I notice how Lincoln's eyes are turned inward, with only the whites exposed, like fluttering oval egg shells. As Jake indicated, Lincoln is mumbling some Seneca words.

"Sigwah, ahsteh, sigwah nyagwaihe..."

"The last time this happened, we were able to use Johnny Snipe as an interpreter. Is he working today?" I ask.

"I think he's working Manchester," Emil says.

"Any chance we can get him to come over here?"

"Just hold on there, boss," Jake snaps. "We have called Dr. Chankra. He'll make the decision on what we need to do."

Jake and I stare at each other. Clearly, he believes the doctor should be in charge of the decision making. No room for independent intellectual problem solving for Jake. The medical model has been in practice for more than a century and will remain intact as long as he is concerned. So we wait for Chankra.

Emil asks Jake, "Think we should wash off some of this crap before the doc gets here? Or would that be tampering with the scent of the evidence?"

"We're not changing one thing until the doctor says so," Jake says, glaring at the grinning Emil.

Lincoln starts to groan and thrash about. Although most of the staff members are wearing disposable gloves, they are reluctant to grab hold of Lincoln's smeared arms and legs.

"Grab his legs!" Jake shouts.

The psychiatric aides pause, then comply.

"Shagowenotha," Lincoln cries out. "Shagowenotha."

"What's he blabbering?" Emil asks to no one in particular.

"Maybe Dr. Chankra will be able to tell us," I say, looking down the hallway. Chankra enters the ward, wearing one of his assorted turbans, this one being taupe.

"Grab his arm, Emil," Jake barks, as Lincoln flails wildly.

Chankra lumbers slowly down the corridor. Waddling his ample bulk, he repositions his turban, which complements his tan summer sport coat and flower-festooned pastel tie. The man, if nothing else, is a dapper dresser.

"Jerome...ah...Dr. Masonheimer, what is that god-awful stench?" Chankra asks, covering his nose with a handkerchief.

"I'm afraid, Dr. Chankra, that Lincoln has smeared himself with feces," I say, nodding toward Lincoln's prostrate body. "It appears he has entered into a disso-ciative trance state, like he did last year."

"Good god. Where's the nurse in charge?" Chankra asks, nervously looking about.

"I'm right here, Dr. Chankra," Jake says, twisting his head up in Chankra's direction.

"Give this man five milliliters of IM Haldol, then take him to the showers and hose him down," Chankra orders.

"Don't you want to check him out before we do that, Doctor?" Jake asks.

"What is to check out? As Dr. Masonheimer has indicated, the man is in the midst of a possession trance. Just wash him down with warm soapy water, which should relax him. After he is cleaned and medicated, bring him back to me."

Chankra grabs my arm and pulls me aside. In a low voice, he says, "Being an American Indian, Mr. Crowfoot shows the same proclivities for trance as do some native Latinos. Except in Puerto Rico, it was called *ataque de nervios*. Really just a brief psychotic spell, a short flight into madness. Nothing permanent or life threatening."

"I've read about that but never encountered it. Incidentally, because Lincoln is talking in his native tongue, would you have any objections if we called in the interpreter to help me talk with him, after he gets cleaned up?"

"Do whatever you want. Until he is on more medication, it won't matter what language you use."

"Point taken. I'll still give it a try," I say, moving out of the way as Jake and the aides struggle to get Lincoln to his feet and guide him down the hallway.

"You would never see an Asian abase himself in such a manner," Chankra says. He shakes his head in disapproval as Lincoln is pulled into the shower room. "Particularly not a Pakistani."

I guess Chankra doesn't consider the caste system to be an abasement of the human spirit.

∽

Open Wide

The corridor leading to the dental office in Dix Building is long and narrow. Lining both sides are offices where clerical staff busily work at their computers. Even though he is manacled to his wheelchair, Overton turns his head to capture a snapshot of each office as the two security staff members wheel him down the hallway to his dental appointment. With office doors either ajar or wide open, there are many easy opportunities for a designing person to have access to letter openers, staple guns, and scissors. None of the workers seem aware of security dangers. It is as cozy as being at home.

Reaching the dental office, the security staff members stop and begin releasing Overton from the wheelchair. Leaving his hands and ankles shackled, they assist him to his feet. Unsteadily, he shuffles into the waiting room, where he is greeted by the dental assistant, Reva Schantz.

At fifty-five, Reva is gray haired and stout with a serious professional demeanor. For the past thirty years, she has seen the worst of dental hygiene and patient behavior. She is not phased by Overton's history. In her mind, she has seen it all.

"How do you do, Mr. Overton? I am Mrs. Schantz, senior dental assistant to Dr. Riley, who should be with us momentarily," Reva says.

"Mrs. Schantz," Overton replies with a bit of a bow in her direction. "It is reassuring to see someone who exudes an air of professionalism." He's referring to her white starched uniform and courteous demeanor.

Reva offers the thinnest of smiles. "Please have a seat until the doctor arrives, Mr. Overton." She turns and enters the inner office, which contains the dental chair and its appliances.

The security staff members grab Overton's arms, and in unison all three men shuffle, turn, and sit on a wooden bench. Sandwiched between the other men, Overton surreptitiously scans the room, searching for any areas that might offer a means of advantage or escape. The only window in the office is by the dental chair. It appears to be free of bars or the typical galvanized wire screening, thus affording relatively easy egress. The countertop surrounding the dental chair is lined with various pointed dental instruments, again within easy reach. There is a door in the inner room, which probably leads to Dr. Riley's private office area.

As if on cue, the door opens, and Dr. Riley announces that he is ready. "Who's next, Mrs. Schantz?" Dr. Riley asks, rubbing his hands. He is a tall man, thin and balding, with sharp, angular features. His large hands extend unfashionably beyond the sleeves of his white frock.

"Mr. Garner Overton is our next patient, Dr. Riley," Reva replies.

"Well, bring him in, and let's get rolling. Overton? I once knew an Overton. I believe he was studying to be a priest. Any relation to...?" The doctor asks, falling quiet as Overton is escorted to the dental chair, his hands and feet bound. "Probably not, probably not," the dentist says.

"Actually, one of my cousins did enter the priesthood, Doc. Me, I never made it past being an altar boy," Overton says, smiling.

"You do say. Have a seat, Mr. Overton." Dr. Riley slips on a pair of protective gloves. "Open wide," he instructs.

Within short order, the exam is completed, and Dr. Riley announces that another appointment will be needed to fix some caries and to remove an impacted wisdom tooth.

"Set him up, Mrs. Schantz, on a day that doesn't conflict with my country club's golf tournament. Don't worry, Mr. Overton, we'll get to putter with your teeth within due time," Dr. Riley says, smiling.

"I don't have much choice, Doc, but to put the welfare of my teeth in your hands. I'm sure you'll be thinking about my not-so-pearly-whites when you're sitting in the clubhouse with all your cronies," Overton says.

"That, I will, my good man. That, I will," Dr. Riley replies, no longer smiling.

~

Brief Encounters

Gently closing the door behind me, I leave Cora Ruth's treatment team meeting pleased that they agreed to let me provide individual therapy to her. Now on to my next task—tracking down Daniel Killebrew and setting up individual therapy appointments with him as well.

Crossing from the women's ward to the men's is an easy walk. From the south side of the hospital to the north side, it's a short distance of sixty feet between ward doors. But before I can reach the men's ward, I encounter several patients waiting for the elevator to take them downstairs, probably to the snack shop to fix their cravings for fats and sweets.

One of the patients waiting for the elevator is Broderick Maveron, who considers himself a wizard of spells. Unfortunately for me, a few months ago I came upon one of his "spells" at a funeral ceremony, where I became disoriented and woozy. I don't want to encounter any more of his wizardry. I attempt to skirt his eyes by sidling behind him.

I get no more than a few feet before another patient notices me. "Hey there, buddy. Got any money today?" he asks, extending his palm in my direction.

I shake my head and keep walking. But Broderick spots me. Rubbing his hands vigorously, a devilish grin emerges on his narrow, pointed face. "Dr. Masonheimer, come over here; I want to show you something," he beckons.

I want to ignore him but don't. I approach him. "How are you, Broderick?"

"I want you to meet my new doctor," he says.

Broderick turns in the direction of the slight man standing next to him, who continues to stare at the elevator door. The man is attired in a crumpled, black, cheaply made suit that is at least one size too small for him. The sleeves fall way above his bony wrists and the pants are high-waters, exposing two different colored argyle socks. He is wearing a blue baseball cap with a Yankees emblem.

"This is Dr. Burda," Borderick says. For emphasis, he snaps his fingers at the man who remains transfixed on the door.

I don't recognize Dr. Burda, or his name. I had heard that several doctors were recently hired but I haven't met any of them, Dr. Yusuf being the exception, and only via the phone. Dr. Burda doesn't look like a doctor, not based on his appearance, yet I have met many doctors over the years who have dressed oddly or inappropriately. I also have met several patients who delusionally believed they were doctors and insisted they be addressed as such. So, who is this guy? Is Broderick playing me?

The elevator arrives, and everyone rushes in, including the mysterious Dr. Burda, whose eyes now appear riveted on the interior control panel. As the door closes, Broderick spews, "Watch my fingers, Doctor, watch my fingers. See the vortex of fire?" The doors close, and I stare at them far too long.

Get your head back where it belongs.

Merely another weird moment at Kinzua State to store away into memory. Shaking my head and moving on, I eventually reach the steel door of Men's Closed Ward. Opening it, I cautiously peer inside before entering. The ward appears empty. Most of the patients who have privileges are probably downstairs. As I walk down the hallway, I notice a staleness in the warm air, tinged with various body odors, common when slovenly men congregate in a closed setting. Except for Eliot and his infatuation with foreign aromas, most people would dread this place.

Passing the nursing station, I wave at Emil, who is alone, and make my way to the back wing to find Daniel. I find him sprawled out on his bed apparently asleep. This time I decide to wake him.

Placing a hand on his shoulder I gently shake him. "Daniel. Daniel. It's Jerome Masonheimer. I need to talk with you." I shake him harder.

He stirs, then turns his head in my direction; however, his eyes remain shut. "Jerome? Where have you been?" he says in a groggy voice.

"I did come by a few days ago, but you were zonked out, so I didn't bother you. This time I thought I would wake you. Can you get up?"

"No problem."

But he remains prostrate. Apparently, he is sedated, too much so. I'll mention this to Dr. Gobind. "I can give you a hand," I say.

"Looks like I could use one."

Daniel rolls over, swings a leg onto the floor and extends his hand. I give him a yank and find myself leaning over, losing balance and toppling on top of him. Daniel laughs heartily, and it becomes contagious. We both lie there laughing. Daniel throws his arms around me in a bear hug.

"Good to see you again, Jerome. You gained weight there, Captain," he says, squeezing my waist.

I become self-conscious of how this might look to any passerby and force myself out of Daniel's grasp. Erecting myself, I use both hands to help hoist him out of bed. "Speaking of gaining weight," I say.

"Yeah, I don't push any plates aside. And what with a McDonalds right down the street from the Personal Care Home, I just keeping packing it on. Talking about food, I think I slept right through snack time. Any chance we can get something to eat while we talk?" Daniel rubs his eyes and rakes his fingers through his black curly hair.

"Well, let's see what nursing has to say. You may want to tuck in and zip up before we head out." I point to his fly.

"Keep leaving that gate open for some reason. Wouldn't want to give nursing the impression we were back here doing something funny, would we?" he says, grinning.

"No, that we wouldn't. If you're ready, let's see what we can do about your appetite."

After tucking in his triple-extra-large Jimmy Hendrix shirt into his jeans and zipping up, Daniel lumbers unsteadily out of his room. We reach the nursing station, and I ask Emil about opening up the dinette area for Daniel and me.

"Sponging off the taxpayers again, Rome?" Emil chides.

"Nothing for me, Emil. Just Daniel," I reply.

"Yeah, right. I noticed you put on a few pounds, Rome. Probably helping yourself when I'm not looking."

I guess I have been eating better since Despina and I have gotten back together. I've got to say no to her baklava. I follow Emil and Daniel into the dinette area and grab a table while they scrounge up some carbs and juice. Daniel plops down several boxes of cereal, a milk carton, and two containers of orange juice. While he digs in, I ask some questions.

"So, Daniel, I don't really know why you came back here this time. What happened?"

Replying through a mouthful of Frosted Flakes, Daniel explains that he had been ditching his lithium and smoking weed again. Within a short time, he was becoming intrusive and getting into trouble. He tells me that he had gone to a local bank, and when they wouldn't cash a check that he had stolen from another resident at the home, he started yelling at the teller and accusing her of being prejudiced. The police were called, and Daniel was hauled off to jail. Of course he has a long history with the police, who treated him well and eventually put a call in to the mental health clinic. Subsequently, Daniel was transferred to the local hospital's psychiatric ward and eventually sent here.

"Now I'm back on my meds and then some," he says, wiping milk off his chin with his sleeve.

"I can see that. Have you mentioned to Dr. Gobind that you are pretty sedated?"

"Yeah, but she said I need to sleep it off."

"Well, Dr. Gobind wants you to meet with me one on one, and in order for that to happen you need to be awake. I think I'll talk to her."

"Sounds good, Captain. You think we can get Emil to come back here and make me some toast?"

"Daniel, lunch will be served in less than two hours. You think we can skip the toast?"

"Still hungry, man. But I guess I could go back to bed and sleep for a couple hours. When will you be coming again to see me?"

"I'll try to come back in a couple of days. Hopefully by that time, you'll be more alert."

When I get up to leave, Daniel stands and puts another bear hug on me. My back cracks, and I gasp for breath.

"Uncle," I say, patting him on his shoulder. Mercifully, he lets go, and I breathe deeply. "For a guy who doesn't exercise, you sure are strong," I say.

"Good thing I like you, huh?" he says with a big grin.

"I'll say. Look, I'll see you in a couple days. Okay? Take care, Daniel."

"See you, Captain." He plops back in his chair, and with a swipe of his finger, collects the remnants of cereal sticking to his bowl. Sucking his finger clean, Daniel seems satisfied.

Massaging my neck as I walk away, I decide to stop in to see how Lincoln is doing. It has been two days since his dissociative episode, and since then he has been confined to the ward. Hopefully he is alert and talking again. I was present when the nursing aide who knew some Seneca language attempted to speak with Lincoln. According to the aide, Lincoln was dwelling on monsters and spirits. Although he was talking incoherently both in English and his native tongue, Lincoln was able to understand words spoken to him by the aide. Lincoln seemed to take comfort when told that there were no monsters visible to any staff, and that staff members were staying in his room to protect him. We didn't add, to protect him from himself.

As I approach his room, I can see that his door is partly closed, so I knock. "Lincoln, may I come in?" When he doesn't respond, I push the door completely open and ask again. "Lincoln, may I come in?" I can see that he is sitting upright on his bed looking out the window.

He turns stiffly toward me and nods his head. His long black hair is pulled back in a ponytail, and he is cleanly shaven. His denim shirt looks recently pressed.

Entering, I notice a strong disinfectant smell permeating the room. Apparently, it had been scrubbed down just like he had. "I wanted to stop by and see how you are. Are you all right?"

Without looking at me, he responds, "My spirit has returned."

"I see. Well, that's good. Do you want to talk about what happened?"

Lincoln returns his gaze out the window before speaking. His words are drawn out, slow and reverent. "I couldn't ignore the cries of my people. Their voices were too loud. Their wails too heartbreaking. They called for my spirit to join them, and it left me. But they sent my spirit back. It wasn't pure enough to be with them. I have not fought honorably for my people, and my spirit has suffered. I need to restore honor to my spirit."

I want to ask him how he plans on restoring honor to his spirit, but instead I match his silence, waiting for one of us to say something appropriate or profound.

Rain begins noisily splattering the window, drawing our attention.

"The sky cries for my spirit," Lincoln says.

"So it seems."

The rain falls more steadily.

The Seeds Of Paranoia

Luther typically works the men's wards, but like other hospital aides he is occasionally assigned wherever there is a need. Today, it is on Women's Closed Ward. Since he relocated from Morgantown to Cornplanter County three years ago, Luther has only had to work on a female ward a half dozen times or so. And that is fine with him. He isn't comfortable around women, let alone women who are prone to hysteria and screaming. They aren't anything like his mother and grandmother. Those were strong women. Women who wore dresses and aprons and spent their time in the kitchen. They didn't rant or cry or throw fits. They cooked, cleaned, bore children, and made sure their husbands were satisfied. They read the Bible and didn't give a hoot about feminism and women's rights. His mother and grandmother cared about him and the other children and made sure the house was clean and respectable for visitors or other family affairs. All this commotion about women's careers and equality and sexual freedom is why family values have gone to hell. It is why the country has fallen apart. That and America's immigration laws.

Luther looks around and sees the evidence for America's deterioration right in front of him. These women patients. There are more blacks, Hispanics, and Asians than whites, it seems. And the white ones are either half undressed or acting like slather-asses. The doctors aren't much better. All foreigners. Few, if any, are Christians—that, Luther is pretty sure of. Where has this country gone? How did everything turn so badly? Luther longs for the days of Eisenhower and Kate Smith.

"Sir?"

Luther stops his pacing and looks down at a small Asian girl. She looks Vietnamese, except she is wearing jeans, no silk pajamas. Disgust and suspicion color Luther words. "What do you want?"

"Could you give me some soap powder so I could use the washing machine, please?"

Definitely Vietnamese. Same accent. Luther had heard their way of speaking from the army's educational classes that he had been given during his basic training. A sneaky way of talking. Pretending to be weak or helpless, all the while setting up a soldier to be booby-trapped. The whole country was a trap.

"I don't work this ward. You'll have to ask one of the nurses where they keep the laundry soap."

Leaving the girl with her mouth agape, Luther walks further down the narrow hallway, to an alcove where he can press his face against a window and not be bothered by shifty-eyed foreigners. The rain has stopped, but there is a gloomy cast over the land.

৵

Too Smart For Her Own Good

Elsa has never liked being told what she could or couldn't do, or how something had to be done. As a child she was precocious, strong willed, and difficult to manage. She had been repeatedly told by her father, "You're too smart for your own good, Elsa. One day you'll find that out." But except for one lapse of judgment—a brief high school infatuation with a lead singer in a punk band—Elsa had been smart enough to graduate magna cum laude from both high school and college, maintain a sizable balance in a savings account, avoid pregnancy, and stay focused on her goal of being a forensic psychologist. Despite this internship at Kinzua State, being a necessary step to apply to a doctoral forensic program, no one, including Dr. Masonheimer, was going to tell her how to behave.

That is why Elsa didn't tell Masonheimer that she was going to the Forensic Unit this morning. Undoubtedly, he wouldn't have approved. But why should he be concerned about the simple act of collecting information? Overton won't be anywhere near the chart room.

Standing at the Forensic Unit's exterior steel door, Elsa presses the intercom buzzer.

"Yes, how can I help you?" a male security staff member asks.

"This is Elsa Heinzelman, psychology intern. I'm here to peruse Mr. Overton's chart."

"Peruse his chart? Well, that sounds more important than just reading it. All right, Elsa Heinzelman, I'll buzz you in."

After being scanned at the sally port, and found to be "clean," Elsa moves through several locked doors to the chart room. There she locates Overton's chart and begins copying background information, to complete his psychological test evaluation.

She finds recent reports from the community that indicate that Overton graduated from high school with honors but never went to college. Instead, upon graduation he worked as a laborer for a masonry company, eventually becoming a bricklayer and stonemason. Never married. No military history. No hospitalizations other than the current one.

Family history indicates that both parents are deceased. One older brother, who is in prison for a bank robbery. His father also had been in prison, but no information as to why. Overton's criminal record consists of an imprisonment in 1981 for battery, kidnapping, and terroristic threats. There also was a previous charge of stalking in 1979, but no conviction. According to the records, Overton was released from prison in 2001 after serving his minimal sentence with good behavior. He then relocated in Lake Corner and found work as a construction laborer. Apparently, Overton stayed out of legal trouble until this year when he abducted a college woman and held her against her will.

Overton has no reported history of substance abuse, which Elsa finds unusual for a person with his antisocial history. So his judgment is impaired by something other than drugs.

She pages to the psychological history section of Overton's chart and finds several assessment reports. A Wechsler Adult Intelligence Scale (WAIS) indicates an IQ of 130. And a Minnesota Multiphasic Personality Inventory (MMPI) shows no psychotic indications and no depression. However, it does clearly indicate psychopathic deviancy and, remarkably, tendencies to appreciate art and aesthetics. Elsa surmises Overton to be of above average intelligence, socially deviant with little regard for the rights of others, and, strangely, somewhat artsy. A bright psychopath with an appreciation of beauty. An interesting combination of traits. She wonders what her professors would make of this clinical profile, and what would Masonheimer think?

She collects her notes, returns the chart to the rack, and proceeds to leave the unit. As she approaches the sally port, Elsa knocks on the station door to alert one of the staff that she's ready to leave. No one answers. She walks to the dayroom door, peers through its Plexiglas window and spies several security guards playing cards with some patients. She raps the window to attract their attention. One of the guards, Kirk Bleu, waves at Elsa and raises a finger indicating he'll be with her momentarily. As she waits, Elsa cautiously looks behind her, then returns her attention to the window pane. Abruptly, Overton's meaty, unshaven face fills the Plexiglas.

Startled, Elsa jerks back. Overton grins. He appears delighted with Elsa's reaction. He begins mouthing something, but his voice is muted by the pane. Elsa draws closer. She strains to hear what he his saying. it sounds like he's asking, "Would you have time to talk with me?"

She shakes her head and points to her watch.

Overton appears to be mouthing, "One minute, please." He holds up his index finger.

She cocks her head and points at her watch.

Suddenly, the sound of the door being unlocked surprises Elsa. She again quickly steps back. "Hey there, psychology intern, you trying to get in here?" Kirk asks, holding the door open.

"Well, I was hoping..."

"She was hoping that she could talk with me, Kirk. If that's okay with you, of course," Overton interjects.

"Yeah, sure, no problem. Come on in, little lady, unless you're afraid of all these bad men," Kirk adds.

"No, I'm not afraid," Elsa asserts. She steps into the dayroom, and the guard lets the door shut with a bang.

"So, Ms. Heinzelman, would you like to have a seat by my table?" Overton asks, pointing toward a small table in the corner of the dayroom.

Elsa hesitates, but then walks smartly to the table. Twenty sets of eyes follow her every step.

❦

Unpacking The Grief

After finishing some documentation, I phone Elsa's office. No answer. I make several phone calls to other ward areas in Dix Building, but no one has seen her. *I wonder where she could be.* Leaving the wards, I decide to head back to my office and tidy it up before Cora Ruth comes for her first individual therapy session.

Journals, articles, and sundry papers are piled high everywhere. So much information and hardly any time to organize it, let alone read it. I create a new stack behind my desk, hoping it doesn't teeter over. Hastily dusting off the small table located between two chairs in a corner of the room, I move a small ivy plant from the window shelf to the table. I straighten out the cheap Oriental rug that breaks up the terrazzo floor and cinch up my tie. Everything looks a bit neater.

I take a seat and reflect that I am making this effort to impress Cora Ruth. Why? Probably because she reminds me of my mother. Pre-countertransference. I wish Karl were around so I could hear his viewpoint. Clinicians like Karl can't be found anymore. The trend is towards neurocognitive therapies with little regard for therapeutic dynamics. Even face-to-face sessions are being slowly replaced with tele-computer meetings. Soon nanotechnology may even enable therapeutic robots to traverse our neurosynapses. Evolution and technology march onward.

A fragile knock on my door brings me around. I get up and open the door.

"Good morning, Dr. Masonheimer," Cora Ruth says, entering. She is wearing a faded calico dress, house slippers and no makeup. She looks washed out, devoid of any life. Although needing a cut, her gray hair is carefully combed and parted, a small effort to look presentable for her first therapy session.

"Good morning, and thank you for coming, Cora Ruth," I begin. I gesture for her to take a seat by the nook. "Before we start, I need to quickly go over some basic information." I sit down across from her. "First, I need you know that I am required to enter progress notes in your chart. However, I only need to provide information regarding your progress toward your treatment plan goals. Any other personal information that we talk about I can keep confidential. However, should you be in danger of hurting yourself or hurting someone else, I am obligated to not only document that, but also alert other staff as to your risk. Does that make sense to you?"

"I hope I would never ever think of hurting anyone," she answers, sounding aghast.

"Including yourself?

"Yes, including me."

"Okay, that's good to know. Well then, let's begin. Although I have read your chart, I need you to educate me about you—why you are here and what you are struggling with. Also, it would be helpful to know what you expect from our sessions together."

"I'm not accustomed to talking about myself, Doctor. I just wasn't brought up that way.

"So, it would be uncomfortable for you to talk about personal matters."

"Yes, it would."

"Would you be willing to try, though?"

"Maybe if we could talk about something else at first, I might get around to talking about other things."

"Okay, I can appreciate what you are saying. Well then, tell me something that you like to do."

"Well, I don't hardly like do anything anymore, except garden and work with plants."

"Working with plants is a healthy activity. Have you always been a gardener?"

"Ever since I was a child. I grew up on a small farm. Besides livestock, we always had a garden."

"When you say 'we,' who do you mean?"

"Well, my mother and father, my grandmother, and my brother and sister."

"Your grandmother was whose mother?"

"My father's."

"I see. Were you close to her?"

"Oh, yes, of course. Gram was a wonderful woman. Kindhearted but strong. She worked right up to the day she died."

"Did she work with you in the garden?"

"Oh, yes. She loved to garden. Except for my brother, we all loved it."

"What did you grow?"

"Why, just about everything that we would need to get through the year. Although we weren't poor, my father worked at a foundry during the day, we bought only what we couldn't grow ourselves. I guess it is in our blood to be self-sufficient. We are Swiss, you see. That is, my grandparents came from Switzerland. My parents were born in America."

"Did you learn a lot from your grandparents?"

"From my grandmother, I did. I never knew my grandfather. He died before I was born. Influenza, I was told. My grandmother taught me to pay attention to animals and to notice how plants grow. She said all we need to know about life can be learned by watching animals and growing our food. I remember her saying that the nature of life is pretty much like a garden." She pauses to stare out the window.

"What did she mean by that?" I ask.

Turning her gaze away from the window, Cora Ruth continues. "Well I think she meant that one can till and till to keep the weeds from taking over all the precious plants, but one can never lay down the hoe to rest, for weeds sprout quickly, as is their nature. To keep a tidy garden, one must work constantly, until a frost comes and winter sets in. Only then can a gardener finally rest."

"So, we need to work constantly to keep what we don't want from overwhelming us. That seems to parallel what I have discovered in working with people."

"In what way, Doctor?"

"Well, for many of us, unhealthy thoughts will crop up and begin to take root unless we stay vigilant and continuously challenge them."

"So you believe we are prone to unhealthy thoughts?"

"Some of us are. Whether it's because we experienced too many hurts and disappointments, or because we never developed a positive view of life. We can let the weeds smother out all the beautiful, affirming thoughts of life."

"Sounds like a lot of work."

"Pretty much like the work of a gardener."

"Hmmm," she replies, turning again toward the window.

Since her admission several weeks ago, Cora Ruth has changed very little. She remains mostly depressed and morose. Yet, she attends all her assignments, which now includes seeing me. Her personal hygiene remains good, and although her grooming is not commendable, it's respectable. Unknowingly, she is putting forth energy, even if it is on a low-kilowatt level. I give her time to form a thought by remaining quiet.

After her contemplation, Cora Ruth turns her attention back to me. "Are you married, Dr. Masonheimer?"

"Yes, I am."

"I wasn't sure, since you aren't wearing a wedding ring."

Glancing down at my left hand, I reply, "I had to take it off after I injured my finger chopping some firewood a while back, and never attempted to put it back on." That had been two years ago.

"Don't you think it would fit?"

"Well, the knuckle is still somewhat swollen," I point out.

"You could get it resized," she says, looking rather sharply at me.

"Yes, I guess I could. I notice you are still wearing your wedding ring."

She stares at her ring. Her thumb moves it slowly around her finger. "I still feel married," she says.

"How long were you married?"

"Fifty-four years. Hans—that was my husband—died two months ago. He was seventy-eight years old." Her attention returns to the world outside the window.

I wait several seconds before asking, "How did he die?"

Cora Ruth flashes a fleeting angry look. "The medical reason was COPD, but I believe it was because his heart was broken."

Her records have indicated that she is referring to the death of her sons. "Do you mean he never got over your boys?" I ask.

"Yes." She again peers outside. "We both never got over that they are gone."

"So, your heart is broken as well," I say.

"Yes, my heart remains broken." Cora Ruth seems to be watching the clouds slowly pass by.

I stay quiet, waiting, and studying her body language. Her breathing ranges from faint inhalation to heaves and sighs. Her hands are resting on her lap, balled and reddened. Anger appears to be coursing through her veins. Which may be a good thing.

If anger edges next to sadness, then sadness is not alone. Anger can move sadness out of the way long enough for one's libido to emerge. Anger can be your ally.

So, apparently Cora Ruth is angry about her sons' deaths. Their deaths undoubtedly devastated her. What mother wouldn't be? Yet there must be something about the way they died that has her so angry. That is what I need to discover. But not today. Today we have come far enough.

When Cora Ruth finally turns her attention back to me, she realizes time has passed. "I'm sorry, Doctor, what were we talking about?"

"Your husband and how he died."

"Yes, that's right. I guess in truth it was too many cigarettes, and of course his pipe. He loved his pipe."

I conjure an image of him smoking his pipe and its aromatic smoke wafting lazily in the air. "It must be hard to be without him."

"Yes, it is. Very hard. Harder than I ever imagined it would be."

"You said a lot today, Cora Ruth. If you would like to stop, that would be understandable."

"Yes, if it is all right with you, I would like to stop," she says, sighing.

"Certainly. Actually, you disclosed more than I expected. Thank you."

"I said more than I expected I would, too. It didn't seem that hard to do."

"Well, let's do it again on Thursday, same time. Are you going to be okay?"

"Yes, thank you. I will be fine."

"I'll walk back with you."

"Thank you, Doctor. That would be nice."

As we exit the office and amble slowly back to the elevators, I notice that Cora Ruth is walking more upright. Maybe some of her burden has been lifted.

"Jerome. Jerome, my man. Wait up," Amerika Rasheed, a patient, says loudly.

Both Cora Ruth and I stop and turn in Amerika's direction. I haven't seen Amerika in nearly two months, and she appears to have lost quite a bit of weight...still obese but much less so. Her short height and rotundness add to her overweight appearance, and her bibbed denim overalls do nothing for her figure. But with a broad smile and lively brown eyes, this forty-year-old African-American radiates happiness and good will.

"Hey there, Amerika," I say.

"Jerome, I need to tell you some good news," she says breathlessly.

"Oh, what's the good news?"

"Hort is coming for a visit." Hort, being her husband of only a few months. Amerika and Hort were wedded back in March in the hospital's chapel. The first marriage between resident patients since the hospital's inception 124 years ago. It was quite an event.

"That is good news, Amerika. Do you know when he will be coming?"

"He said he could catch a ride with the bus coming down here for the Summer Festival. That's in a few weeks, right?"

"Actually, it's scheduled for the third week in August. So, that would be four weeks away."

"I wish it were tomorrow."

"I bet you do." I become mindful that Cora Ruth is being ignored during this exchange. "Amerika, do you know Cora Ruth?" I tilt my head in her direction.

"Yeah, she's the plant lady. Got plants in your room, right?"

"Yes, I do have a few plants on the window shelf."

"That's what I hear. I don't know anybody else who has any in their rooms. Guess staff's afraid we're going to eat them," Amerika says laughing.

Now that Amerika has brought this up, I wonder why more patients don't have plants in their rooms. It might help raise spirits, and it would give them something to care for. "Well, we need to be getting back to the ward," I say.

"Okay, Jerome. See you when I see you," Amerika responds. "Bye there, Cora Ruth."

"Bye," Cora Ruth replies.

"Thanks for sharing the news about Hort, Amerika. Now we have something to look forward to," I say.

"He's my man," Amerika replies. She turns and sashays down the hall, her dreadlocks slapping against her shoulders.

"Nice lady," I say, nodding in Amerika's direction.

"Yes, she seems to be," Cora Ruth says. "I noticed she was wearing a leather ring and not a gold wedding band."

"Yes, that's right. Hort and Amerika couldn't afford gold rings, so Hort made their bands out of leather."

"That's different. I don't know anyone who ever did that."

"Well, Amerika and Hort are a different kind of couple. That's for sure," I say, deciding not to say anything more about how different Hort truly is.

෨

Entering The Spider's Web

Elsa has managed to elude Masonheimer for the past two days. Today, being Saturday, she planned to get away from the hospital and avoid answering any of his probing questions until Monday. However, before driving home for some rest and relaxation, Elsa types up the information she has found out about Overton.

In the first paragraph, Elsa lists Overton's criminal record and then cites his family's history of antisocial behaviors, suggesting a causative association. She follows this with Overton's educational and work data. Next, she lists his past psychological test findings. Lastly, Elsa adds a paragraph containing the information Overton personally disclosed to her in the Forensic Unit's day-room yesterday.

Elsa was both awed and thrilled that Overton revealed to her that he had been rejected by girls as well as bullied and intimidated by boys during his school years. He also divulged to her that when he had told his parents of his torment, his father had belittled him for being overly sensitive and not manly. Instead of receiving sympathy and support, Overton had been given a good thrashing. This taught him that he needed to become hard like his father and indifferent to the feelings of others. He learned from that point forth that taking advantage of others wasn't bad or wrong. It showed that one was taking care of one's needs.

To Elsa this information helped explain why Overton wasn't concerned about how his victims felt. It also verified her belief that he was probably still a sensitive man if only he were shown some kindness and empathy. That is why she agreed to help him during his next visit to the dentist, which apparently he was dreading because of his sensitivity to pain. All she needed to do was give him some support and understanding. Elsa was certain that any man given a modicum of thoughtfulness would respond in a civil manner. Remove a thorn, and even a lion would purr.

◦◦

Strange Occurrences

M onday comes too soon for most of the staff. Not only is it back to the grind, it also brings on a barrage of patient encounters. Patients generally are more demanding on Mondays since they have had few activities over the weekend and fewer opportunities to receive staff attention. And with more staff about, there is a greater chance of receiving treats and cigarette breaks.

I'm pretty sure that Daniel will be eager to see me, especially if there is a chance we will stop by the Snack Shack. I log off my computer and grab a few bucks out of my wallet before locking it in my desk drawer. But before I can reach the door, Woody slops his mop on my floor and begins a rant.

"Well, Rome, I guess you found out firsthand about the greenhouse, didn't you?

"Ah, yes, I guess I did, Woody."

"And did you find out how the spineless worms will respond to its closing?"

"If you are referring to Dr. Daltry et al., I don't think they're going to respond, Woody. I just think they're going to make preparations to close it."

"Craven midgets. Always caving in to the bean counters. No moral principles. No temerity. Let the patients suffer as long as pension plans aren't jeopardized. The budget is balanced on the backs of indigents and the afflicted, Rome. Plenty of money for staff trips to workshops and conventions to learn how to use the Internet, but is there any money for the patients? Of course there isn't. Capitol City keeps the roads and turnpikes paved and flowing for the affluent, while the downtrodden and homeless whimper and wheeze in infested encampments. Reprehensible. You can judge the moral rectitude of a society by how its misfortunate members are cared for, Rome. And from where I'm standing, our country is morally bankrupt."

I wonder if Woody and Luther could be related. "Well, what could be done about the greenhouse closing?" I ask.

"We could gather signatures, from the top on down. That's what we could do. And the public could be asked to sign a petition. So could our state representative and community leaders. A people's movement, Rome. People need to speak out and demand that we don't abandon our helpless brethren. That is what is needed from our timorous paper tigers in the front office."

For some reason, I'm struck by the righteousness of what he is saying. "Okay, Woody. If you want to start a petition, I'll join you."

Woody stares at me. He appears thunderstruck. "Are you serious, Rome?"

"Yeah, I'm serious, Woody. What you said makes sense to me, and I'm willing to support you."

"Well, bravo for you Rome. Bravo. I'll compose a document, and we can nail it to their polished doors." With that, he gathers his mop and cart and proceeds down the hallway. My floor is a wet soapy mess, but at least Woody is rejuvenated and I can finally get to see Daniel.

When I reach the ward, I am immediately surrounded by several patients seeking favors. "Hey, Grandpa. Have any small change to spare today, Grandpa?"

"You a doctor there, buddy? Can you get me some privileges?"

"Hell, that's Dr. Masonheimer, boys. He's almost a doctor, ain't you, Masonheimer? What's that Ph.D. stand for Masonheimer...post-hole-digger? He's got more than change jiggling in his pockets, boys. I hear he carries a wad bigger than Chankra's. Let's empty his pockets and see for ourselves."

"Okay, gentlemen. Enough is enough," I say swatting away pestering hands. I manage to twirl away from this gaggle of panhandlers, only to have them follow me step for step. Luckily, they mean no real harm and are merely nuisances. As I enter the nursing station, Emil sees my dilemma.

"See you brought your fan club, Rome. Can I have your autograph?" He quips.

"You have anything we can give them to stop their pestering?" I plead.

"Only a threat, Rome. Fellas, if you don't let the poor psychologist alone, no cigarette break for you guys," Emil informs the men.

With that, the men move away, grumbling as they go.

"Ah, the power of the spoken word," I say.

"The power of nicotine," he retorts. "So, what are you doing up here, Rome, besides attracting a crowd?"

"I'm going to take Daniel down to my office."

"The Killer? You better take your vitamins. Gobind lowered his medications, and he's back to his old self."

"A bit hyper?"

"A lot manicky."

"Oh, boy. Well, at least that's the guy I'm familiar with instead of Mr. Hibernation," I say, backing out of the station. I begin heading to the back ward, but stop in my tracks when I hear what sounds like a galloping herd of bison approaching me. As the pounding footsteps grow louder, I move closer to the wall. Turning the corner and barreling toward me are Daniel and Delbert in an apparent foot race. I flatten myself and hope I'm not hit as they tear by.

"Hey, knock that off, you two," Emil yells.

Abruptly, Daniel and Del stop running. Gasping for breath, they pat each other on their shoulders and laugh heartily. After a moment, Daniel turns and spies me. Extending his arms, he hurriedly draws near. "Jerome, my captain. Come here, fella." He hooks his hands under my armpits, lifts me up, and we twirl around like a carousel. We spin, nearly careening into the wall.

"Daniel, that's enough! Stop! Put me down," I blurt out. Daniel's head is tilted back, and he seems to be growing more ecstatic with each turn.

"Put him down, Killer. Now!" Jake shouts. He steps out of one of the treatment rooms carrying a tray of instruments. "Now!"

Daniel slows his spin, and my feet catch the floor, which dizzily moves under me.

"What do you think you're doing, Masonheimer? Do you think this an arcade room?" Jake asks, clearly annoyed.

"Of course not," I say, struggling to fix my eyes on him. "I didn't expect that Daniel would pick me up." Although this isn't the first time that he's done this.

"Ain't his fault, Jake. It was my doing. Just having a little fun, that's all," Daniel says.

"This is a hospital, not an amusement park. We're not here to have fun. Your psychologist should know that."

"Like I said, Jake, it was my bad, not his," Daniel says, looking more contrite.

"We'll get out of your hair, Jake. I'm taking Daniel down to my office for our therapy session," I say.

"You got an order to do that?"

"Signed by Gobind, in his chart." I nod toward the chart rack.

"I'll check," Jake says. Apparently surprised and somewhat disappointed to have found the signed order, he reminds me to have Daniel back in time for his mid-morning medications.

Relieved to leave the ward, Daniel and I take the stairs down to the Snack Shack. Along the way, Daniel chatters away about various topics that are loosely associated. I realize now that he is back to being manic. Sitting and talking in a therapeutic manner will be just as difficult as when he was sluggish and groggy. If only there were a happy medium.

At the Snack Shack, Daniel orders a taco salad with extra blue cheese dressing, and a large Coke. I get a small cup of black coffee. Instead of finding a table, I decide that we should eat and talk in my office where we will have privacy, and where Daniel's booming voice will be hidden from curious ears. At my office, I settle in my usual chair while Daniel sits at my desk and digs in.

"So, Daniel, tell me what you could have done differently to stay out of Kinzua State."

Speaking through a mouthful of salad dripping with dressing, Daniel says, "Could have stayed away from the weed, I guess."

"So, you were smoking quite a bit."

"Yeah. No. Well, maybe. Depends what you think is a lot," he says wiping his mouth on his bare forearm. "I guess I was doing three or four blunts a day. Not too many for me. Maybe too many for you, Captain, but not for me. But then again, here I am. Ain't I?"

"Yeah, here you are," I say, tossing him a small package of Kleenex to use as napkins.

"Maybe if I had a girlfriend to keep an eye on me like your wife does for you, I might have smoked less. You still have your wife, don't you?" He points to the photo of Despina on my desk.

I nod affirmatively.

"You're lucky, Captain. With a wife like yours, I would be salivating every night waiting for her to come home...or in your case heading home to her. Any which way, she's a looker, Captain." He takes another forkful before continuing. "A woman is a good thing, Jerome. Except when you're on the woman-wheel, then they can be an addiction, just like weed. And that's the key... to manage your addictions...your poisons. Too many poisons and your mind gets screwed up. You're probably are one of those people who likes how their minds works, aren't you?"

I nod affirmatively and point to my chin, trying to alert Daniel that blue cheese is covering his chin.

He swipes the dressing with his palm and licks it clean. "I heard that God's mind is vast and deep, somewhere a guy could get lost and never find his way out, kind of like my mind. You know, Captain, a person really can't lose their mind; believe me, I've tried. My mind is driving me crazy. I would like to lose it for a while. But you probably know more than I do about what makes a mind worth having." He stops to wash his food down with his Coke.

"Actually, modern psychology doesn't talk much, if at all, about the mind, Daniel. A lot safer to talk about neurons and synapses."

"Well, I think that's stupid. You guys are out of your heads if you think that a person's mind isn't important. Look around this place. Don't you think people are having troubles with their minds? But then again, what do I know? I didn't even graduate from high school."

"Can we get back to why you were hospitalized?" I ask, hoping to reign in his rambling thoughts. "Besides smoking too much dope, was there anything else you did?"

"Stopped taking my medications, I guess. Some days I take them, others I wouldn't. Got tired of going for blood work. My arm began to look like I was a heroin addict."

He extends his arm in my direction for me to inspect. I can't really see much, but his skin is very dark, and I'm pretty far away. "People think it's easy taking medication. Just pop them in and wash them down. They don't know that you got to sign up for them, take them home in a huge freezer bag, count them out, remember to take them morning, noon, and night. And then there are the side effects. Dry mouth, constipation, dizziness, no energy. Then there's those warnings: Don't use any alcohol, make sure you drink liquids, but not too much, don't use with other medications. Who can keep up with all that?"

As he scrapes the sides of the nearly empty Styrofoam bowl, I offer a reflection. "So, you got tired of it all after a while."

"You got it, Captain. But the magic dragon helps me out. And like I said, I don't use it much anymore...just a little to get through the day. I'm not using it because I'm a hippie or lazy or a head-banger. Just trying to have some simple pleasure. Actually, I consider myself to be Zen-Amish you know...just a simple guy living a simple life," Daniel says, grinning widely.

"Zen-Amish, huh? Never heard anyone describe himself that way before. No bling for you then?" I chide.

"No bling or grills for me, Captain. Too expensive. Plus, you attract the wrong brothers wearing that stuff. I'd rather just float around trying to follow my mind wherever it leads me. And right now, it has led me back here." Daniel stretches out his arms in a gesture of embracing the room.

"Home sweet home," I say.

"A poor man's Florida," Daniel replies, smiling.

"Not bad for the winter months, but it's July," I point out.

"Yeah, I know. My timing has always sucked."

After finishing off his Coke, Daniel asks if we can to go outside for some fresh air. So I grab my bucket-cap to shield my pate, and we exit the building. As we walk, Daniel spots several male patients he knows and asks permission to go over to the picnic table where they are sitting. He hits up one of the men for a hardy pinch of snuff, and with his lower lip bulging like an inner tube, starts freely associating as we resume walking.

"You know, Captain, ever since Dr. Gobind lowered my medications, I can dream again. Had a dream last night about flying alongside a jet plane. People were looking out their windows at me and waving. I couldn't wave back 'cause I needed to keep my arms stretched out or else I would have crashed. What do you think about that? You think it means anything important?" he asks.

Before I can reply, Daniel spits out some juice and continues talking.

"I think it means that I can do more than I think I can...up to a point, I mean. Of course, dreams are really just visitations from angels. You know, white angels and black angels. A dream that makes you feel good is when a white angel visits you. A nightmare is when a black angel touches you with one of her black wings. Even though I'm black, I don't like those black angels. They're no good. Messengers from the devil is what I believe. You believe in the devil, Captain?"

This time I don't attempt to answer, and wisely so, because Daniel continues with his flight of ideas, ranging from the devil's ability to assume human form to the reason why falling snow doesn't make any noise. I fade out of his stream of consciousness only to be startled by someone yelling "Blacky! Blacky!"

About fifty feet ahead, Wilma Sours is running toward us, looking up in the sky calling out "Blacky." This is very odd given that I never heard Wilma Sours ever speak, nor have I ever seen her off the ward. Both Daniel and I look up to where Wilma is directing her shouts, and we see a large crow slowly flying above. Further above it is a contrail from a jet streaking across the blue sky, and the crow seems to fly parallel to it. Wilma stops in front of us and points to the bird and says, "That's Blacky."

"Blacky, huh?" Daniel utters. "For a second there, I thought it was me."

Wilma stares at Daniel in bewilderment. I wonder if the passengers can see us, and if they are waving.

◌୭

An Unexpected Choice

After returning both Wilma and Daniel to their respective wards, I head down to Elsa's office, which is at the far end of the hallway where my room is located. Approaching the dental office, I see Reva Schantz unlocking the door.

"Morning, Reva."

"Jerome, morning to you as well." She turns to face me. Her starched white uniform seems to lift her off the ground. "You know, Jerome, your intern is such a sweet young woman."

"Oh? How so?"

"Well, on Friday afternoon, she came by and offered to help me with any patients who might be afraid of having dental work. She said that she knew of some technique—EDR or something—that she said would help patients relax and not be so scared. I thought that was very nice of her to offer. What's her name again?"

"Elsa. Elsa Heinzelman."

"Elsa. What a lovely name. What a lovely young woman. To be so concerned about patients at such a young age."

"Yes, she goes out of her way, quite often. I'm heading down to her office. I'll tell her that we spoke."

"Please do."

Taking my leave, I start wondering. *EDR? Elsa probably said EMDR, and why would she even offer to use that approach? Then again why would she even offer any services before checking with me? Lovely, indeed.*

I knock on Elsa's door, but apparently she isn't in. On a scrap of paper, I write that I want her to call me via my pager, ASAP. I slide it under the door and head to my office.

After throwing my keys on my desk, I pick up the phone and check my voicemail. The first message is from Elsa.

"Dr. Masonheimer, it's Elsa. It's nine a.m. on Monday, and I need you to know that I'm going to be late. I had a flat tire on my way to the hospital and am getting it fixed. I hope to be on the road in another hour or so. I should arrive at the hospital by noon. I'll let you know when I do. Thanks. Bye."

I'm surprised that she even bothered to call. Perhaps I have been overreacting and too critical. Definitely one of the traits I inherited from my father, being overly critical. I'm always combating his traits, not wanting to accept them as my own.

There is a second voice mail. It is from Ophelia. Another surprise.

"Jerome, this is Opie. I need to talk with you."

Ophelia has never called me before. There must be something pressing for her to call. I decide to head up to her room.

Arriving on the women's ward, I walk into an ongoing quarrel between two patients, Hazel Fenster and May Tavormino. I stand away from the fracas, which now includes Paige and another nursing aide. From what I can discern, the conflict is over a jar of hair remover.

Apparently, May is accusing Hazel of going into May's room and stealing her jar of Nair. Hazel is denying the charges, but there are telltale signs she may be lying. Hazel, being sixty or so, and in that stage of life where facial hair can become noticeable (and in her case quite evident on her chin and upper lip), has a swatch of her moustache partially devoid of hair, apparently as a result of Hazel being interrupted by May during the act of spreading on the creamy white goo. Hazel is claiming that her mother sent her the depilatory, which isn't believable given that her mother is deceased. Paige is attempting to resolve the conflict by confiscating the cream and returning it to May, but Hazel is having none of it.

"Hazel, give me the jar," Paige says. "Please, Hazel, give me the jar."

"No. It's my cream, and I'm keeping it," Hazel responds.

"Liar. You know it's not yours. You're a liar and a thief," May states. May grabs Hazel by the arm and starts yanking her out of her bedroom in order to get to the sought-after jar.

"Let her go," Paige says, grabbing hold of May's free hand. May is short and pudgy, but younger, and is showing her strength by wrestling free of Paige's grip and pulling hard on Hazel.

I lend a hand by grabbing and twisting the back of May's collar, pulling her out of the room. May starts to stumble but maintains her grip on Hazel. I'm now in danger of falling to the floor with May and Hazel on top of me. To prevent a potential pile up, I let go of May and brace her back with my shoulder. Stabilized, May starts kicking Paige. She responds by grabbing both of May's arms and swinging her around. This breaks May's grip on Hazel but positions May in front of me. She kicks me hard in the shin.

"Ow!" I shout out in pain, jumping about on one foot.

Now amused, May starts laughing. Paige yanks May farther away from Hazel's room while the other aide grabs May's arm for added security. Meanwhile, Hazel has retreated into her bedroom and is quickly slathering on a coat of Nair all over her face.

Emma and a nursing aide are briskly coming up the hallway. "Now, what is this all about?" Emma asks.

But before anyone replies, Emma spies Hazel and exclaims, "Hazel, stop that. Stop that right now."

With her face completely layered in cream, Hazel relinquishes the hair remover to Emma. Realizing the danger of what Hazel has done, Emma quickly whisks Hazel down to the bathroom to remove the white mask. Emma shouts out orders along the way.

"Paige, let May go, and put a call in for Doctor Rabenold to come up here, ASAP."

I rub my sore shin and stay off to the side.

Paige carefully lets go of May, who turns and positions herself ready to deliver another kick. The aides back up out of the way.

"We're not done with you, May. Merely taking a break. We'll be back," Paige says.

As the aides hustle toward the nursing station, May goes to her room, offering an apology as she passes by me.

"Sorry about your leg. I always was good at kicking. Next time don't stand in front of me when I'm mad."

"Advice well taken," I say.

I lift my pant leg and lower my sock to inspect the damage. Luckily, I see no blood or broken skin, just redness and tenderness. I decide not to file an injury report. I know from past experience that there is a good chance someone from the safety office will conclude that my injury was the result of an unsafe act on my part. That would add insult to injury. Instead, I painfully resume my trek toward Ophelia's room.

It is nearly noon, and soon patients will be escorted to the dining room, eagerly filling the hallway. I hope I don't get caught up in that crowd. Reaching Ophelia's room, I find her lying on her bed seemingly asleep on top of her covers. I knock on the door's casing.

Ophelia's eyes open. "Come in, Jerome. I'm not asleep," she says, swinging her feet onto the floor. She is casually dressed in jeans and a black tank top, which reveals a series of old scars on her inner forearms. None are red, which indicates she hasn't been recently cutting herself...at least not there.

I step inside and move some clothing off the lone chair before sitting. "I got your phone call," I say.

"I didn't think I would actually call you, but I did." Ophelia runs her fingers through her short, uncombed hair, ruffling it about with no purpose. "I...I haven't told anyone about my past, but I think the time has come that I should. I trust you, Jerome. But I'm not sure if I can talk with you. You being a man that is."

She lets her hand drop to her lap and looks intently into my eyes. Her boyish features strain and harden.

"I can see why that might be difficult for you. What about one of our female psychologists?"

"The ones I know, I don't like."

"What about Paula Cotton? Do you know her?"

"I've seen her, but I don't know her."

"Well, she is a good person, Opie. Someone I trust, and maybe you could as well."

"Maybe. I still haven't ruled out talking with you. I've been around you. You listen and seem to pick up what others are feeling. That is important to me. It's just that...most of my problems are because of men." Ophelia casts her eyes downward, compressing her body into a tight mass.

"That could make it hard for you to open up," I say. "I am here for you, Opie, if you decide you want to work with me. But maybe you should first meet with Paula and see if she and you connect."

"Okay, I can do that. Would you set that up?"

"Sure. Whoever you decide is the best person for you, we will need to run it by your treatment team and get their permission."

"I see."

"Lunch time!" Paige shouts down the hallway. Almost instantly the creaking of box springs and the scurrying of feet fill the air.

"Well, I better let you get to lunch," I say, standing.

"Thanks for coming, Jerome."

"Glad to, Opie."

She extends her hand in my direction. I reach out, and we shake. It's the second time in a week that I have held her hand. A visible sign of progress. I nod as I release my grip and move into the corridor where women are scampering by on their way to the dining room. I shoulder the wall, keeping out of the way of their hunger.

∾

Hearing Is Not Listening

Eating lunch in one's office is frowned upon by the administration. I assume it's because of sanitation reasons. One of those rules that I never questioned. There are too many of them—rules and administrators, that is. Generally, I eat on the run, but today I plan to eat a generous slice of leftover spanakopita at my desk while I read some snail mail. I lock the door to ensure no one interrupts me, particularly Woody.

I have polished off half the spinach pie and read several letters when someone knocks on my door. I decide to ignore whoever it is and continue with my repast. A sheet of paper slides under the door. Curious, I get up and read the note. It's from Elsa.

I open my door in time to see Elsa entering her office. Wiping my mouth with a Kleenex, I run my tongue over my teeth to ensure no spinach is protruding, swish a swig of water, and proceed to her office. I knock on her door.

"Come in," Elsa says.

I enter and see the phone receiver cradled against her ear. She waves me forward. "Dr. Masonheimer, I just slipped a note under your door."

"I know. I just read it." A scent of lavender lingers in the air.

"Oh, I thought you weren't in." She hangs up the phone.

"I was. Just occupied at the time you knocked. So, I assume your tire is fixed?"

"Yes. What an inconvenience. Sorry about being late. I didn't miss any therapy appointments. I only missed a treatment team meeting and an infection control training class."

Elsa smiles nervously. She appears genuinely remorseful about being late.

"Well, then it sounds like you didn't miss much. So, I haven't seen you since...let's see, I think Wednesday. What did you do Thursday and Friday?" I ask.

Elsa moves from behind her desk and sits in a chair facing me. She is attired per usual in a sleek black suit, her hair pulled back in a tight bun.

"Please, have a seat, Dr. Masonheimer." She gestures to a chair across from her. I close her door and sit.

Sitting erectly, with her hands folded on her lap, Elsa maintains steady eye contact.

"As I recall on Thursday I taught two classes at the stimulation track, conducted three individual therapy sessions, and did corresponding documentation. On Friday, I taught another class, did chart work, and walked the grounds with several patients. That was pretty much the extent of it. Oh yes, I also went to the library to do some research."

"Oh? What were you researching?"

"Sadism and its relationship to childhood abuse."

"Let me guess. Overton?"

"Yes. That's okay, isn't it? That I did some research on his behaviors?" She remains very much composed with nary a muscle twitch.

"If you completed all your assignments as expected, you can freely use your time to do research at the library...whether it is on sadism or anything else you find interesting."

"Don't you find his sadistic behaviors to be interesting?"

"I admit that I do. There are many characteristics and behaviors of his that are fascinating. And as long as we are fulfilling what we are expected to do with Overton, then we can set aside time to study other features about him."

"And specifically what are we expected to accomplish?"

"What I am expected to accomplish with the help of others—this includes Dr. LaFleur and yourself—is to administer and complete psychological assessment procedures, then submit a report."

"So, you don't think learning more about his sadistic behaviors will help you with the psychological evaluation?"

"It would be supplemental, not essential, to the test data. But let's be more specific about what we are talking about, Elsa. Although I find Overton's particular brand of sadism to be intriguing and baffling, and can only imagine it is for you as well, I want us—you and me—to follow protocol when dealing with him. I don't want us to become so captivated by his pathology that we place ourselves in a compromising or unsafe position."

"Going to the library and doing research is unsafe?"

"No. You know perfectly well that doing research isn't unsafe. It's becoming absorbed in Overton's pathology that isn't safe. We need to ensure that he doesn't get into our heads, that we don't lose our ability to detach ourselves from him."

"Why do you always imply that I don't know what I am doing?"

"What I'm implying is that you have a strong independent streak, Elsa. And as a result, you push the envelope on boundaries that hold back your autonomy. Not to mention that someone telling you what to do activates a defiant part of you. Not being in the lead doesn't mean you aren't smart, Elsa. It merely means that sometimes you need to be a follower. And in your role as an intern, you need to accept that position, at least for now."

Elsa's jaw muscles flex and strain. She appears to be biting her tongue...holding back an urge to let fly what she is feeling. Instead she remains mute.

Awkward seconds seem to stretch into minutes. I break the tension.

"We have our supervision tomorrow afternoon at four. We could talk more about this matter then, along with how we will be wrapping up our assessment of Overton." I rise to leave. "You may want to review Millon and Klerman's thoughts on sadistic personality. I believe they subsumed it under an aggressive personality style. I'm pretty sure our library has their book *Contemporary Directions in Psychopathology*," I say turning to leave.

Elsa remains seated, appearing unmoved. Grudgingly she says, "Thank you for that suggestion."

"You're welcome. See you tomorrow at four."

Going Beyond Complaining

Still reflecting on the brief meeting with Elsa, I don't immediately notice that Woody is waiting at my door. He is without his ubiquitous cleaning cart and is dressed differently. Instead of jeans and a rumpled T-shirt, Woody has on a clean pair of chinos and a dress shirt. He's freshly shaved and has had his hair trimmed. I'm impressed.

"Hey, Woody. What's up?"

"Got our petition," he says, holding up a manila folder.

"Okay, good. Let's go into my office and have a look at it."

"It took me a while, but I got it finished. I think it's written rather well, but see what you think." He hands me the folder.

I start reading it as I walk toward my desk. While still reading, I draw out my chair and sit.

"Well, what do you think?" Woody asks impatiently.

"Other than it reading like a legal brief and every other word being impossible to decipher, I would say it has promise."

"What do you mean?" Woody looks crestfallen.

"What I mean is that it is written in a very complex manner. I don't think it will be easy for a layperson to understand it. And the signatures of regular people are what are needed to make this document work," I say. "For example, this line '...forthwith, ersatz representatives of the citizenry cannot and shall not promulgate an incursion into the inherent rights and privileges of the afflicted members of society...' etcetera, etcetera. Who will understand that?"

"I will."

"That's because you wrote it, and that is how you think. Most people don't think or talk that way, Woody. Most people want matters to be said simply."

"Simplicity is complex, Rome."

"I agree that it can be difficult to say something simply. But that is what you need to do if you want this petition to succeed. If you would like, you could leave it with me, and I'll make the necessary revisions so that it is easier to understand."

"All right, Rome. If you don't mind?"

"I don't mind. Give me a few days, and I should have something to show you."

"Ok, Rome. Thanks." Woody, still looking dejected, turns and walks down the hallway.

"Woody," I call. "Thanks for taking the time to put forth the effort to get this petition started. Our patients need advocates like you. Our society needs you as well."

"Thanks, Rome. I appreciate that." Smiling, his spirits are buoyed once again.

I watch him move along before returning my attention back to my unfinished lunch and ever-present inbox. From the looks of it, I'll be here until quitting time.

༄

Speaking From The Heart

Tuesday morning and I'm already running behind schedule. Too many demands and too little time. I jog to the group room and find everyone standing around, waiting for me to let them in.

"Sorry for being late," I say. "I got sidetracked with someone, and couldn't comfortably break away."

"You should be sorry," Harvey says. "I've been waiting for you to show up so I can read my poem."

"Shut up, Harvey. You were holding up the wall, sleeping before Jerome even got here. So don't act like the idiot that you are," Ophelia says.

Apparently, Ophelia is feeling like she needs to defend me. Which is different than where we were less than a week ago when she was peppering me with snarky remarks.

"Opie, would you be willing to let Harvey start with his poem?"

"Whatever."

"Thank you." I turn to him. "Harvey, do you want to read now?"

Abruptly standing, Harvey shuffles through some scraps of paper and starts reading.

"Excuse me, Harvey," I interrupt. Let me put you on the timer. Harvey stares at the egg timer as I place it on the table next to where he is standing. His long uncombed dark hair flops over his face.

"Five minutes?" Harvey asks.

"Five seconds," Kendra blurts.

"One minute," Ophelia says.

"How about three minutes, Harvey?" I ask, precipitating a group groan.

Harvey approvingly nods and clears his throat. "Get ready, get set, here I go. The devil's tongue lashes and latches onto my gametes that were stolen before I was born..."

And off we go. I try to listen to the string of nonsensical words that reflect Harvey's loosely associated thoughts, but I can't maintain a coherent focus. It's like trying to avoid the ruts and holes on a muddy country road. Logical thinking is jarred and upended, while images are strewn, scrambled, and recombined into grotesque shapes. Even the flow and cadence of his words are unsettling. Unquestionably, Harvey's verbal ramblings are genuine manifestations of a psychotic process. Beyond his will. Beyond all of us.

When the timer finally sounds off, everyone but Harvey appears stupefied. His face radiates a relief as if he were unburdened from a prolonged constipation.

"Well, what can be said about Harvey's recitation?" I ask.

"Thank Buddha it's over," Kendra replies.

"Amen to that," Ophelia adds.

Lincoln's strong voice speaks next. "I have traveled in a night dream very similar to Harvey's poem."

We all look at Lincoln for some clarification. Sensing our collective need, he continues.

"I have ridden with wild horses being chased by a black wind blown from the mouth of a lake monster. It was strong and overwhelming. I was tossed and thrown about, held aloft by an eagle clasping my hair. Only by being dropped in a virgin forest was I safe."

I stare at Lincoln wondering if he really has recovered from his regression last week. He appears stable, but that may be an illusion. Lincoln remains composed and quiet. He seems satisfied with his explanation with no concern to say anything more.

Hoping I can bring the group back to our classroom reality, I say, "It sounds like you know how troubled a mind can be, Lincoln."

Except for one brief eye blink, he remains impassive.

I take the ensuing silence as an opportunity to change our focus. "So, does anyone have a poem to share?"

No one immediately speaks. The group's silence seems to allow Harvey's and Lincoln's bizarre disclosures to fade from awareness.

Silence can be an incubator. Be patient and observe. Something will emerge, Karl would say.

To my surprise, it is again Lincoln who speaks up. "I have something more to say about monsters."

"And what would that be?" I ask apprehensively.

Lincoln stands tall and reaches into his denim coat pocket to retrieve a small notebook. Slipping on his reading glasses he says, "This is called 'Thorns at Dusk.'"

Where goldenrods turn a hairy fawn
Rutting bucks can readily hide
Until they are roused, testing
One's fearless nerve

During clear bright days
Red berries gleam, easily seen
At dusk, their thorns fade from view
Pricking and drawing blood

A fire of locust wood
Keeps the dark edge
From swallowing
The breath of Life

As cautious eyes close
Sleep darkens one's mind
While monsters roam about
Leaving warning tracks for the morning

Another walking day
To follow the signs left behind
Worn spirit paths
Meandering, searching for justice.

Again, the group seems dumbfounded while Lincoln appears satisfied.

I am about to speak up when Autumn scoots her chair in Lincoln's direction and gently asks, "Are you saying that you can never be at peace, Lincoln?"

"Not in the world of the white man."

"Not even in this group?"

"This group is not of nature. This building is not of nature. The medicines I take are not of nature."

"What about me? Am I not of nature?"

"Your spirit is of nature. Your thoughts are not."

Autumn looks intently at Lincoln. "When I think of you, I feel close to you. Is that not of nature?"

Turning toward Autumn, Lincoln ponders her features and presence. I wonder if he sees something more than I can perceive in her pale face and vulnerable, woebegone expression. Autumn looks so fragile and weightless, as if she could be easily swept away by an insensitive comment. I give her credit for speaking her truth and putting herself—actually all of us—in this awkward position.

Everyone, except Harvey, who is scribbling on his slips of paper, is looking at Lincoln and Autumn. As long as the group remains quiet, I wait and say nothing to break the tension.

God, I love these moments, even if they are excruciating.

"Speaking from your heart is of nature," Lincoln finally says, continuing to lock his eyes on Autumn.

A relief seems to flow through Autumn. Her eyes brighten. "I'm glad you see what I feel as being natural."

"You're not going to kiss him, are you?" Harvey blurts, still scribbling away.

"Shut up, Harvey!" Ophelia says, throwing a wad of paper at his head.

Kendra laughs. And although smiling, I say, "No throwing anything at anyone, remember? One of the rules of the group."

"He deserved it," Ophelia says.

"People are not for hitting."

"That's a good one."

"Can we get back to the moment we just let slip away?" I ask. "It feels to me that we might have some closure between Lincoln and Autumn, but I want to check it out. How are the two of you doing?"

Autumn's head is lowered, but I can see that she is smiling and flush. Lincoln is sitting stoically erect as usual, but he is blinking and seemingly thinking about what just happened.

"Is there anything more that needs to be said?" I ask.

Autumn raises and gently shakes her head. Lincoln turns in my direction, and with a solemn expression, shakes his head as well.

"Anyone else?" I look around the room. No one speaks up. "All right, then. We still have fifteen minutes left. Does anyone else have a poem to share?"

"I can read one," Cora Ruth says. Abruptly, she stands righting a wobble before slipping on her taped-up reading glasses. She clears her throat. "I call this ditty, 'Mammie Groller.'"

Mammie Groller came knocking
Around midmorning
While I was putting up
My stewed plums.
She said she was making
Her boys a peach cobbler
And ran short
A sugar cup.
Would I mind sparing some?
Would I mind?
After going nearly the summer
Without her talking once
Would I mind?
For Mammie Groller this year
I wouldn't spare a spoonful.
But for her boys
I would give
The whole bag."

Before sitting, Cora Ruth looks around the room perhaps wondering if she did the right thing, casting her pearls.

"Thank you, Cora Ruth, for sharing your poem. Would you care to explain what it means to you?" I ask.

"I suppose it is a sinful poem. One that I am not proud to say was true for me. That I was jealous and bitter. In need of some sugar, I suppose."

"Do you mean you were jealous that Mammie Groller had boys to bake for you and you didn't?" Autumn asks.

"Yes. I am ashamed to say that is true."

"My mother made a good peach cobbler," Harvey interjects.

"So did I. At least that is what my boys told me," Cora Ruth says. With her lips trembling, she appears on the brink of crying.

"What happened to your boys?" Harvey asks.

Cora Ruth turns to take in Harvey. He is scribbling and not looking her way. I imagine she is wondering if he is seriously interested or merely being insensitive. "They died," she says softly.

Everyone turns in her direction...all but Harvey, who continues to scratch away.

"Oh," Harvey says without looking up, adding, "sorry."

I'm taken aback that Harvey not only is paying attention but that he is able to respond appropriately to someone's loss. Tears drip down Cora Ruth's cheek. She reaches in her pocket for a handkerchief and wipes her face.

I wait to see if anyone will offer support. Autumn moves her chair closer to Cora Ruth and places a hand on her shoulder. This gesture produces more tears but also an expression of appreciation from Cora Ruth.

I lend my support. "Your loss seems to be felt by the people in group today, Cora Ruth. That means your poem was poignant...moving us to understand you better."

"I was beside myself when I wrote it. I never thought that it would amount to anything good, only that it would bring me shame."

"Looks like it brought you something other than shame. Your words brought you compassion," I say, extending my arm around the room.

Another silence. Perhaps this is a point where I should declare closure and end group.

"We still have a few minutes, but I'm wondering if this might be a good place to stop."

I look around the room, and everyone appears somber. I briefly contemplate engaging everyone in a centering exercise but decide to let them sit with their feelings since no one seems overwrought with psychic tension.

The balancing of tension is a delicate matter. Sometimes it requires faith that each person's internal gyroscope will right itself.

I lean toward faith. "Well, then, let's get back together on Thursday and remember to write down your thoughts and feelings in as poetic a manner as you can."

We all exit, silently keeping our thoughts to ourselves.

༄

Honoring The Past

Over the course of the hospital's first eighty years, all religious services were held in the old chapel located in the center section of Dix's third floor. Voices of the afflicted filled the sacred cavity beseeching God that he would lift them out of their mental and existential plight. Prayers, which, unfortunately, went painfully unanswered until science provided a series of dubious elixirs beginning in the 1950s.

The old chapel's enormous walls ascend nearly twenty-five feet before they reach the upper ceiling of Dix. Now in sad disrepair, the chapel's tall windows are comprised of assorted shards of opaque colored glass. They form diverse abstract patterns that allow wandering eyes to imagine objects of comfort, or horror, depending on one's state of mind. Some broken window panes have been replaced with bare plywood boards or aluminum strips. Practical materials, but devoid of inspiration. Despite this patchwork of repairs, a kaleidoscope of light still manages to penetrate the nearly barren chamber that once housed polished oak pews and a marble altar. It is a mystical light that seems to be searching for human souls.

Off to one side of the room is a cubicle constructed of folding gypsum board panels where a large metal table and a dozen metal chairs are positioned. It is here that our Historical Preservation Committee meets to ponder how to deal with all of the hospital's artifacts, some of which are boxed and stacked in corners of this once grand house of worship.

"Well, I don't think anybody else is coming today. So let's begin," Dr. Winston Pierce says. Dr. Pierce is the chief of psychiatry and the chairperson of the Historical Preservation Committee. "Winnie" has been at Kinzua State over forty-three years and has an intimate knowledge of nearly all aspects of the hospital, particularly its history and artifacts. A tall, handsome man with a striking shock of white hair, combed back into a mane, Winnie is urbane by lineage but proletarian by choice. Unassuming, he speaks to everyone in a common manner.

"Jerome, would you be willing to take minutes for this meeting?" Winnie asks.

"Certainly," I reply. "Should I record who is both present and absent?"

"Merely list who is here. After all, this isn't an executive-level meeting...only some staid historians getting together to hold on to the past."

"Not all of us are staid, Dr. Pierce," Otis Hessinger says. Otis is the director of occupational therapy and fairly young, as hospital staff goes. He is slender as a reed, with a hatchet face, somewhere in his midthirties. Otis only recently had been promoted to the director position after his predecessor, Louise Handwerk, suddenly expired while demonstrating how vestibular processes could be measured by twirling rapidly in a suspended chair. Needless to say, Otis curtailed any further measurements of vestibular functioning via the twirling chair method.

"Note that in the minutes, Jerome," Winnie says. "Anyone else objecting to being called staid?"

Although I consider myself to be a young fifty-four, and generally lighthearted, I kind of like being thought of as staid. There's a solidness to the term. And our only other committee member present today, LaDean Keglovitz, probably won't object either. LaDean, our librarian, is about my age, decidedly overweight, and the antithesis of vibrant. Squat, with a puggish face that is caked in makeup, ostensibly to disguise the deep creases running down to her jowls, LaDean dresses, acts, and thinks drearily.

"We are who we are, Dr. Pierce," LaDean says.

"Indeed, LaDean, we are," Winnie replies. "So, let's begin. At last month's meeting we discussed our options of how to dispose of all of Dr. Hole's brain specimens. As you recall, I had volunteered to contact the American Medical Association (AMA) to find out if they would be able to identify any university medical department that might be interested in our collection of deranged minds."

Winnie is referring to the brains of those hospitalized patients who died prior to 1960 and who had willed their organs to science, or whose next of kin gave such permission. Over a fifty-year span, Dr. Willard Hole and his predecessor, Dr. Roosevelt Shell, were responsible for harvesting, preserving, and studying the brains of patients who suffered from intractable schizophrenia. The doctors had published their studies in renowned journals of their day and brought Kinzua State to the cutting edge of neurological inquiry, so to speak. However, with Dr. Hole's death, and the elimination of funding for scientific studies at the hospital, scores of jars containing gelatinous gray matter floating in formaldehyde are stashed away in a storage room in Manchester building.

Winnie continues. "I received a complimentary phone call from an administrative assistant at the AMA's office kindly reporting that our request for a home for our brains has been placed on the agenda of the next meeting of its executive committee. Quite an honor, isn't it?"

"I'm touched," Otis remarks.

"This assistant said she will call me back when a decision has been made. She estimates sometime toward the end of this month. Any questions or comments?" Winnie looks at us. "None? Well then, that's one agenda item down and two to go," Winnie says, scratching one of his bushy eyebrows with the cap of his pen. "Next, we need to discuss what to do with that trunk." He extends his finger in the direction of a large wooden chest resting on a pallet in the corner of the room.

"What's in it?" I ask.

"Lives," Winnie replies. "The proofs of lives."

"You mean that trunk contains patients' birth certificates?" LaDean asks.

"More like life certificates, LaDean," Winnie says. "My dear committee members, that treasure chest contains all the photographs ever taken of patients at this hospital over the course of the last hundred years."

That gets our attention.

"How do you know every possible photograph is in there?" Otis asks.

"I was hoping someone would ask that question." Winnie wears a mischievous smile. "As you may know, I am somewhat of a shutterbug, not good enough to quit my day job but good enough to recognize excellent work of accomplished photographers. And over the last century, we at this hospital have had our share of very good cameramen. Our last photographer, Warren North, was in my opinion on par with Ansel Adams. As strange as it may sound, that trunk does not contain one colored photograph. They are all black and white, which was the best choice for capturing the presence of our patients. And Warren was the best man I have ever met to have done just that. Prior to his retirement two years ago, I directed him to collect every photo ever taken by his department and to scour every office and closet in this hospital for any wayward patient photos, including our library, LaDean. It took Warren nearly six months, but he assured me there wasn't any room or desk drawer with a photograph of a patient remaining. We placed them in that chest, locked the latch, and stored it up here. Would any of you care to see one or two of them?"

Even Otis's cynicism is overcome by curiosity. So, we all get up and walk with Winnie to the wooden trunk. Whether for dramatic effect or merely because he is up in years, Winnie fumbles with his ring of keys, searching for the right one. "How many blasted keys does a person need to work at this place?" Winnie asks, to no one in particular.

Finally settling on a small skeleton key, Winnie inserts it into the brass lock and slowly raises the chest's lid. I almost expect to see some ghosts fly out, but only a musty odor emerges. Apparently, Warren had arranged the photos in antiquated binders that were artifacts themselves. Winnie lifts one of the binders out of the trunk and opens it for all of us to see. There before us is a picture of several bearded men, presumably patients, in denim work clothes and straw hats holding shovels while standing next to the edge of a trench. None of the men are smiling, and most are looking warily at the camera.

"That I believe is a photo of some patients taking a break from digging a section of our tunnel system," Winnie says.

"The patients were used to dig the tunnel system? I didn't know that," I say.

"They worked alongside of the staff and horses and mules. It was part of occupational therapy back then," Winnie says.

"Occupational therapy back then was known as occupational work," Otis remarks.

"And back then, work was considered therapeutic," Winnie adds.

"When was this photograph taken?" LaDean asks.

"Well, let's see. I had asked Warren to put the dates on the back of them," Winnie says, pulling out the photo from the binder. "This one doesn't have a precise date. Just a circa of 1925."

"Almost eighty years ago," I say. "Still in good condition."

We spend the next ten minutes or so keenly looking through several more binders. Photos of patients working in fields picking beans, milking cows, canning vegetables, baking bread, washing laundry, sewing clothes and many other labors of existence. Chores that needed to be done to keep the hospital going. It was hard work. Tiring work. Therapeutic and meaningful work that no longer is available to patients. Instead, we have medications, activities, and treatment practices based on talk therapy. But no work, except a small workshop and the greenhouse, which is now scheduled to shut down. Where do patients find meaning in their lives in the twenty-first century? Certainly not at Kinzua State and, tragically, in few places of our modern society.

After locking the photographs back in the chest and tabling any decision regarding their disposition, Winnie leads us to agenda item number three: hydrotherapy apparatuses. Apparently, there are several stalls and tubs with metal pipes and hoses held in storage bins in the basement of Dix. Between 1910 and 1940 these units were considered to be effective treatments for depression, mania, psychosis, and curing chronic inebriates. Along with soaking tubs and wet packs, patients with intractable conditions could expect during their hospitalization to receive several treatments of hydro-therapy massages, a continuous spray of water, to either calm or stimulate their state of being. Since there are no available testimonials from patients of how effective these treatments actually were, we can only rely on archival reports from the psychiatrists who supervised their use:

...Patient appears to be less volatile with fewer expressions of lunacy since her last hydrotherapy treatment...Patient has begun eating again after four days of hydrotherapy massage... After two wet pack treatments, he (patient) is less agitated and more cooperative with nursing directives...

"I can tell you from firsthand experience that wet packs brought about a submissive posture, if not outright obsequiousness," Winnie says.

"You mean you were wet-packed?" I ask

"Indeed I was. I asked to be back in 1961. That's when I first arrived at Kinzua State to do my residency. Even though patients were no longer submitted to wet-pack treatment back then, I still wanted to know what it was like. Dr. Knappenberger was my supervisor, and although he thought I was a nutty young man to want to be swaddled in wet sheets, he agreed to let me undergo the procedure. I recall being somewhat embarrassed to strip down to my underwear in front of the nursing staff, which included one damn cute redhead, to whom I have been married for the past forty-two years. However, my embarrassment quickly evolved into resignation at being powerless for the next three hours. Wisely, I never fought my helplessness. I was told that many patients who had undergone the treatment had struggled mightily to break free, which was truly impossible. After about ten minutes their bodies were exhausted, and after about an hour their minds as well. Eventually, one comes to accept one's predicament. 'God grant me the courage to accept the things I cannot change...' I can't say that undergoing hydrotherapy made me a better psychiatrist, but it did increase my empathy for anyone enduring forced treatment." Winnie pauses and looks up at the colored light radiating through the windows. "I also got his permission to take Thorazine and ECT," he adds, chuckling

"Thank goodness he didn't agree to letting you try out a lobotomy," I chide.

"Thank goodness, indeed. And thankfully he didn't hold any of my self-experiments against me. Dr. Knappenberger was very tolerant of me and other young psychiatrists as well. As long as everyone—psychiatrists and other staff—were trying their best to improve the welfare of patients, Dr. Knappenberger was one hundred percent behind them. He was a wonderful man and a tremendous role model for all of us. I sorely miss not having him around."

"So, what about all this hydrotherapy equipment? Do we keep it or do we sell it?" Otis bluntly asks.

"Ah, back to the matter at hand. Thank you, Otis, for beaming me back to reality," Winnie says. "Yes, what to do about these antiquated treatment devices. Any suggestions?"

"I propose we put them up for auction. Those surplus barber chairs brought a pretty penny last year.

I bet there are some plumbers out there that would want these water fixtures. Old parts and all," Otis says.

"I think we should keep them and find a place for visitors to view them. Just like that old horse-drawn plow that sits out front as a lawn ornament," I say.

"You want the water treatment equipment out on the lawn?" Otis asks.

"No, not on the lawn. That was merely a comparison. What I imagine is a room somewhere in the front hallway that could display some of our artifacts. Such as the badges that staff at one time wore, or the uniforms that patients at one time were required to wear."

"What about the leather gloves that male nursing staff wore to protect their hands when a punch or two was needed to subdue a patient?" Otis retorts. "Do they get displayed as well?"

"Really, Otis, be civil, won't you?" LaDean says.

Winnie reenters the discussion. "Unfortunately, Otis makes an sobering point, LaDean. If there ever would be a display room, how would we choose what does and doesn't get included? Quaint ideas only, or all the relics of ignorance?"

"I vote for displaying all aspects of our history...good and bad," I say. "We have decidedly advanced beyond brute force, if not experimentation."

"Some would say that the use of psychotropic medications are just that...brutish and experimental," Otis says.

"Before we drift too far afield into a critique of modern psychiatry, I think we should keep our discussion to the topic at hand...the hydrotherapy appliances. What should we do with them?" Winnie asks.

"Where do you envision a display room being located, Jerome?" LaDean asks.

"I'm not sure. Perhaps where Mary Jonas has her office in the front hallway. It's large enough for items to be displayed and for visitors to walk freely about."

"And what would happen to Mary, Jerome?" Otis asks. "Does she get stuffed and become an exhibit in your imaginary room?"

"She already is pretty stuffy isn't she, Otis? Maybe, she could just stay right where she is and wave at the passersby. Kind of an animated exhibit," I reply dryly.

"We are drifting again, gentlemen. Back on topic, please," Winnie says.

"I think we should devote more time to exploring the practicality of Jerome's idea of a display room," LaDean says.

"That sounds like a motion to me. Any objections to tabling this topic for more discussion? None? Good. We now have successfully tabled all our agenda items and thus have preserved history in the same place we found it. This committee is indeed living up to its name. So, for our next meeting we will review all current agenda topics and also our next concern."

"And what would that be?" Otis asks.

"What to do about the ECT equipment that is stored in this room."

"Do we get the opportunity to try it out?" I ask.

"I'm afraid I am losing my memory fast enough, thank you," Winnie replies. "However, if you would like to try it out Jerome, I'm sure Otis wouldn't mind spinning the dials, would you, Otis?"

Otis mimes an expression of a mad scientist pulling levers. "Welcome to my laboratory," he says with a sneer.

"Something tells me to skip the demonstration," I reply.

"And to think that I was questioning your judgment, Jerome," Winnie says with a smile. "All right, folks. See you in one month. Same place. Same time."

As we exit the old chapel, LaDean voices a concern to me.

"Jerome, your intern is spending quite a bit of time researching the psychological abstracts and placing requests for articles. Not that I mind assisting her if all the information is job related. Is she working with quite a few psychopaths?"

"Actually, Elsa isn't officially working with any psychopaths, other than myself."

"Well, then why is she collecting so much information on that condition?"

"Perhaps because I had asked her to help me with a psychological evaluation over in the Forensic Unit. It probably piqued her interest in the subject. However, there are limits to one's interest. I'll talk with Elsa and see if I can stop the number of trees being cut down, LaDean."

"I don't want to be seen as a bad guy, Jerome. I just got to watch out for expenses, that's all."

"No problem. Elsa needs to know when enough is enough. Part of the learning experience. Thanks for letting me know."

The question is, will Elsa ever realize when enough is enough?

∽

The Trap Is Set

The interior of the Forensic Unit is as dark as the night sky. But its exterior is aglow in an eerie blue radiance emitted from towering mercury vapor lamps positioned every seventy-five feet around the building's perimeter. Inside, the patients are soundly asleep; medications provide a welcome sedating effect. All are undoubtedly oblivious to the artificial light enveloping them. All except Garner Overton, who stares out his window at the ethereal glow, scheming his escape.

Next week Overton has a dental appointment. He is confident that Elsa will meet him there. His pathetic story of him being fearful of dental work and his plea for a hand to hold seems to have drawn her in. She doesn't suspect that he intends to use her as a shield to break free of the guards and the confines of Kinzua State. With only a modicum of charm, Overton was able to determine that the intern has a car, and it is usually parked in the front lot of Dix. Getting her keys may require more than charm, however. That is where a persuader will be needed. Overton is self-assured that he can find some type of instrument in one of the nearby offices to use as a weapon, and although he doesn't intend for anyone to get hurt, if violence is needed to ensure an escape, well, then too bad for the intern or anyone else getting in his way.

The only uncertainty is whether he lets her go free.

∾

What She Needs

This morning I plan to track down Elsa. But before I do I have scheduled a brief meeting with Paula Cotton to share with her what I know about Ophelia. She agreed to give Paula a chance, only if I act as a liaison between them. Paula's office is on the first floor of the south side, and along the way I stop at a coffee break room frequented by office staff. Slipping a buck in the collection box, I pour a cup of the black brew and start to head back out but find myself blocked by Dr. Chankra who is squeezing his mass into the small room.

"Jerome, what a surprise. I see you are getting your caffeine fix. Bad for the blood pressure and sexual drive, Jerome. Why don't you empty that down the drain and try some of my green tea? It is imported from an exclusive tea plantation in Pakistan. A gentle flavor with hints of coriander. Soothing and a mild aphrodisiac, I might add. You do enjoy sexual intimacies, don't you, Jerome?" Chankra smiles broadly, waving the canister of tea in my face.

I don't know if it is the body heat being generated by Chankra in this cramped room or his talk about sex that is making me warm and uncomfortable. I back further into a corner hoping that he will move past me to the carafe of hot water that he is seeking.

"Don't really need an aphrodisiac, Pratap. Thanks anyway," I say.

"What are you men doing in here? Probably talking about women, aren't you? I know how you men think. You are all alike," Priscilla Dolak says, nudging her way into the room. Pricilla is a human resource specialist, middle age, fairly attractive but insufferably verbose. "Don't you look particularly handsome today, Dr. Chankra. That paisley tie goes so well with that sport coat. Silk, isn't it? What a rakish dresser you are, Doctor."

Chankra is beaming and no longer interested in me. "My dear, you are as intelligent as you are lovely. Would you like to share some of my tea? It has some very special properties."

"That is so sweet of you, Doctor. What type of tea is it?"

"Excuse me, folks, I'm going to wriggle my way out of here," I say, sucking in my stomach to avoid brushing Pricilla's backside.

I gently close the door behind me thankful to be free of these overbearing personalities. In less than a minute, I reach Paula's office and apologize for being late.

"Sorry, Paula, for not being here earlier. I got caught in between two blooming egos."

"Huh? What does that mean?" Paula asks.

"Forget it, just a figure of speech. Sorry for being late." I take a chair next to her desk. "So, Ophelia has agreed to meet with you?"

Paula removes her glasses, stands up, and moves to a chair across from mine. She is a moderately tall, handsome woman who needs very little make up. With short auburn hair combed back in a natural wave, high rugged cheek bones, dark eyes and a full sensual mouth, Paula imparts a solid balance of feminine and masculine features. She immediately comes across as strong and stable. A person one can trust.

"Yes, she says she is willing to try. However, she wasn't very convincing. In fact, she seemed pretty unsure of herself."

"I think Ophelia is genuinely struggling to come to terms with what she is experiencing. She is having a very hard time accepting that she needs help. But she appears to be at a point where she can't do it alone."

"Well, her chart doesn't indicate very precisely what she is dealing with. I read it yesterday, and the only thing I picked up was that prior to being hospitalized she was homeless, undernourished, barely responsive, and suffering with a staph infection from all the cuts she afflicted on herself. And since being here at our hospital, she hasn't talked much about herself to anyone, and has been caught self-mutilating at least a dozen times."

"That's our girl. I forget if we did any testing. Did you find any?"

"Only an IQ test. That's all she agreed to do. Full scale of 115. Not too shabby for our population."

"Or our staff," I quip.

"Yeah, right. So can you fill in the blanks, Rome?"

"Well, yes and no. Ophelia hasn't been all that forthright with me, either. I know that she doesn't have any family. At least she doesn't talk about any. She had been homeless like you said. Apparently she was drifting from one hangout to another. Given that she's only twenty-two, that means she was living on the streets for at least four years. And as you know, in order to do that, you are either caught up in the social agency network or bartering for your meals and drug highs. And I suspect the latter."

"Why's that?"

"During our poetry group, Ophelia has made quite a few allusions to being mistreated. I suspect that she was either in one or several abusive relationships, or even prostituting herself to survive. She has insinuated several times that she is fearful of what is 'out there.' So, one can only imagine what she has been through in her young lifetime."

"Is that why she didn't want to talk with you? You being a male?"

"Yes. She came right out and said so. That is why I suggested she give you a chance."

"So, you think I should focus on her past?"

"I don't think you have a choice. Ophelia is bursting at the seams with her past. She wants to be free of her nightmares. After you establish a working alliance with her, I think you would need to help desensitize her traumas and torments. Although she may be free of staph, Ophelia is still infected, with the effects of human psychopathology."

"Sounds like I have my work cut out for me."

"It should be interesting."

"Well, thanks, Rome. I hope you are willing to be a consultant should I need you."

"Most certainly. Just a reminder, you will need her team to approve individual therapy before you start. Not that there would be any objections. Lord knows they have been at a loss to find some way of helping Ophelia stop her self-destructive behaviors. You could be the therapeutic factor that has been missing for the last six months."

"I just hope she will relate to me, and we can get her to stop cutting herself."

"Definitely a worthwhile first goal. Well, I should be off. I need to find Elsa and have a little supervisory chat."

"That sounds ominous."

"I better work on the tone in my voice, huh?"

"Dialing it down a notch might be a good idea, Rome."

"Thanks for the suggestion, Paula."

"You're welcome, and thank you for helping me with Ophelia. I may be calling you more than you might want."

"Never too much for her or you. Take care, Paula."

⚬

Danger Looms

"Can you believe this bullshit!" says Jarrett Finken, a psychiatric aide. He crumbles up the letter and attached leave slip that were in his mailbox, and throws them in the wastebasket next to the coffee urn.

"Four months ago, I put in to have next Saturday off so I could attend my brother's wedding. Now they've got the guts to say it's being denied because of staff shortage. Well, screw them. I feel a bad case of the flu starting to come on."

"They did the same thing to me last month," Emil says, not looking up from his magazine. "Had a fishing trip all planned out—chartered boat, cabin rental, the whole bit. Got nixed at the last minute because of staffing problems.

"I wonder if the hags in the front office ever get their weekend manicure appointments cancelled because of staff shortages."

"Doubt it. Got to keep those nails sharpened to dig into our hides, my man."

Luther listens to his fellow aides carp about nursing administration and how they are being treated like a bunch of refugees. Merely another example of how some career women are making the lives of hardworking men miserable. Luther loses his appetite and puts his sandwich back in the break room refrigerator. He grabs his coffee cup and heads to the staff bathroom.

The sign says "Unisex Restroom." Luther can't seem to get away from reminders of how affirmative action has changed everything at the hospital, and throughout America as well. All this equality and women's rights despite the Equal Rights Amendment never having been passed. As he lifts the lid and relieves himself, Luther continues to despair about the loss of male power and biblical relationships as well as America's decline. In his mind, America was not only once a superpower but *the* superpower, which dominated the world. Now it has become a cruise ship filled with immigrants skippered by a woman.

A knock on the door brings Luther around. "Take your time in there. Just wanted you to know someone is out here waiting to make her bladder gladder." A woman with no modesty.

After zipping himself up, Luther flushes and turns toward to the door. He pats the Colt .45 strapped to his calf. He feels its power radiate through him strengthening his resolve. Luther stares straight ahead as he exits the bathroom. Zoned-in to his power, he doesn't hear a thing being said to him.

Inconsiderate

Ophelia has an urge to cut. She doesn't want to, but like a maddening itch the impulse has her attention. During her first session of individual therapy, she agreed to make a commitment to change her old habits, like cutting. And Paula will ask about it. And Ophelia doesn't want to lie to her. A couple of tokes might help take the edge off. So, Ophelia goes to Kendra's room. She isn't there. Ophelia then goes to Kim Huong's room. The door is shut. Ophelia knocks.

"Wait. I will be right there," Kim says through the closed door. Sounds of drawers closing can be heard. The door opens. "Oh, hi there. Opie, right?" Kim says, smiling.

"Yeah, that's right. Kendra is my friend. But I can't find her right now. So, I thought I would come to you," Ophelia says.

"I see. You want something?"

"I have money."

"So do I."

"I mean, I can pay.

"You think I have something to sell?"

"All right, forget it." Ophelia turns to leave.

"You know why Kendra and I get along?" Kim asks.

Ophelia stops and faces Kim. "Why?"

"She is nice to me. Knocking on my door and waving money isn't being nice. Do you see?"

"Yeah. You're right. My bad." Ophelia again turns to leave.

"Want to get a Coke?" Kim asks.

Ophelia nods, "Okay, sure."

"Good, let's sign out."

∽

Memories That Heal

I start my day in the staff library. I want to find Cleckley's *The Mask of Sanity* and search his bibliography. If my memory serves me correctly, I believe he references a seminal article on psychopathology by Karpman, wherein Karpman argues that psychopathic behaviors are comprised of several subtypes, at least one which may be amenable to psychotherapy. If Overton falls into that category, I could at least offer it as a recommendation in my psychological report.

After a few minutes of having no luck locating Cleckley's book, I finally cave in and ask LaDean for help. She informs me that with the last purging of holdings all books prior to 1960 that weren't discarded are now stored in the back storage room of the library. I shudder to think *The Mask of Sanity* was thrown out like some pulp fiction.

Entering the small storage area, I encounter boxes of books stacked several high on small pallets. I open one box and find that there is no order to its contents. Books of Freud and Jung are mixed with those of Eysenck and Menninger. Cleckley could be in any one of these scores of boxes. Although I would love to spend the rest of the morning digging through these treasures, I need to break away and head downstairs for my session with Cora Ruth.

"Did you find what you were looking for, Jerome?" the librarian asks.

"No, I didn't. Ran out of time. I'll try later this week. Right now I need to get back to my office for an individual therapy session," I say, heading for the door.

"Well, the books back there aren't going anywhere soon. No one finds old tomes that interesting it seems."

"I do. To me there's something exciting about reading the observations and theories of clinicians who devoted their lives to a specific subject."

"Maybe you should be working up here in the library, Jerome."

"If I didn't enjoy working with the patients so much, I'd gladly become your assistant. There's something comforting about being surrounded by books and ideas. So protective. Sheltering, really. For me it is like being in church."

"Careful, Jerome. You're making my heart flutter. You better be on your way before I come over there and start hugging you."

"LaDean, you're a married woman. Get a grip on yourself," I tease.

"At my age, the last thing I need to do is to get a grip on myself. You better get going, Jerome. I mean it," she says walking toward me.

"Okay, I'm going. But I'll be back."

"That's what they all say," she says, pretending to be jilted.

I make it to my office at the same time Cora Ruth does.

"Good morning, Dr. Masonheimer."

"Good morning. How are you?"

"All right I suppose."

She stares at the floor waiting for me to unlock the door. Her attire hasn't changed much: plain patterned shirt-waist dress, slippers with white ankle socks. Her face is freshly washed, with no makeup. Her hair parted and brushed to either side. Simple, old fashioned, devoid of any color.

I close the door, and we take our customary seats. Per usual, Cora Ruth waits for me to say something.

"So, you had quite an impact during our last group session," I begin.

"I think I made a fool of myself."

"Why do you say that?"

"Crying like a baby and everyone fussing over me. That isn't me. It wasn't right."

"You aren't comfortable receiving so much attention."

"No. Not in that way."

"It happened naturally...spontaneously."

"To me it was unexpected and unnecessary."

"It seemed like you needed to express yourself."

"I don't know if it did me any good."

"It might take some time to know. Expressing feelings is a bit like fertilizing a tree. The first couple of days the tree doesn't look any different, but in a couple of weeks or months, the tree starts noticeably changing...growing."

Cora Ruth remains quiet, but her eyes are blinking, apparently considering my comment.

I venture a question. "How do you feel talking about your sons?"

She peers at me long and hard before answering. "I don't like talking about my boys, Dr. Masonheimer."

"When do you talk about them?"

"I don't." Her expression hardens into an unspoken warning.

"It seems that it's very hard for you to openly grieve their deaths."

She casts a disapproving scowl.

I wait for the tension to build before speaking. Frequently, patients defend against feelings of helplessness and vulnerability by consciously or unconsciously avoiding dreaded topics. Raising emotionality can overcome resistances and expose the source of their anguish.

"What can you tell me about them?"

Cora Ruth continues to look hard at me. I half expect she might get up and leave. She moves her tongue against her cheek before speaking.

"They were twins."

"Twins? They must have had a special relationship, being twins."

"Yes, they did. They were together most of the time."

"What were their names?"

"Heinrick and Johannes...Henry and John."

"Good strong names. May I ask when they died?"

"Nineteen seventy-two."

"In the same year?"

"In the same week." Cora Ruth is no longer looking at me. Her eyes are closed, and she is sighing heavily.

"Were they involved in an accident?"

She buries her face in both of her hands and bends forward, shaking her head. She softly repeats the word "accident."

"Accident? Unless you consider being born at the wrong time in history an accident, Doctor...no, it wasn't an accident."

I'm confused but wait for her to make the next move. The lid on the box is open. *Will she show me what is inside?*

Cora Ruth stares vacantly through me. Her mind is somewhere other than with me. I have seen this empty look before when talking with deeply psychotic patients who couldn't extricate themselves from their perceptual labyrinths. They would be physically present but only as a shell. Cora Ruth isn't psychotic, only momentarily consciously lost, perhaps processing images of Henry and John, recalling private conversations, tender, meaningful moments.

She focuses her eyes on mine. "After school and during summer, they would love to play imaginary games. We had a large backyard that bordered a field that was used to grow corn and such. There they would pretend to be soldiers, crawling and hiding, shooting and dying..." She stops to sigh. "I would scold them for getting so dirty and spending so much time playing war. I had had enough of war, and I didn't like them pretending war to be fun. Hans had been in the army as had my brother and uncle. They all were in the war, WWII. My brother and Hans came back home, but my uncle Pete didn't. Then there was the Korean War, and Hans was thinking of signing up. I begged him not to, with me being pregnant and all. He finally agreed. And everything was fine for awhile...until the next war came along." Again, Cora Ruth stares into space.

"The next war being Vietnam."

"Yes, that war. A war that cost so much and for what purpose? I ask that question over and over. Day in and day out. For what purpose?" Cora Ruth once again pauses to gaze out the window. After some time passes, she resumes her account. "The boys turned nineteen in 1971 and were drafted into the army shortly thereafter. I tried to put on a brave front and show support for their commitment to our country, but I was a nervous wreck every day they were away. When they completed their infantry training, they came home to spend a few days with their friends, and Hans and me, before being deployed. They looked so different...thinner and harder. More like men than boys. It was during their visit when we had learned there was a military rule forbidding brothers serving in a combat zone at the same time. Which meant that Henry was being sent to Germany, while John was going to Vietnam. I don't know which one of us felt worse, Henry or me. He wanted so badly to be in Vietnam, not just to be with his brother but also to be part of the fighting. They both had prepared for being soldiers for so long, and now the time had come, but not in the way they had thought it would." Cora Ruth coughs, clearing her throat.

"Would you like some water?" I ask.

"Yes, that would be nice."

I retrieve a bottle of water from a stash that I keep in my lower desk drawer. "I'm afraid it's room temperature," I say handing the bottle to her.

"It will do, thank you." After a few sips, Cora Ruth resumes her story. "I remember being so torn. So relieved that Henry was going somewhere safe and so upset that John was being sent into danger. I couldn't even touch him or look into his face when he left for the airport. I was so beside myself. I hid in my bedroom, crying, lost in self-pity. I'll never forgive myself for not saying goodbye to John. Now he's gone. They both are gone."

Tears well up in her eyes. I reach for a box of tissues and hold them in front of her. She takes the box, wipes her eyes, and blows her nose.

"Watching them leave overwhelmed you," I reflect.

"Not being able to stop them from going, from leaving me, and fearing never to see them again, that overwhelmed me. The dread of watching your children being taken from you, from this earth, was more than I could bear. I felt like I was dying, and perhaps I did." Cora Ruth stops momentarily, then continues.

"While John was in Vietnam, Henry was stationed in Fulda, Germany. He hated it. He wanted to be with his brother, not in a quaint town with neat-as-a-pin streets. Hans and I would write telling Henry how fortunate he was not to be in danger, but he wouldn't hear of it. Only much later we had found out that he was coping by drinking and taking drugs. Drugs and war. How I detest war, Doctor. It took my boys. That war. That wretched war killed both of them."

"I'm not sure that I know what you mean, Cora Ruth." I say.

She breathes deeply before explaining. "When Hans and I received word that John had been killed while on a mission, I immediately called Henry and told him. It was one of the hardest things I had ever done. We all were devastated, but Henry was beside himself. We couldn't console him. The next day we received a phone call from his base commander informing us that Henry had died. We were told that he had overdosed on heroin. And just like that, both our boys were gone. Just like that, gone, forever and ever." She stares out the window as tears flow down her cheeks.

Be aware that one's mind can process only so much pain before it shuts down. Grief needs to be measured in dosages that are digestible.

"I can see why you have been having so much difficulty moving on. Losing both your boys so suddenly was too much to bear. It overcame your spirit."

Turning back to me, Cora Ruth says, "I never fully recovered from that horrible time. Then when Hans died, it was the last straw for me. I stopped living as well."

"And how did you stop living?"

"By not eating. Just sitting and staring at the pictures on the wall."

"Is that when you were taken to the community hospital?"

"Yes. One of my neighbors called the police, and they took me to the psychiatric ward, which sent me here."

"I'm glad you're here, Cora Ruth. And willing to work through your grief."

"Is that what I'm doing, Doctor?" she asks, wiping her face.

"Each time you talk about your loss and allow yourself to feel the heartache, you're moving the process along. I believe you are further along because of today's session."

"How can you be sure? How can you tell?"

"Without becoming too technical, I believe each time we bring forth painful memories we change them. There are fancy terms like desensitization through covert exposure, but simply it is a matter of expressing our pain until it disappears and allows the positive memories of our loved ones to emerge and comfort us. Today you expressed the pain associated with your losses. Perhaps now there is room for a positive memory to emerge. Before we end today, why don't you try to see if you can recall a comforting memory of one of the men in your life?"

Cora Ruth pauses and breathes deeply. She remains quiet, apparently taking time to conjure a memory. She drifts to another place and time. Slowly a faint smile emerges on her face.

"I do recall a summer when we were all together at our cabin here in Cornplanter County. It was August, I believe, hot and muggy. The boys were about ten or eleven. To get away from the heat, we had walked down to where a spring flowed out of the base of one of the hills, where we got our drinking and cooking water. Hans had brought a metal milk container to fill with water and then haul back to the cabin. I don't know if you know what I mean."

"Are you talking about one of those large heavy metal canisters that dairy farmers use?"

"Yes, those are the ones we used to store water. When they were filled to the brim, they were very heavy and very difficult to carry. Anyway, we were all standing around watching the water pipe fill the container. When it started to overflow, Hans told the boys to cap it and start carrying it back to the cabin. Well, each of them grabbed a handle and struggled to lift that container off the ground. They hadn't gone more than a couple of yards or so, groaning every inch, before they stumbled and tipped over the container, spilling the water on the ground. I remember that they sheepishly looked back at their father fearing he would be upset with them, but Hans was laughing out loud. Then he swooped each of the boys up in his arms and sat them right under that spring pipe. And before I knew it, he had me in a bear hug dragging me down with him right next to the boys. We sat there soaking wet, laughing and laughing. We were like a family of frogs. Life didn't get much better than being under that water pipe," Cora Ruth says, smiling, but with a bittersweet strain.

"It sounds like a wonderful memory, Cora Ruth. You are so fortunate to have recalled it so clearly. Thank you for sharing it. How are you feeling?"

She breathes deeply and exhales loudly. "Like an angel has carried some of the weight off my chest."

"A little less heavy."

"A little."

"Do you feel ready to go back to the ward?"

"Yes, I do."

"What will you do when you get back?

"I don't know. Maybe lie down for a while, until group starts."

"Do you want me to walk back with you?"

"No, there's no need for that. I'm fine, Doctor. Thank you. And thank you for being patient with me. I know I can be stubborn."

"Not a problem. Your resistance is a way of protecting yourself. I can appreciate that. My job is to recognize it and gently find ways of moving it aside."

"You are a good man, Doctor."

"I try. Sure you're okay?"

"Yes, I'm fine. See you at our next session." Cora Ruth walks down the hallway with her head up. I take that as a good sign. I decide that after jotting down a brief case note, I'll use the next hour to work on Woody's petition. That is, if nothing unexpected comes up.

Reaching His Limit

"**L**uther! Come here. I've got something for you," Jake yells down the hallway.

Luther trots down to the nursing station, his camo-boots loudly scuffing the floor. "What do you got for me, Jake?"

"I got some news concerning your work assignment. Seems that you are being transferred indefinitely to the women's ward. You'll be working with my sister, Emma, starting this morning. In fact, she wants you there right now to escort some patients."

"Is this one of your jokes, Jake?"

"No joke, Luther. With the number of male admissions being down and female being up, there's less need for staff up here. So, you are heading downstairs my friend."

"Can I appeal this decision?"

"To whom? To Mrs. Blass? Good luck with that. She can put us wherever she wants to. That's the privilege of being in management and the lousy luck of being a line worker."

"I can't last down there, Jake. Those women drive me crazy. I won't last a week."

"You'll need to find a way, Luther. Until you and I sign our own pay checks, we do what we're told to do."

"I'm not being told much longer."

"What? What do you mean by that?"

"Nothing."

"Another thing, Luther. Take this mail down to Emma when you go. Seems like it got mixed in our mail," Jake says, pointing to a stack of envelopes and a copy of the morning newspaper.

Luther grabs the bundle of mail, pulls his fatigue cap down over his forehead, and dejectedly marches to the exit door. As he leaves the ward, he spies the front-page headlines on the paper. "USA Whites in Minority by 2040." The dark cloud hovering over his head gets darker.

~

The Last Chance

Friday starts out quietly. No demanding patients, no pressing work assignments, no Woody intrusions, and no e-mails to answer. As soon as I think that this will be an easy day, my pager sounds off, indicating a crisis on Men's Closed Ward. I rush down the hallway and up the nearest staircase to the third floor. No need to unlock the door; it is being held open by the psychiatric aide, Mamie Mae. She looks terrified and points me down the hallway to where a mass of staff members surrounds a male patient that I don't recognize...probably a new admission. He's around six feet, dark hair, muscular, and wild eyed. Emitting a guttural snarl, he beckons staff to come forward even though they have him backed into a corner. As I approach him, I can see that he is clad only in his underwear and is standing on a heap of clothing. Upon closer inspection, the pile is not clothes but a person...Emil. He is lying still, his arm twisted in an odd position.

"We need to get him off Emil before he suffocates," Jake says to the staff.

"Can he be talked down?" I ask.

"He's way beyond talk, Rome. He's psychotic and out of control. We've got to act now before it's too late," Jake says, moving toward the wild man.

In unison we descend upon him. He lifts his head like a wolf and howls, thumping his chest and stomping his foot on Emil's back. Emil moans but doesn't move. Jake is the first to grab an arm; another staff member follows suit. Both are flung backwards against those who are hesitant to latch on to this brawler. He lashes out with fists and leg kicks, repelling all attempts to secure him. Several staff members fall to the ground and are promptly trampled. I manage to reach Emil and yank his crumpled body away from the fracas. My eyes are riveted on the feral face of this possessed soul, and for a brief nanosecond he locks his eyes on mine. A flash of ferocity shoots through me. Cringing, I remove both Emil and myself farther away from the melee.

After minutes of raucous grappling, the staff members finally succeed in subduing the man. A strong dose of IM medication is administered before he can be carried into a seclusion room and strapped to a mattress. The situation clearly calls for making an exception to the use of leather straps, which is generally forbidden. An ambulance takes Emil to the emergency room, while first aid is given to other staff members with abrasions and sprains. Although exhausted, Jake starts the necessary documentation to record this terrible tussle. I, too, fill out an incident report that will be compiled with the rest of the staff's accounts. All to be used by reviewers to ensure proper procedures were followed, with little consideration that we were fighting for our lives.

"I don't even know this guy's name," I say, looking to Jake.

Jake looks up. His cheek and forehead are red and bruised. "Bram. Bram Kratzer."

"Did he just come in?"

"Yesterday. He was pretty quiet all day, but this morning he showed his true colors and strength," Jake says, gingerly rubbing his forehead. "I hope he wakes in a different mood. Don't want to go through another meltdown anytime soon. Getting too old for this."

"Yeah, I know what you mean," I say, twisting my aching neck. We both resume our paperwork, and the rest of the morning quietly goes by.

When I return to my office, I scan my e-mails. One post indicates that because the greenhouse will be closing today, all plants will be given away for free. I decide to head over there and see what I can pick up. The walk over is exceptionally pleasant. Sunny, mild temperature, and a soothing breeze. Inside the greenhouse, it's a different atmosphere. All these glass panels capture and retain every ray of the sun. I decide to look around quickly and get out before I start sweating. The place is packed with scavengers from both the hospital and the surrounding community. Apparently, free is a bargain no one wants to miss out on. I spot Cora Ruth placing planters on a long mesh table. She has on a work apron and a pair of cotton gloves. I approach her.

"Hello, Cora Ruth. How are you?"

"Dr. Masonheimer. I didn't expect to see you over here," she says, wiping her gloves on her apron.

"Free plants even got me out of the office. Any that you would recommend?"

"These geraniums are very healthy and quite pretty," she says, pointing to the table next to me.

I take a moment to examine the red flowers. "This must be a sad day for you," I say without looking directly at her.

She sighs deeply. "Very sad. I'll miss this place and these plants. I don't know what I'll do come Monday."

"Perhaps you could work in the sheltered workshop? Kind of like factory work, but it might help structure your time."

"The greenhouse staff suggested the same thing. I don't know. Factory work never appealed to me. We'll see."

We fall silent. She busies herself with the plants on the table. I watch her, mindful that openly discussing personal issues isn't appropriate in this setting. Our silence is interrupted by Luther and two patients entering the greenhouse.

"I told you we had to hurry. Now look. Most of the good plants are gone. You staff are a bunch of douche bags," May Tavormino says to Luther, who is chomping on his huge lower lip, apparently holding back his anger. "And why are you dressed like G.I. Joe? You pretending to be a war hero or something? I swear you staff are as crazy as we are," May adds.

Luther reaches down to pat his calf. It appears to be a compulsive movement similar to what autistic children might do when stressed. Then again maybe May kicked him, and he's rubbing his bruise. I still have a black-and-blue mark where she kicked me a week ago. Regardless the reason, Luther seems to have received some comfort from his maneuver and appears less tense. He moves away from May and lets her rant on.

"Well, I think I'll take your advice and get two of these geraniums," I say to Cora Ruth.

"One for you and one for your wife?"

"Two for my wife. She's the one with the green thumb."

"You shouldn't give up trying to grow plants, Doctor."

"I won't give up, if you don't."

She scowls at me. "It's not the same."

"No, you're right. Your life is more important."

"You're twisting my words, Doctor."

"Your life is important enough for me to do almost anything, Cora Ruth."

"Don't forget to water your plants, Doctor Masonheimer."

"I wonder where you'll be when you value living again."

"It won't be in this greenhouse."

"You never know," I say, picking up my plants and leaving her to her work.

After completing a ton of documentation and assorted other tasks, I am ready to head home. And, of course, someone raps on my door. I sure hope it isn't Woody. Opening the door, I'm surprised to see Sherm.

"Can we go outside?" he asks, holding up his cigarette.

"Does the staff know you're down here?"

"I don't know. Maybe. I don't know."

"Well, let me call upstairs to tell them you're with me," I say, heading for the phone. After letting staff know that I will be meeting with Sherm and returning him around four, I grab a Zippo from my desk and follow him outside. Lighting his cigarette, Sherm heads to a nearby picnic bench, where we sit across from each other.

"So what's going on, Sherm?"

He exhales a large plume of smoke before speaking. "I'm pretty sure something's going to happen."

"What do you think is going to happen?"

"The Chinese. They're doing something to change the jet stream."

"The jet stream? How could they possibly do that?"

"By heating the troposphere."

"And how would they heat the troposphere?"

"With solar panels on satellites."

"And how would anyone know if that was really happening?"

"Changes in the jet stream. Weather changes. Aircraft accidents."

"Well, at least there is a way of testing out your worries, isn't there?"

"We got to warn the president about what they're up to," Sherm says, gravely.

"You feel the government needs to be alerted."

"The president. Not the government. The government can't be trusted."

"Alerting the president is a huge step, Sherm."

"Damn it, Masonheimer, it's gotta be done!" he shouts, reaching for another cigarette from his crumpled pack of Camels.

"I hear you feel strongly about this, Sherm, but I think we need to sleep on it."

"Why? All we'd be doing is giving the Chinese more time to wreak havoc."

"Maybe you don't need more time, Sherm, but I do. Let me think about what you are saying, and we can get together on Monday."

"Monday? Why not tomorrow?"

"Tomorrow is Saturday."

"So, I'm not going anywhere."

"Well, I typically don't work Saturdays, Sherm."

He stares at me incredulously, his cigarette dangling precariously on his lower lip.

"Well, I guess I could come in for an hour or so," I say, reluctantly.

"What time?"

"What about nine a.m.?"

"Bring your lighter."

"Right."

Virga

"All right ladies, strip your beds and drop off your dirty sheets, if you want to go out for privileges," Paige shouts down the hallway. Saturday morning, linen day. Time for old sheets to be shipped out for laundering and the new to be tucked in. "Let's get that laundry bag over here, Luther," Paige says.

Luther, sullen, seems to not have heard Paige. He stares down the hallway at nothing in particular.

"What's with him?" Paige asks Emma Worman, who is writing in a patient's chart.

Emma peers over her reading glasses at Luther, who seems cemented to the floor. Even though Luther has primarily worked on men's wards, Emma knows him, knows that he is a strange agent, but overall a compliant worker. However, since he has been reassigned to the women's ward, Luther has been more distant and removed from everyone, more than she can recall him ever being.

"Luther. Please give Paige a hand with the laundry bag," Emma says loud enough to stir him.

He turns toward the salt-and-pepper-haired nurse. His eyes appear glazed. "I'm going home. Don't feel well," he says flatly. Without a further word, he turns and ambles down the corridor toward the exit door.

"Good riddance," Paige says to Emma. "That guy is as useless as teats on a bull. I can handle the work without him, Em. No need to try to find a replacement."

Emma wonders if Luther is going to be okay. She'll need to call downstairs and let them know he went home without approval. But before she does, she will need to help Paige with the laundry and make some phone calls to doctors. The job seems to get harder each day.

"Here are my bed sheets, Mrs. Worman," Kim says, clumsily holding on to the bundle of bed linen that hides most of her torso.

"Take them to where Paige has the laundry bag," Emma says.

"Thank you. Can I please go out for privileges then, Mrs. Worman?" Kim asks.

"After you pick up your new sheets and make your bed. Just remember to sign out." Emma remains wary of Kim's politeness. As a nurse for the past thirty-five years, Emma has been schmoozed too often; polite agreeableness raises a red flag to her.

As patients straggle to the laundry exchange room, Emma and Paige work in tandem to deposit soiled linens and dispense new ones. They ignore the phone, which has rung several times, thinking that if it's important enough the caller will call back. Meanwhile, a queue of patients is forming by the exit door, all waiting to be let out for privileges.

"A humid one this morning, isn't it?" Paige says, wiping her brow. "I bet we get rain."

"Go ahead and let the women with privileges out, Paige. I'll finish this," Emma says.

When Paige opens the door and visually inspects who's leaving, she asks, "All you ladies have signed out, right?" A chorus of yeahs rings out. "All you have written down where you're heading, right?" Again, a group affirmation is heard.

But several patients aren't being truthful. Ophelia and Kim have whereabouts they don't want to reveal on the sign-out sheet. And one other, Cora Ruth, hasn't indicated where she is going as well. Highly unusual for her not to follow rules, but today she has a good reason.

∽

It feels strange to be driving to the hospital on Saturday, and not to have shaved or put on a tie. I find the parking lot nearly empty. I slip my truck into a space marked "Physicians Only." Not much chance that any of them will be coming in this morning. I lock up but then remember that I'll need a lighter, so I unlock and search for one. Given that I don't smoke, I wonder if I will find any. Then I remember I have some matches in a camping bag that is stuffed under the seat. Securing the matches, I head out to pick up Sherm. Dark looming clouds jostle overhead. Looks like rain. I wonder if

I should bring an umbrella. I decide against it knowing that Sherm wouldn't accept its protection, and I would feel silly using it as we walk together. Besides, I'm wearing old clothes and sneakers. A little rain isn't going to hurt.

I avoid the front entranceway to Dix by unlocking a side door to access a staircase to the third floor. Signing in at the front desk is the normal procedure, but I'll only be here a few minutes. Besides, I'm feeling too self-conscious being unshaven and dressed so casually to be seen by familiar faces.

When I get to Sherm's unit, there is a hubbub of activity with patients hauling bed sheets around. *So, this is what a Saturday morning looks like.* I head in the direction of the nursing station when Sherm turns the corner. He's filling his tattered shirt pocket with a pack of Camels. His fly is open, and his shoes are untied.

"Hey, Sherm. Ready to go?"

"Yeah."

"What about your shoelaces?" I ask, pointing to his feet.

He stares at the laces like he never saw them before. Eventually, he bends down and ties them.

"Don't forget your barn door," I say, shooting a glance at his fly.

He zips with annoyance. "You want me to comb my hair, too?"

"No, let's get going before it starts raining," I say, opening the side door. As we near the first floor, I remember to ask, "Did you tell nursing where you were going?"

"Yeah, when I got my cigs."

I wonder if he really did. But I don't want to waste any more time heading back upstairs again. When we open the exit door, the air smells swollen with moisture.

❧

In the front parking lot, Luther sits in his truck listening to the rant of an ultra-conservative talk-radio jockey...*America is on the road to ruin my fellow Americans. Its lifeblood is being drained by the welfare programs at the federal level. Its values are being destroyed by the immigration invasion at its borders. Terrorists are designing their next assault while prayer is banished from our schools. Where has the respect for American principles gone, my fellow Americans? Where has it gone?*

The words resonate deep in the marrow of Luther's bones. The time has come to take a stand and put an end to this hell. He turns off the radio, locks his truck, and walks smartly to his destination.

❧

"Come on, I know a safe place." Kim motions to Ophelia. "The greenhouse closed yesterday. No one will be there. We can enjoy this herb without anyone bothering us." She waves a perfectly rolled blunt in front of Ophelia's face.

"Sounds good to me. Maybe we should try to find Kendra. I'm sure she would like to get high with us," Ophelia says.

"Didn't you hear? Kendra went home for the weekend with her boyfriend."

"Her boyfriend? What boyfriend?" Ophelia is genuinely stunned.

"Didn't she tell you? She met him at the outpatient clinic last year."

"Are you sure? She never mentioned any guy to me."

"Yeah. I think his name is Joe."

"Joe? Wait a minute. Did you see this Joe?"

"No. Kendra just told me about him."

"Joe ain't no Joe, Kim. Joe is a she...Josephine, Kendra's old caseworker. So she's coming around again? I bet it's not to fill out social security forms." Ophelia is clearly irritated.

"Hmmm. Sounds like you need to relax, Opie. This little fella will help." Kim holds out the doobie in front of Ophelia.

"Yeah, but stop waving that joint like a flag. Someone might spot it. We better circle the greenhouse a few times to make sure no one is around. Then we can sneak into the side door. It's easy to force open. Kendra and I have done it before. But forget her, I got you," Ophelia says curling her arm around Kim's shoulder.

The wind picks up and pushes against their backs.

ॐ

Clutching the key she had taken yesterday from the greenhouse, Cora Ruth walks anxiously around the northern wing of Dix building. She has never done anything like this before; never has done anything dishonest. Accordingly, she is feeling both nervous and excited about stealing some private time among the remaining plants that were left behind at the greenhouse. She also is feeling somewhat shameful to be breaking a rule and for which she will be punished should she be caught. But she doesn't want to give up on what is good for her. So much good has been taken from her already. She is not going to give up on her plants and soil.

After turning the corner of Dix, Cora Ruth starts to walk on the sidewalk adjacent to the chapel. She goes only a short distance before she sees Dr. Masonheimer and a male patient approaching on her left. She decides to reverse her course and walk behind the chapel until they are out of sight. Again she feels shameful about being sneaky, and avoiding Dr. Masonheimer, who has been so nice to her. But she is determined to spend time with her plants.

After the men move past, Cora Ruth quickly crosses the inner hospital road, pausing at the old cannery, which is adjacent to the greenhouse. She scans the area. There are a few patients walking about, so she decides to sit on a nearby bench and wait. When the coast is clear, she will go to the backdoor and use her ill begotten key to gain entry.

❧

Slate-colored clouds build rapidly as Sherm and I approach Manchester building. I'm concerned about them, but more so about Sherm. He has been chain smoking ever since we started walking, and rambling on about the malevolence of the Chinese. He has progressively become more churned up like the threatening clouds surrounding us. Moreover, Sherm has given me few opportunities to challenge his logic or to guide his attention elsewhere. He is fixated on the impending doom associated with the possible alteration of the jet stream by the Chinese. As unlikely as that is, I am looking for a way to build on this fear in order to maneuver him to more rational ground.

"They have the technology to build satellites that could reflect the sun's rays into the stratosphere above North America. That could change the jet stream. They would have to experiment with it for a while in order to find the right amount of energy to steer an air mass, but it wouldn't take long. Hell, they've probably figured it out already, and these clouds above us are part of their design. Made in China, Masonheimer. Just like everything else." Sherm stops to cough and spit.

"Sherm, why don't we take a break from this and get a soda. You sound hoarse and dry. What do you say?"

"You buying?"

"Yeah, I'm buying. Come on, let's stop at the vending machines in Manchester."

Sherm grows quiet. He reaches for another cigarette but stops short. Instead, he sinks his hands deep into his pants pockets. We walk in silence.

◌◠◌

The lock on the rotting door easily gives way to Ophelia's shove. Once inside, Kim and Ophelia head to a corner worktable and crawl underneath. "You have the lighter, right?" Kim asks.

"I thought you brought it?" Ophelia replies.

"What? You don't have a lighter?"

"I thought you were going to bring one."

"Now what are we going to do?" Kim says, looking crestfallen.

Ophelia nudges her. "Only kidding, Kimmy. Here. Don't burn yourself," Ophelia says, handing her a red plastic lighter.

"Kidding is good, but a lighter is better." Kim takes a long drag off the joint before handing it to Ophelia.

They pass the doobie back and forth, feeling more at ease with each hit. As the marijuana gradually relaxes them, they are taken by surprise. A key is opening a lock. Kim looks wide-eyed at Ophelia and starts giggling. Ophelia cups her hand over Kim's mouth. Ophelia shakes her head and holds up her index finger to her lips, signaling Kim to be quiet. Fighting back her laughter, she crushes out the roach and sinks deeper into the corner. Prostrating herself on the dirty concrete floor, Ophelia carefully peers in the direction of the back door. She sees the legs of a woman wearing a faded calico dress and white slip-on sneakers entering the room. *Odd.*

Relocking the door, Cora Ruth walks toward the planting table where a mound of dark, rich humus is piled high. But before reaching it, she stops and sniffs the air. A pungent yet aromatic scent fills the room. Cora Ruth wonders if someone forgot to turn off the coffee pot from yesterday. She goes to the kitchenette but finds the coffee pot unplugged. She walks in the direction of the burnt aroma, fearing that the green-house is on fire.

As she nears the table where the two girls are hiding, Ophelia shouts, "Hey!"

"Whaaa!" Cora Ruth cries out.

"What are you doing here?" Ophelia asks, rising from the floor.

Cora Ruth gasps for air holding a hand against her chest. "Good lord. You scared the devil out of me." She leans against the table trying to regain her composure.

"What are you doing here?" Ophelia asks.

"I'm tending to some plants. What are you doing here?"

Before Ophelia can say anything, the sound of a key in the door is again heard. Ophelia sinks to the floor as does Cora Ruth, and they scurry under the table. "I thought you were here to work," Ophelia whispers at Cora Ruth.

"Shush," Cora Ruth whispers back.

∽

With two cans of pop in hand, Sherm and I walk back outside and immediately are greeted by an ugly gust of wind. We definitely are going to get rain.

"Let's walk back, Sherm, before we get caught in a downpour," I say.

"Can we sit for a second, Doc? I want to study the clouds." Sherm strikes a match to light up his cigarette.

"All right, just for a second or two. I don't like the looks of this weather."

I lead us toward the ball field bleachers that sit between Manchester and Dix. I wonder if Sherm isn't tired out after chain-smoking for the last twenty minutes and just wants a chance to catch his breath. But when we sit down on the bleachers, true to his word, Sherm scans the sky.

"These are different clouds than we usually get around here. I wonder if the Chinese are seeding them," he muses.

"Now, how could they do that?"

"Balloons. Radio controlled. Small enough to slip by radar but big enough to unload silver iodide. See those reddish hues in that patch of clouds?" Sherm asks, pointing to a bank of lead-colored clouds streaked in bands of orange and red. "Could be because of the iodide."

"Yeah, I see them. They look like they were smeared with mercurochrome," I respond.

"Mercurochrome and iodine are pretty similar."

"Regardless of how similar they are, I don't like the looks of them. They spell trouble to me."

"That's what I've been saying. Sounds like you are coming around to my way of thinking, Doc."

"Let's not go that far, Sherm. What do you say we get going?"

"Give me a couple more seconds." He takes a swig of pop.

"Only a couple, Sherm. Then we got to go."

༄

After carefully closing and locking the greenhouse door behind him, Luther stops to sniff the air. His bulbous nose inhales deeply. "Smells like oregano," he says aloud. He figures it must be growing somewhere in here, but it really is of no concern to him. Instead, he reaches down and lifts his trouser leg above his calf. He removes his Colt .45 from its holster, then lowers the pistol to the side of his leg. Slowly, he begins walking between the work benches.

Peering from beneath the table, Kim sees camouflage boots approaching. She recognizes them as those belonging to the male aide who doesn't like her. She leans forward and whispers to Ophelia, "It's that weird aide with the army clothes. I think he is coming to get me."

Ophelia crouches down low and sees what Kim is talking about. Besides the boots, Ophelia spots the pistol that Luther is holding by his leg as he approaches them. "What the hell is he up to?" Ophelia whispers to Cora Ruth.

Cora Ruth shakes her head. She, too, sees the pistol and is dumbfounded as to why an aide would be coming for them with a weapon. Breaking into the greenhouse deserves a punishment but nothing like this.

The women squeeze closer to one another expecting to be called out. Instead of stopping, Luther walks by. He proceeds to the end of the work table. He pauses, removes his cap, and pulls out of his pocket the polyester American flag. He drapes the flag on an overhead wire. Slowly, he salutes it. Then he raises his gun to his temple.

"Don't you dare! Don't you dare! Don't you dare!" Cora Ruth shouts, struggling to lift herself from under the table.

Luther stares in bewilderment at the old woman. His pistol remains frozen at his head. "What the hell," he mutters.

"Put that gun down. Do you hear me? Put that gun down," Cora Ruth says, walking toward him.

"Cora Ruth, for God's sake, come back here!" Ophelia yells. "You're going to get yourself killed."

Luther bends down and spies Ophelia and the Vietnamese girl. "What the hell."

"Don't you dare shoot yourself. Don't you dare take the life that your mother gave you," Cora Ruth admonishes, waggling her finger at Luther. "What would your mother say to you if she knew you were pointing a gun to your head?"

Luther becomes more confounded. He is struck by how Cora Ruth's voice reminds him of his own mother's. How the tone is so similar. She even looks somewhat like his mother. Could this be her apparition?

"Don't you ever think you have the right to kill yourself. Your mother struggled to give you life, to raise you, to make sure you were safe and had the opportunity to be happy. You can't ignore all that she did for you just because something isn't going right in your life. Now put down that gun."

"It's not a gun...it's a pistol," Luther mumbles, slowly lowering the weapon to his side.

"Well, whatever it is, unload it," Cora Ruth demands.

Luther is stunned. He doesn't know what to make of this woman and the spell she has cast upon him. He feels as if he were a child being upbraided for misbehaving. Surprising himself, he unlocks the Colt's magazine and hands it to Cora Ruth.

"I don't want to touch that thing. Put it on the table. Is it safe now?" She asks, pointing to the pistol.

Luther looks at the muted steel .45 laying so foreign in his hand. He pulls back the action, and a cartridge ejects. "Yeah, it's safe now."

"Well then, put it away."

Luther slides the pistol into his leg holster. He picks up the cartridge and lays it next to the magazine, and looks to the woman waiting for her next command.

Cora Ruth legs begin to wobble. She leans against the table to steady herself. Ophelia crawls out from beneath the table and puts her arm around Cora Ruth, who begins to sob.

"You're going be okay. Just take your time," Ophelia says softly, embracing her.

Kim also emerges from underneath the table. She stares at Ophelia and Cora Ruth, then at Luther. She wonders if she is hallucinating all this when a lightning bolt lands outside illuminating the whole greenhouse.

Bam! The ensuing thunderclap shakes the glass panes and startles everyone.

"What a trip I'm on," Kim says, holding her hands over her ears.

"This ain't no trip, Kimmy. We got to get out of here before it's too late," Ophelia says.

"I'll get the door," Luther says, seemingly regaining his wits. He pockets the flag and the ammo, then turns to the women. "What should we do about what happened in here?"

The women look at one another shaking their heads. "Bump it," Ophelia says.

"Meaning what?" Luther asks.

"Meaning we were never in here. None of us. Agreed?" Ophelia proposes.

"Fine with me," Cora Ruth says in a drained voice.

"I imagined the whole thing anyway," Kim says.

"Okay. I owe you," Luther says, opening the door.

Outside, the wind is whipping the trees and punishing anyone who dares to walk through it. Another lighting strike hits nearby, and thunder slams the greenhouse.

"Come on. We can make it to the back entrance of Dix," Luther shouts over the wind.

As they scurry toward the stone fortress, a massive gust of wind knocks Kim and Cora Ruth to the ground. "I'm going back to the greenhouse," Kim says, picking herself up.

"No. We're not going back there," Ophelia shouts. "Come on. We can make it. Keep walking."

"No. I'm going to get blown away," Kim cries. "I'm going back to the greenhouse."

"Damn you, Kimmy. We're not going back there!" Ophelia shouts.

"Well then, I'm going in there," Kim says, pointing to the Love Nest. She runs slipping and falling until she reaches the giant rhododendron bush. She scampers underneath its protective branches.

"Kim. Damn you," Ophelia says, giving chase.

Luther assists Cora Ruth along as they follow Ophelia. When they reach the Love Nest, Ophelia is trying to drag Kim out but with no success. "Go. Go on. I'll stay with her," Ophelia says to them.

The wind increases to a gale force, blowing Luther's cap off his head and ripping away at Cora Ruth's dress.

"We can't leave them," Cora Ruth says to Luther.

He looks toward Dix. It is only fifty yards away. He knows he can get inside and be safe.

"All right, you go first. I'll follow you," Luther says to Cora Ruth.

She crawls into the nest. Luther looks toward Dix before burrowing into the warren with the others. They huddle close as the wind increases its intensity.

∽

A dust devil descends on Sherm and me as we struggle to make our way back to Dix. With lightning and thunder all around us, even he is beginning to worry about whether we can reach our destination safely.

"Those Chinese know how to whip up a storm, don't they, Doc?" he shouts. "They must have heard me talking about them, and now they're trying to silence me."

"Let's keep moving. We're almost there," I shout back.

As we approach the rear of Dix, Sherm suddenly stops and stares at a large rhododendron bush off to our left. "What are you stopping for?" I yell.

"You see what I see?" He points to the bush.

"What? I don't see anything but branches flapping in the wind. Let's get going before these clouds burst open and drown us."

"Look." He says, pointing. "Look, there's an American flag in there."

Although certain that this is another of Sherm's distorted perceptions, I nevertheless squint at the bush. To my surprise, I do see a flag. It seems to be hanging inside the base of the shrub. Probably blown by the wind.

"Yeah, I see it, but let's forget about it. We got to get inside."

"We can't leave the flag out here. I'm going to get it," Sherm declares.

He marches off leaning into the wind with every step. I shake my head and follow him. When we reach the bush, I can't believe my eyes. Huddling inside is Luther hoisting his polyester Old Glory over the heads of Cora Ruth, Ophelia, and another young woman.

"What the hell are you guys doing in there?" I shout.

"We're riding out the storm. Want to join us?" Luther says.

"Why would you want to take shelter in there when the building is only a few minutes away?" I ask.

"Kim won't go, and we aren't going without her," Ophelia says.

"Well, that's bighearted of you, but you're going to get soaked," I say as the rain unloads on us.

"The flag will protect us," Luther says flatly.

Shaking my head at that notion, I nevertheless crawl inside and huddle with them. Although we are tightly packed together, I'm surprised how accommodating the bower is. Realizing that Sherm is still outside, I yell at him, "Come on in, Sherm. There's enough room."

Sherm ignores me, staring at the sky. Angry colors are clashing with the brutal wind and falling rain.

"Sherm, come on in. Get out of the rain. There's enough room in here."

"It's a virga," Sherm says, looking up at the sky.

"What?"

"A virga," he says, pointing at the sky.

"What's a virga?" Luther asks.

"I have no idea what he means," I say, crawling back outside to join him.

Sherm points to the sky immediately above us. "I can't believe it, but damn, there it is. It's a virga."

I still don't know what he means, but notice that the rain has stopped. Well not stopped, but somehow is being drawn back up into the sky, instead of falling down. I've never seen anything like it. And the wind seems to be swirling upwards, too.

"This generally doesn't happen around here," Sherm says. "It mostly happens out West."

Luther and the women come out to see what Sherm is talking about. We all gawk at the strange sight of rain evaporating back into the marbled sky.

"It was the flag," Sherm opines. "The Chinese were repelled by the stars and stripes."

Everyone stares at Sherm. Then at me. "It's a long story," I say.

∽

Planning Ahead

Cameron pensively inspects the appointment board. Overton is scheduled for another dental appointment tomorrow at the same time that she is scheduled for a series of ultrasound tests. Cameron is tempted to cancel her appointment but knows that if she does it will be at least a week before another test could be rescheduled. Can she trust her back-up to assign enough staff to safely escort Overton to Dix? She decides to call Myrna Blass and make sure tomorrow is handled properly. It's not normal protocol calling the director of nursing to discuss how to arrange escort services, but then again, Overton is not a normal patient.

"Hello, Mrs. Blass."

"Myrna, it's Cameron over in forensic."

"Yes, Cameron. What can I do for you?"

"I hate to bother you with this concern, Myrna, but I want to err on the side of caution. It has to do with Garner Overton."

"What about Mr. Overton?"

"Well, tomorrow he's scheduled for a dental appointment, and I'm scheduled to attend a medical appointment."

"And what's the connection?"

"Since I won't be here tomorrow to arrange the escort services for him, I want to make sure someone will get him there and back again without any blunders."

"You assume there will be a blunder? Why?"

"I'm not assuming that anything will go wrong. I only want to ensure nothing does go wrong."

"So, you want me to personally be involved in arranging how Mr. Overton gets to his dental appointment?"

"Yes, I guess I am asking you to personally oversee it, Myrna. I know it should be my back-up's responsibility but I don't know who that will be, whereas I know who you are."

"And I am...?"

"A responsible person...whom I trust."

"If it will put your mind at rest, Cameron, then I will personally oversee that Mr. Overton gets safely to his dental appointment."

"Thanks, Myrna."

"Incidentally, what medical procedure will you be having done?"

"An ultrasound...my carotids...they might be clogged. Years of smoking finally catching up with me, Myrna. That and my addiction to sirloins.

"And here I thought you were a vegan, Cameron."

"Hah. Up 'til this point, I've been getting my daily vegetable via four-legged grazers or inhaling tobacco leaves. Of course all that may change after tomorrow," Cameron says more seriously.

"Don't worry about tomorrow, Cameron. We still have to get through today."

"So we do. Thanks, Myrna."

"Good luck, Cameron."

Myrna hangs up the phone. She turns her attention back to the union grievance lying on her desk. Defending Capitol City's edict of mandatory overtime for nursing staff is giving Myrna a headache. This is one of those times when she wonders if her six-figure income is really worth all the stress that comes with her position. At least tonight is her casino club and a chance to unwind.

Spellbound

As night falls, security globes send a surrealistic blue beam streaming through Overton's window. Lying on his bed, he imagines the illuminative light to be magical and meant to empower him in his quest for freedom. Ever since he was an altar boy assisting priests with spiritual rituals, Overton has been fascinated with supernatural experiences. He especially enjoys the mystical transformation that happens to women when they succumb to his command over them. Admittedly, they surrender to his physical strength and domination, not his amorous powers, but for him it is the relinquishment of their will that results in that scarce moment of beautiful tenderness. For the briefest twinkling of time, vulnerability radiates, transcends, then silently withers like a plucked flower—the face of God peeking through the veil before disappearing. Exhilarating.

Overton picks up his sketchpad and examines his drawing of Elsa. It is a good rendition of her features, but it is stilted, lacking life. Tomorrow he believes he will finally see her without her boldness. Wounded and helpless. Then he will know what she truly looks like. Then he will sketch her.

~~

What Can Go Wrong

At seven in the morning, day shift nursing staff members meander into ward offices to hear the reports of the night shift, who eagerly await the end of their rotation to go home and get some sleep or get their kids ready for school. Kirk is drifting in and out of the night shift report when the phone next to him rings.

"Hello, Forensic Unit," he says in a sleepy voice.

"Who is this?"

"Kirk. Who's this?"

"This is Mrs. Blass, Mr. Bleu. Apparently, you need a refresher course on how to answer the phone. I'll make sure you are registered for one. Now, put the charge nurse on the phone, Mr. Bleu."

"Yes ma'am. One minute." Kirk waves at the night shift nurse. "Phone's for you, Joanne, Kirk says thrusting the receiver in her direction.

"This is Mrs. Lakowitz."

"Joanne, it's Myrna. Is the day shift charge nurse there?"

"No, not yet. Cameron is off, and I don't know who is substituting for her."

"I'll fix that problem right now. But I want you to make sure you tell the staff that Garner Overton doesn't leave the ward without at least three staff members being available to escort him. He has a dental appointment this morning, and Cameron wanted to make sure it goes off without any problems."

"All right, Myra. I'll pass that information along in my report before leaving this morning."

"Also, Joanne, Mr. Overton is to be shackled every inch of the way, back and forth."

"Understood. Anything else, Myrna?"

"No, that's it. I'll be sending a nurse over there as soon as I can."

"Okay, Myrna. Thank you."

Hanging up, the night shift nurse resumes her report, and relays Myrna's message. Kirk has nodded off and several of the other day shift staff members are fading in and out as well. Kirk awakes in time to hear Overton's name and something about a dental appointment.

∽

The Stage Is Being Set

Jake Worman takes a sip of his coffee before entering the nursing administrative office. He wonders where he'll be assigned today. Yesterday was Manchester building working with patients he barely knew. It's hard to develop a working relationship with patients when you're bouncing all over the hospital. Jake looks into his mailbox and pulls out his assignment sheet. Forensic Unit. Terrific. From the geriatrics to the sociopaths.

Jake heads back to his car and drives to the Forensic Unit. At the unit's sally port he is met by Kirk, who is scanning the oncoming staff.

"Hey, Jake. See you got stuck being Camie today."

"Where is the beast of the east?"

"I think she's at a medical appointment."

"So she's human after all!"

"Camie's really not that bad, Jake. Not that I would want to live with her, mind you...but overall she's not that bad."

"If you say so, Kirk."

"Come on through, Jake. Looks like you ain't packing anything dangerous today," Kirk says, buzzing the electronic lock to the ward door.

Jake and Kirk walk to the ward office. "So, what's on the schedule for this morning?" Jake asks, looking at the assignment board.

"Not much. The shrink has some patient reviews at nine forty-five. And we've got to take Overton to the dental office for his eleven o'clock appointment. Other than that, just the routine stuff. Should be an easy day."

"I have yet to have an easy day at this place. I don't see why today would be any different."

"Got to look on the bright side of things, Jake. That's what my horoscope said this morning: 'Today, the light will shine on you.'"

"Don't go blind staring at all that light shining on you, Kirk," Jake says. He scopes out the staff roster. It indicates there should be three more men other than Kirk. "Where are these guys?" Jake asks, pointing to the roster.

"I think Banks called in sick. I guess Gus and Ernie are out back with the inmates getting them roused for breakfast."

"Inmates? Is that what you call them over here, Kirk?"

"What do you want me to call them, Jake? Consumers of forensic services?"

"And Cameron is okay with that?"

"When she's around, we call them patients. But when the cat is away..."

"Well, let's get going with breakfast. That is, if you can break away from all that light shining on you.'"

"Your wish is my command, Master," Kirk says, mockingly bowing at Jake.

Jake heads to the break room for another cup of coffee. He grabs one of the walkie-talkies and hooks it onto his belt. It screeches painfully, and he turns it off.

∾

An Unfortunate Distraction

"**B**ring in the next man, Nurse Worm," Dr. Yusuf says.

"That's Worman, Doctor. Not worm. My name is Jacob Worman," Jake says with a strained voice.

"And a good name it is, Nurse Worman," the doctor replies. "Bring me the next man."

Jake goes out of the interview room mumbling to himself that retirement can't come soon enough.

"Ernie, get me Yost. The doctor wants to see him."

"Okay. The air's pretty thick, Jake. Okay with you if I turn on the fan?" Ernie asks, pointing toward the large free-standing fan at the end of the corridor.

"Go ahead. Moving the air around has got to help with this heat."

In short time Ernie has Buster Yost in tow, but he doesn't appear to be in a good mood.

"What's the doctor want to see me for? I ain't done nothing." Buster lumbers along. With his knobby shaven head angled and stretched in front of his three hundred pound torso, he resembles an angry snapping turtle ready to bite.

"The doc only wants to check on how your meds are doing, Buster. Nothing more," Ernie says.

"Okay, Ernie, I'll take him in," Jake says. "This way, Buster." Jake extends his arms toward the interview room.

Buster noses into the room but balks. "I ain't talking to that damn foreigner. Can't understand what he asks me. Ain't you got any real doctors?"

"Come on, Buster. Let's go. The sooner you get in here the sooner you get out," Jake says, grabbing onto Buster's arm.

"I told you I ain't going in there." He forcefully rips his arm away from Jake's grip.

"Damn it, Buster. What's wrong with you?"

"Get out of my face. Or I'll show you what's wrong with me, you Nazi nurse," Buster glowers at Jake.

"Buster. My bud. Come on now, let's be reasonable," Ernie says, trying to placate him.

"You get out of my face, too. I ain't your bud, buddy."

Buster turns and stomps down the hallway, stopping by the floor fan. He lifts it up by its post and smashes it against the wall. The motor sparks, and the blades flail against the fan housing. Buster slams the clanking fan to the floor as if it were a vanquished victim.

"All right, Ernie, let's restrain him," Jake says, removing his glasses and walking briskly toward the angry patient.

Ernie looks shocked at the idea of attempting to subdue Buster, who has the strength of a Neanderthal. "Wait a minute, Jake. We're going to need more muscle to put him down."

"Buzz for Bleu and Meckley. They should be in the dayroom," Jake orders, slowing down his pace as he approaches Buster.

Ernie hits a wall alarm that buzzes throughout the unit. Within seconds, both Kirk and Gus Meckley rush into the corridor to assist Jake and Ernie.

"Okay, boys, we're going to do a wall restraint, and if that fails then we put him on the floor," Jake says.

"Once we have him pinned down, then what are we going to do with him?" Kirk asks.

"We'll syringe him. But keep your pants on. First we got to get a hold of him,"

Buster beckons the four men toward him.

Sharing More Pain

After making a number of corrections to Woody's petition, I hustle to the group room where Autumn and Lincoln are waiting quietly for me to open the door. They take their usual seats, and within a few minutes Kendra, Ophelia, and Cora Ruth join them. Everyone is here except for Harvey, which is unusual. He rarely misses group.

"Well, folks, I think we can get started. Hopefully, Harvey will be along shortly."

"Or hopefully not," Ophelia says.

I ignore her comment. "So, last group we left off with Cora Ruth reciting her poem which was entitled..." I search my memory but am coming up short.

"Mamie Groller," Lincoln says.

"That's right. Thank you, Lincoln. At least someone has a good memory. So, does anyone have any thoughts or comments about her poem?"

I look around, but no one is making any sign that they have something to say. "Okay, then let's move to something current. Does someone have a poem to share?"

Again, no one responds. Harvey's absence is evident. I notice Cora Ruth looking about. Uneasy with the group's non-responsiveness, she speaks up.

"I could share one, I guess."

"That would be wonderful. Please do."

She slowly stands and removes her fractured glasses from her pocket along with her notebook. She looks straight at me.

"When my husband died, I shut down and didn't care whether I lived or not. I only took care of my plants. But once in a while, I wrote down what was stuck in my mind. This ditty is from one of those times. I call it 'His Lunch Pail.'"

> He wakes before me, every day,
> Washes his face, shaves.
> I hear the water running
> The razor clinking the sink.
> I duly rise
> Put on my housecoat and slippers
> And trudge to the kitchen.
> I stopped long ago asking what he wants
> I just pack, every day.
> A summer sausage sandwich,
> Pickles, cookies, and his thermos.
> Every day.
> I close the lid
> Snap the clasps and wait.
> He dons his cap and coat.
> I turn a cheek for his peck

Then watch him take his lunch pail
Into the darkness of the morning
Sure that he will return
Every day.

Instead of sitting, Cora Ruth remains standing, staring at her notebook. She appears transfixed, lost. Then suddenly she shakes her head, realizes she has finished, and takes her seat.

"Your poem, Cora Ruth, captured how we expect the familiar to stay the same," I say.

"It didn't stay the same," Cora Ruth replies.

"No, sadly it didn't for you. Nor in the long run does it for any one of us."

"And for some of us that would be a blessing," Ophelia says.

"Amen to that," Kendra interjects.

"I wish nothing had ever changed," Cora Ruth says. "Every change in my life has brought me pain."

"Losing your husband is like my people losing their land," Lincoln says.

I can see how Lincoln could make that connection. I wonder if Cora Ruth will accept his analogy or find it to be offensive. She scrutinizes Lincoln before speaking.

"I can understand how losing your way of life is like losing a loved one. For me my husband and my boys were my way of life. Without them I am wandering about, lost, without a home. I guess that is what you and your people have been feeling as well," she says looking at Lincoln.

"By your words you understand," Lincoln says.

"By my heart I understand," Cora Ruth replies.

The Best Of Intentions

Elsa checks her lady Rolex, almost ten thirty. In thirty minutes she will slip over to the dental office to give Garner Overton the support that he needs to get through his dental work. She has prepared for Garner's appointment by reviewing the psychology department's treatment manual that provides instructions on how to do relaxation training. If Garner follows the relaxation steps that she will teach him, he can reduce his anxiety and calmly allow the dentist to provide the dental services that he needs. Psychology work really is pretty simple. All those old-fashioned psychodynamic notions and beliefs that Dr. Masonheimer keeps referencing are merely havens for psychologists who don't know how to apply behavioral principles.

❦

Falling Into Place

"Let him sleep off that Haldol," Dr. Yusuf says to Jake. "And put him on one-to-one watch."

Buster groggily moans and slowly rolls his head across his pillow. After fifteen minutes of putting up a valiant struggle with the four forensic guards and two administrative assistants, he now has succumbed to the tranquilizing effects of Dr. Yusuf's psychotropic injection. For the next six hours, Buster will sleep and be as harmless as a baby.

Jake sits, exhausted, and realizes the morning is only half over. He wonders what else can go wrong after this shaky start. Restraining Buster has sent one guard downtown to the emergency room with an arm injury, and now another is tied up on one-to-one observation. Jake glances at the wall clock. Ten forty-five, time to take Overton to the dental office.

"Kirk, let's get Overton and strap him in his set of wheels," Jake barks into the dayroom where Kirk is playing cards with some of the patients.

"Give me a minute, Jake. I'm set to take these guys to the cleaners," Kirk replies.

"Now, Kirk. Let's go. Hubba-hubba," Jake orders.

Kirk groans and forcefully lays down his cards. "Duty calls, gents. I'll get back to you later." He walks to the corner of the dayroom where Overton is reading.

"Let's go, Garner, old boy. You've got a date with a drill and some pain."

Overton grins. "Thanks, Kirk. I've been looking forward to my appointment with Dr. Riley. I'm ready when you are."

"You're in too good of a mood to be seeing the dentist. What's up with you?"

"Getting out of this building can raise a man's spirits. Don't you think?"

"Yeah, I guess you're right. After wrestling with Buster, I need a break from these four walls myself. Let's move it, Garner, before Jake flips his lid. This morning's fiasco has him in a foul mood."

Within minutes, Kirk parks Overton in front of the forensic nursing station and informs Jake that they're ready to go.

"I have Overton shackled and strapped in the wheelchair. All I need is his chart, and at least one or two other staff members to head out with me," Kirk says, entering the nursing office.

"Look around, Kirk. Ain't no one here but you and me," Jake replies, not looking up from the incident report form he's completing. "Do you think you can wheel Overton down the tunnel to Dix by yourself?"

"Yeah, I guess I could. It's not what we normally would do, but then again this hasn't been a normal day so far, has it?"

"As soon as you leave, I'll phone the nursing administration and see if they can send someone to meet you at the dental office."

"Okay by me, Jake," Kirk says, turning his attention to Overton, who is smiling. "You're not going to give me any problems, are you Garner, old boy?"

"I'm just a passenger on this journey, Kirk, old boy," Overton replies.

Jake gets up and inspects the straps securing Overton to the chair. They are tight and buckled properly. With his hands manacled, Overton can't get out.

"Giving me some personal attention, Nurse Worman? How thoughtful," Overton says.

"All right, get him out of here, Kirk. And make sure you have your walkie-talkie with you."

"Got it right here," Kirk says, patting the black device strapped to his belt. He places the chart on Overton's lap. "You can touch but don't look, Garner, old buddy."

"It would be my privilege to assist you, Kirk, old buddy," Overton says, patting his chart.

Kirk pushes Overton in front of the elevator door. Within seconds the door noisily opens, and they head down to the basement and the connecting tunnel leading to Dix. Entering the darkened tunnel, the walkie-talkie starts screeching. Kirk stops to listen. Ernie is screaming something about Buster becoming agitated again. Kirk pauses to ponder what he should do. Turn around and go back or let Jake and Ernie deal with Buster? Kirk massages his aching neck and decides he's had enough wrestling with that bruiser for one day. Overton is an easier assignment, and he's strapped securely. Seems like a no brainer. Kirk turns off the screeching black box and resumes wheeling Overton down the tunnel.

An Unlikely Messenger

"I know I'm late, but it wasn't my fault," Harvey loudly announces before sitting down.

"Wait one second, Harvey," I say. "Lincoln was about to recite one of his poems."

"It was that dentist and that girl...that psychology girl who made me late. I told them I had to go. They had it in for me. They wanted me to get in trouble with you. Can I read my poem now?"

"No, Harvey. I told you Lincoln is about to read his poem. Please sit quietly and give him a chance."

I wonder if Harvey is referring to Elsa. And if so, why would she be at the dental office?

"Sorry, Lincoln. Please go ahead with your reading.

Lincoln stands, shakes his long hair away from his face, affixes his glasses, and opens his notebook. "I call this 'Light and Shadows.'"

Beyond the fallen trees
Away from the gouges
And machine scars
Atop an old village hill
Surrounded by new growth
Light and shadow
Slowly dapple the forest floor
Forming patterns
For future dreams.

Lincoln removes his glasses and sits down. His poem is not as dark and foreboding as what he usually shares. I wonder if he might be moving out of his morbid state.

"I picked up some hope in that poem, Lincoln. Am I right?" I ask.

"Allowing oneself to dream can allow hope to come out of the shadows," he replies.

"Is that what you are doing, Lincoln? Allowing yourself to dream?" Autumn asks.

Lincoln turns in her direction, and for the briefest of moments I detect a loving expression come over his face, and just as quickly disappear.

"I allow myself to dream of land teeming with life. If that is what you mean by dream."

"I have dreams, too," Harvey blurts. "They are written down here." He holds up a wad of rumpled paper in his fist.

"Your dreams are more like nightmares," Ophelia interjects.

"Can we get back to Lincoln?" I ask. "I don't think he was finished."

"Lincoln had his turn. I want my turn," Harvey says excitedly.

"Please, Harvey, I want you to wait your turn."

"If he wants to talk, let him," Lincoln says.

I yield. And Harvey eagerly launches into his stream of loosely associated thoughts and images.

❦

Fate Towers Above

K irk and Overton arrive at the basement elevator. When the elevator door opens the cab stops short, not settling flush with the floor.

"Damn those maintenance people," Kirk mutters. "I reported this last week, and they still haven't fixed it." He struggles to get the wheelchair into the cab.

"I'd be glad to give you a hand, Kirk," Overton says, lifting his cuffed hands in front of him."

"I bet you would, Garner," Kirk replies.

With a final heave, he lifts the chair into the elevator. Creaking, the door closes, and within seconds he and Overton are elevated to the first floor of Dix. Exiting the elevator, they wheel down the hallway toward the dental office. Kirk notices that there aren't any nursing staff members waiting for them, only the good-looking psychology intern. Jake must have been too busy with Buster to call for additional help.

"Hey there, psychology lady. What brings you down here?" Kirk asks

"I'm here to assist Garner with his dental anxiety."

"Dental anxiety? The big bad Garner has a fear of the dentist, does he? Is that right, Garner, old boy? You afraid of the mean old dentist?"

"Ms. Heinzelman is here to make sure I can get by with a minimum of discomfort, Kirk," Overton says, winking and smiling.

"Just having her around makes me feel better, too. Why don't we get you inside and see how well she and you work together."

Kirk pushes Overton into the waiting room and hands the chart to Reva.

"How much time will it be before he gets in?" Kirk asks.

"The doctor will be back in a minute or two."

"I hope so, because I got to visit the little boy's room," Kirk says.

Overton suppresses a grin. This situation is going better than he had imagined.

"I'm starting to feel a bit nervous about the drilling, Elsa. Is there anything you can do to help?" Overton asks.

Elsa moves her chair closer to Overton. "I have some relaxation methods we can try. Would you be up for that?"

Overton doesn't answer. He has never been this physically close to Elsa before. He is amazed at how her complexion is milky smooth and flawless, how her thick hair has a rich sheen, and how delicate the down across the nape of her neck seems to undulate as she breathes. He is taken aback with her body warmth as it carries her scent deep into his lungs, washing his senses with her essence. He forces himself to speak.

"Of course I would be willing to do whatever you ask."

"Who's next, Reva?" Dr. Riley asks, coming out of his office, brushing some crumbs off his smock.

"Mr. Overton is next, Doctor. Should I bring him in?"

"Absolutely...Overton? I've see him before, haven't I?"

"I'll think you'll remember him, Doctor."

Reva signals for Kirk to bring Overton into the operating room. Kirk rises and unbuckles the chest and lap belts. Overton holds his shackled hands up in Kirk's face.

"No way those are coming off my friend," Kirk says.

He uses both hands to grab hold of Overton's jumpsuit and yanks him upright. Overton wobbles a bit.

"Whoa, steady there, Garner, old boy. Get your legs underneath you."

"Thanks, Kirk. I think I got my balance back," Overton says, steadying himself.

"Can I help?" Elsa asks.

"No thanks, little lady. I think we have this situation under control," Kirk says.

Overton shuffles his shackled feet in the direction of Reva, who is waiting to escort him toward the dental chair.

"I'll take over from here," Reva says, reaching for Overton's arm.

"Good," Kirk replies. "I need to run to the bathroom. Are you sure you'll be okay for a few minutes without me?"

"I don't see why not," Reva answers. "Mr. Overton will be very cooperative. Won't you, Mr. Overton? ·

"Scout's honor," Overton responds.

Kirk doesn't like how nice Overton is behaving. But nature is calling. And how much trouble can Overton get into with his hands and feet shackled?

"Be back in a jiff," he says, hustling off to the bathroom down the adjoining corridor.

Overton realizes he has only a minute to act. He hobbles toward the reclining chair, pausing to ask Reva if Elsa can come in, too. When Elsa enters the small room, Overton strikes. He raises his bound arms and swiftly sheathes Elsa tightly against his chest. Without hesitation he lunges toward the instrument tray and grabs several sharp metal picks, positioning them in a threatening manner toward Elsa's neck. Both Reva and Dr. Riley bolt backwards, while Elsa, stunned, mumbles incoherently.

"Both of you get on the floor, now!" Overton shouts.

The dentist complies willingly, but Reva remains standing. "You don't want to harm that girl, Mr. Overton," Reva says.

"If that is what it takes to get you on the floor, I will," Overton says, gesturing the picks more threateningly. "It'll be you who gets her pretty neck cut. So get down. Now!"

Reva sees the terror on Elsa's face and relents.

Overton backs his way into the waiting room. "If I see either of you get up, she gets cut," he warns.

He drags Elsa into the hallway and shambles backwards toward the front entrance of Dix. Overton estimates he has only seconds before Reva calls security and they respond.

"Don't you worry Ms. Elsa, I won't draw a drop of your pretty blood. All I want to do is to get to your car and away from this place. So stay calm. This will be over before you know it," he whispers in Elsa's ear. The aroma of Elsa's hair and sweat mingle in his nostrils, briefly causing him to lose concentration.

"Emergency! Stop that man! Stop that man! Emergency!" Reva's shouts echo down the hallway.

Overton regains his bearings and hurries his shuffling.

Clerical staff members file into the corridor curious to see what the shouting is about. Myrna darts out of her office and can't believe what she sees. Overton has shuffled to the elevator and is only feet away from turning the corner to the front entranceway. Surprisingly, he suddenly stops, turns around, and inches back toward the elevator. Two security staff members have blocked his exit and are quickly approaching him. Myrna calls to the onlookers to join her.

"Get up here with me. We'll cut off his exit down this hallway."

Overton realizes he is trapped and leans against the elevator's casing. He uses his elbow to press the control panel and the distinct sound of the elevator becoming activated is heard.

"Stay where you are!" he screams. "I can get to her jugular before you can get to me."

Everyone heeds his threat and ceases their advancement toward him. Elsa attempts to wrestle free, but

Overton merely coils his arms tighter around her, restricting her movement and breathing. She begins gasping for air.

"Try that again, and I'll choke you out," he says, releasing his hold ever so slightly.

With a metal clunk, the elevator arrives. As the door opens, a small bespectacled man in a black suit and a baseball cap begins to step out. The mysterious Dr. Burda finds himself blocked by Overton and then shoved against the cab's wall as Overton backs into the elevator. "Reach over and close the door," Overton orders.

Dr. Burda complies without a word, and the door creaks shut.

"Hit the button for the third floor," Overton snaps.

Again the little man responds as ordered, and the elevator starts it ascent. "There is no way out on the third floor," Elsa weakly offers.

Overton considers her words. She's probably right. There won't be any way out on any of the floors. His only hope is to find an isolated area and use Elsa a bargaining chip. "What's up on the top floor?"

"The library."

"You have a key for that?"

"At this time of day, you won't need one. It's open. You only need a key to get the elevator to stop on the fourth floor," Elsa says, nodding in the direction of the control panel.

Overton sees that there isn't a button for the fourth floor, only a key slot. "Do you have a key for that?"

"Yes."

"Where is it?"

"In my pocket."

"Reach in her pocket, little man, and get her key," Overton directs Dr. Burda.

Obediently, he retrieves the key.

"Stick it in that fourth floor slot," Overton says.

∽

After Harvey's run-on exposition, everyone, including me, is exhausted. We all agree to end group early and take a break. As I'm locking the door to the group room, several security staff members run by me. Then a couple of nursing aides follow, running at full speed.

"What's the problem?" I shout.

"A patient has taken a staff member hostage," one of them yells back.

That's odd. My crisis pager didn't sound off. Unless it isn't a patient from Dix building. I start walking, then running down the hallway. I don't get very far before I encounter a crowd milling about the dental office. I spot Reva, ashen-faced. "What's going on?" I ask.

"Oh, Jerome. I'm so sorry. That poor girl..." Reva covers her mouth with her hand.

"What poor girl are you talking about?"

"Don't you know? That forensic patient, Garner Overton, abducted your intern."

A wave of nausea courses through my gut. I close my eyes and lean against the wall. "How long ago did it happen?"

"Only a few minutes ago. He dragged her up the elevator," Reva says, pointing down the hallway. "She was so scared. I hope he doesn't hurt her."

I rush to the elevator only to find that security staff has the elevator and the adjacent stairwell cordoned off. I will need to find another way up.

∞

"You wait in that elevator and don't go anywhere with it," Overton orders Dr. Burda. Exiting, Overton backs his way to the medical library's door. He turns around, and with Elsa facing the door directs her to open it. Entering, they find LaDean sorting through journals at one of the circulation racks.

The librarian startles at the sight of Elsa and Overton approaching her. "My God!" she says, dropping an arm full of journals.

Overton looks around. Too much room to cover, even if there is only one door in and out. Moving forward, he spots a small door on his left that appears to be an entrance to a stairwell.

"Where does that door go to?" he barks at LaDean.

"To the roof."

"Is there another way up there?"

"Not that I know of."

"Okay, open it," he orders.

Looking at the horrified expression on Elsa's face, LaDean realizes she mustn't do anything to jeopardize the girl's safety. LaDean reaches for her key ring, finds the right one, and unlocks the door.

"Get back and get me that extension cord over there!" Overton orders, nodding in the direction of an overhead projector.

The librarian retrieves the cord and holds it in front of him.

"Take the cord," Overton tells Elsa, giving her a shake.

With cord in hand, Overton lifts Elsa and stumbles up a few stairs before stopping. He raises his arms over her head, and she falls forward.

"Stay there," he orders, roughly grabbing the extension cord from her hand. He quickly closes the door and lashes one end of the cord to the doorknob and the other to a light fixture above the doorway.

"Okay, start climbing, slowly," he says to Elsa.

Elsa begins to climb the darkened staircase but trips.

"Let's put some light on the subject," Overton says, pulling the chain on the light fixture.

The stairwell comes into full view. Although dusty, it's in good repair.

"Get going." Overton shoves Elsa up the stairs. When they reach the landing, he finds another light that illuminates the area above the library. He's surprised to see that it's a finished attic with planked floors, paneled walls, and tall enough for him to walk around.

"Kind of like a toy box, isn't it?" Overton says. "Take a load off, little lady. It won't be long before we have visitors."

❧

Security staff first rushed to the third floor and waited for the elevator door to open. When it didn't, they realized that it must be on the fourth floor. Reaching the medical library, they find LaDean shaking uncontrollably.

"He went up to the roof. That way," she points to the door. Yanking at it, they realize it's jammed.

"Let's take it apart," Ron Peters says. "Get a screwdriver; we'll remove this knob. Hurry."

Overton's voice booms down at them through the closed door.

"No one comes any further without the girl getting hurt. If you want me to slide a piece of her under the door to show you that I mean business, start messing with the door."

"Okay, we hear you," Ron says, backing away from the door. He turns to the rest of the staff. "We'll wait until the state police get here."

"I'm not waiting for the damn police," Kirk says, rushing in. "That bastard will cost me my job. I'm going after him."

"No, you're not. We are not getting someone hurt just because you want to square off on him. From where I'm standing, you're in trouble enough. If that girl gets hurt, you'll have a hell of lot more to worry about than losing your job," Ron says.

"I knew Overton was up to no good. I just knew it. And that psychology intern walked right into his scheme."

Kirk punches the wall. "It's Jake's fault. This wouldn't have happened had he called for more staff."

"Psychology intern? Is that who she is?" Ron asks.

"Yeah. She's dumber than I am."

༖

Having accessed another stairwell, I race up the stairs. I stop at each floor only to find nothing unusual going on. Only when I reach the fourth floor do I encounter security staff members blocking the library. *Why would Overton flee to the library? There's no way out.*

Ron comes out of the library looking flustered. He reaches in his shirt pocket for his pack of cigarettes but only fingers it before turning to me.

"You shouldn't be up here, Rome. The police will be here any minute, and they'll probably boot you off this floor."

"The woman he has is my intern. I'm responsible for her."

"I know, Rome. But you can't do anything about it now. Why don't you wait downstairs, and if we need you we'll call you."

"Do you know if she's injured?"

"I don't know. There's nothing to suggest that she is, but I don't know. Overton has the door to the roof blocked, so we haven't had a good look at her. Incidentally, what's her name?

"Elsa. Elsa Heinzelman. He has her on the roof?"

"Technically, under the roof. It's the space right above the library. I bet it's got to be a hundred or more degrees up there. Honestly, Rome, go downstairs and we'll let you know how Elsa is as soon as we can."

I reluctantly comply and turn to leave. As I do, I hear the elevator humming. With a jolt, the doors open, and four uniformed state troopers get out.

"Where is he?" one of them asks.

"Follow me," Ron says, turning to enter the library.

❧

"Hot up here, isn't it, Elsa? Perhaps we should remove some of our clothing to get more comfortable?" Overton says.

Elsa doesn't respond. She is lying on the floor tucked in a corner, in shock.

Overton sets the dental picks down on the floor and unbuttons the top of his blue pajama shirt. With his hands manacled, the only way he can remove it is for it to be cut apart. Although Elsa appears to be docile, he isn't ready to trust her to help him. He'll just have to wait for the police to start negotiating with him. Then he can bargain for some water and maybe some ice.

"Garner Overton. Can you hear me?" a male voice calls outside the door.

Overton moves down the steps but only to the point where he can still keep an eye on Elsa.

"Yeah. I hear you. Who are you?"

"This is Sergeant Dylan. I'm here to help resolve this situation, Garner. May I call you Garner, sir?"

"You know, I kinda like the sound of the term 'sir,' sergeant."

"All right. We want to resolve this situation with no injuries to anyone. Are you in agreement with that, sir?"

"No injuries to anyone? Sounds good to me, as long as I get what I want."

"And what specifically do you want, sir?"

"Well, sergeant, here are my three wishes. First, I want some bottled water, a bag of ice, and some towels. Second, I want a key to remove these shackles around my hands and feet. Third, I want a car delivered to the front entrance, with a full tank of gas and its engine running. You can do all that can't you, sergeant?"

"And what are you prepared to do to help me fulfill your requests, sir?"

"Let me think about that for a second, sergeant. Hmmm. Let's see. What could I do to help you out? Hmmm. I got it. I could put in a good word with your captain, or even better, recommend that you be promoted to captain. What about that, sergeant? Would that help you out?"

"What I would find helpful, sir, is you releasing Ms. Heinzelman."

"Now that would be a nice thing to do, wouldn't it, sergeant? A nice thing but a very dumb thing indeed. Without her, you might not even give me any water, let alone a shiny car. No, nice try but she stays right here with me. And, sergeant, Ms. Heinzelman is so very warm and so, so thirsty. If you truly care about her welfare, how about a granting my first wish?"

"I need to know that Ms. Heinzelman is all right, sir. Please allow her to speak to me."

"That sounds like a simple request, sergeant. But before she can talk, she needs to wet her whistle."

"One second, sir."

Realizing that an opportunity could present itself when Overton opens the door to get the water, the sergeant orders his men to fetch bottled water and some ice.

"It'll be a few minutes before we can get that water and ice to you, sir."

෧෨

When I get back to the first floor, I head to Phyllis's office. But she isn't there. I go to my office to check my phone messages. There is one from Phyllis indicating that she is meeting with Aggie about the hostage situation. Phyllis recommends that I call Elsa's university advisor, Dr. Daugherty, and let her know about Elsa's plight. I dread the phone call but know it must be done. Fortunately when I call, I get Dr. Daugherty's voice mail. I leave a message for her to call me as soon as possible. I don't mention anything about the danger Elsa is in.

෧෨

Overton removes the cord from the light fixture and positions himself with his rump on the staircase. With one foot on the door's casement, he grabs the doorknob and leans back. Using his weight and that of Elsa's, who he has re-sheathed in his arms, Overton believes he can prevent the police from yanking the door open when the water is delivered. Elsa is limp and non-responsive. She offers no resistance while they wait for the police to make good on their promise. Her skin is hot and sticky with sweat. Overton likes how she smells and feels against him.

"Okay, sir. We have your water and ice," the sergeant says.

"What, no towels? I distinctly recall asking for towels, sergeant."

"Sorry, no towels."

"That commendation is looking shaky, sergeant. Well, I guess water and ice will have to do. I'm going to crack the door open, and I want you to set it all on the step. The only part of you I want to see is your hand and arm setting down the goods. Got it, sergeant?"

"Yes, sir. One of my troopers will be setting them right on the step like you want."

Overton twists the knob and allows the door to slowly crack open. Suddenly, the door is pulled further open and the trooper's arm reaches around to grab Overton's leg. With an enormous heave, Overton slams the door, pinning and cracking the trooper's arm. The sound of him shrieking in pain echoes through the stairwell. Elsa tries to squirm loose, but Overton squeezes his elbows tighter around her.

"You're definitely not getting that commendation now, sergeant," Overton says, pulling harder on the doorknob as the trooper howls in pain."

"Let him go! Let him get his arm out of there!" the sergeant yells at Overton.

Elsa twists and screams at Overton to let go of the door. He yields enough force to let the trooper remove his arm. Overton then pulls the door closed and leans back.

"That stupid maneuver just got you kicked off the negotiating team, sergeant. I'm done dealing with you. From now on I want someone I can trust to be doing the talking. Get little Doc Masonheimer up. And do it now!"

※

I'm on my way to see Aggie when it hits me to check Elsa's office. I know she has a cell phone that she locks up before going to the wards, but maybe this time she took it with her. Inside her office, I find an unfinished test report on Overton, and right next to it is Elsa's cell phone. *So much for the phone idea.* I scan the report and find the background information section to reveal more data about Overton than I had previously known. It could be helpful. I grab the report and hustle out.

Outside Aggie's office, I encounter a throng of staff members milling about. I push my way into the waiting room where Essie shoos me into the inner office. Already seated in a circle of chairs are Aggie, Winnie, Phyllis, Ron, and Sergeant Dylan, who I had met three months ago at another hospital incident. I take an empty chair and try to pick up the discussion.

"How bad was your man hurt?" Aggie asks the sergeant.

"I think his arm's broken. He's on his way to the emergency room. We got reinforcements on the way."

"And why is Overton demanding to speak with Dr. Masonheimer?"

"What's that?" I interject.

"Overton is demanding to speak with you, Jerome," Aggie says.

"Overton said he trusts you, Doc," the sergeant replies.

"I find that hard to believe," I say.

"Why's that, sir?"

"Well, each time we have been together, he has ridiculed me."

"What do you mean by that?"

"Calling me names. Saying I'm not really a doctor. Insults like that."

"And how did you respond?"

"I didn't. I just noted what he was saying."

"That could be why he trusts you. You stayed calm and didn't retaliate."

"And you showed him that you were in control of yourself. He may realize that someone in control is to be trusted...or looked up to," Phyllis adds.

An odd thing for Phyllis to say given her propensity for behavioral principles over psychodynamic "mumbo jumbo," as she refers to anything Freudian.

"Maybe it doesn't have anything to do with trust or fear. Maybe he believes he can manipulate Jerome," Aggie interjects.

"I don't see any reason for him to believe that, Aggie," Winnie says. "If Jerome had given a sign of weakness or some gesture of conciliation, then perhaps Overton would believe Jerome could be manipulated. But you never showed him that, did you?"

"I was very professional with Overton. During my interviews, I maintained a neutral and objective position, especially when Elsa was with me. It was because of her tendency to shoot from the hip that I was intentionally maintaining a tough stance on boundaries with no special treatment or exceptions shown. I wanted her to see me be all business when interviewing a forensic patient, especially Overton. Looks like that didn't do much good."

"Why was Elsa at the dental office to begin with?" Phyllis asks.

"I believe she thought Overton needed help to deal with anxiety about seeing the dentist. As foolish as that sounds, I think she earnestly thought he needed help."

"Did you grant her approval to be there?"

"No. We never discussed it. She acted independently without me knowing what she was planning."

"Well, we're all responsible now," Phyllis concludes.

"And I'm responsible for negotiating with this man, except I need to use the doctor here to do my talking," the sergeant says, clearly irritated.

"What do you want me to do?" I ask.

"I want you to get him talking and keep him talking. At some point, we get him to see that his best choice is to give himself up. He probably will hang on as long as he can, but we take our time and let the heat wear him down."

"What about Elsa?" Phyllis asks.

"He won't give her up willingly. We can work the sympathy angle, but he knows without her he has nothing to bargain with. What we could use is more information about this guy...background information...psychologicals."

"I got a partial psychological right here," I say, holding up the test report.

"Good, but let's get more. And as soon as possible."

"We can get his chart to you, sergeant," Winnie says.

"That would be good. So, what about this psychological you got? What does it say?"

"It shows his IQ and previous test results."

"Anything that could be of help?" the sergeant asks.

"Well, he's bright, for one thing. Another finding is that he has psychopathic traits, but they're modified by some softer personality features. Which means he isn't completely heartless and possibly could feel some compassion toward another person, particularly if he admires that person...which I think he does Elsa."

"That could be useful, especially if we can get him to have more sympathy about her suffering up there. Does she have any medical condition or some illness we can play on?"

"Not that I know of."

"I wouldn't count on him having very much sympathy, sergeant. The man has a history of assaulting women and torturing them," Aggie interjects.

"He didn't torture them in a violent manner," I respond. "He's more voyeuristic."

"He abducted them, restrained them against their will, and submitted them to cruel conditions. To me, that's torture," Aggie retorts.

"So, this guy doesn't sexually assault his victims?" the sergeant asks.

"No. He exploits and demeans them, but he doesn't sexually abuse them," I reply.

"Which means we don't have to worry about her being attacked by him. He'll try to keep her safe, so he can use her to get out. Then we don't need to rush in. Do we?"

"What do you mean we don't have to rush in?" Aggie asks.

"If your intern doesn't have a medical condition and isn't going to be assaulted by this guy, then we can let him stew in his juices for a while. Let him get real uncomfortable up there. He'll be more apt to demand less and give up more."

"Or be more likely to act irrationally and take his anger out on Elsa," Phyllis says.

We silently ponder that possibility. The sergeant is the first to speak.

"We'll do everything we can to make sure she isn't harmed. We got a call in for a special negotiator from the Lake Corner barracks to join us as soon as he can.

He may come in by chopper. Any problem with landing him on grounds, Dr. Daltry?

"I don't see any problem with that, sergeant. It may get the neighborhood stirred up, but this is a crisis. And incidentally, I want don't want anyone talking with anyone, particularly the media, about this. Everything comes through my office. Understood?"

"Good point, Dr. Daltry. I'll position a man outside to keep any reporters away," the sergeant says.

"So now what?" I ask.

"Well, Doc. We head upstairs, and see if you can do your stuff," the sergeant says, rising out of his chair.

I shake hands with everyone and wait in the hallway for the sergeant to finish talking to one of his men. Feeling anxious, I start wondering if I can pull this off. I turn my thoughts to Elsa and what she must be feeling.

"Ready to go, Doc?" the sergeant says.

His voice snaps me out of my stupor. "Yeah, let's do it."

We walk to the elevator, and standing there with his tool bag slung over his shoulder is Gunner.

"Hey, Gunner. Can we get you to take the next elevator? We're in a bit of a hurry," I say, pointing to the sergeant.

Gunner takes in the sergeant's uniform. "Sure, Doc. I was only on my way back to the shop. Where are you two heading?"

"Up to the top floor. We got a crisis situation up there, Gunner. One of our patients has taken a staff member hostage and is holding her above the library."

"No kidding. I didn't know that. Hope no one gets hurt out of it."

"Amen to that. Well, we got to go, Gunner." The elevator door opens and the sergeant and I step in.

"Above the library, you say?" Gunner asks.

"Yeah. Up on the roof."

As the door closes, I hear Gunner say, "I know how to get up there."

The sergeant sticks out his foot, blocking the door from closing. "You mean the stairwell in the library?"

"No, not that way, another way."

"I didn't think there was any other way up there. Are you sure?" the sergeant asks.

"My first year here I helped put in a trap door to the roof. So, yeah. I'm sure."

"Well, climb in. We need you," the sergeant says, letting the door slam shut after Gunner joins us.

ɔͻ

Overton lies prostrate on the top landing of the staircase, staring at Elsa, who is huddled in a corner, her head resting on her knees. She hasn't said a word since he released her. She should be as thirsty as he is, but she hasn't complained once. He realizes he has very little chance of getting out of this situation. His hopes of driving across a remote area of the U.S.-Canadian border are not looking good. However, he is determined not to go back to prison, so escaping in some manner is his only option at this point. If only he had his sketching materials, he would capture the tragic helplessness of Elsa's form. Her vulnerability is striking.

⌖

Gunner leads us to the library's storage room, where only hours earlier I had been searching for a book that might have helped me work with Overton.

"Right up there." Gunner points to the corner of the drop-ceiling. "Above those panels is a small catwalk that accesses a hatch to the roof. Never thought I would have anything to do with it again after I helped build it forty years ago."

"We need a ladder. Is there one nearby?" the sergeant asks.

"I think custodial keeps one in the bathroom," Gunner says.

The ladder is retrieved and put into place. One of the troopers climbs up and removes several of the ceiling's panels.

"Yeah, I see what he's talking about. But we're going to be a few feet short of reaching it with this ladder," he says, climbing back down.

"What if we build a platform with all these boxes of books? That would give you the extra height you need," Gunner says.

"It might work," the sergeant says.

All of us pitch in to stack boxes as quietly as we can, creating a tiered platform. Cleckley's book is going to come to good use after all. After repositioning the ladder, we cobble together a new strategy to deal with Overton. The sergeant proposes that I deliver the water and ice to Overton and then convince him to let me in to see Elsa. Once I'm in, I'll find a way of alerting her to go to the back of the roof, where one of the troopers will lead her to safety. I'll need to keep Overton distracted while Elsa is spirited away, and give the other troopers time to sneak in and subdue him. Simple but fraught with what-ifs.

"Okay, Doc. Let's head over to the door and see how well this plan flies," the sergeant says.

With two bottles of water and bag of ice in hand, I knock on the barricaded door.

"Who's there?" Overton asks, his voice dry and raspy.

"It's me. Jerome Masonheimer. I've got the water and ice."

Ah! The distinguished Dr. Masonheimer, at last."

I hear his heavy footsteps descend the stairs.

"We are going to try the same routine that the sergeant managed to screw up. I'm going to open the door a wee bit and you are going to place the refreshments on the step. You think you can do that, Doctor?"

"I would rather come up and see both of you face to face."

"What's with you guys? Do you find me so attractive that you gotta see my puss? You realize, Masonheimer, that if you get on this side of the door you might not get back out again?"

I pause only briefly knowing there is no way to get Elsa out but for me to go in.

"Yeah, I understand that once I'm in I might not get back out."

"And how can I be assured that the sneaky sergeant won't barge in right behind you?"

"I give you my word. The only person coming in will be me."

"Your word, huh? And how do I know your word is any good?"

"You don't. But I know my word, and when I give it I mean it, no matter what."

For a few seconds, there isn't any response from Overton. Then I see the doorknob slowly turn, and the door cracks open just wide enough for me to squeeze in before he kicks it shut. With the metal picks clasped between his teeth, he quickly secures the cord around the knob and the light fixture, then leads me up the staircase. When we reach the top landing, he pats me down. I look around for Elsa but don't immediately see her.

"That water is going to go down real easy," Overton says, grabbing one of the plastic bottles.

As he chugs the water, I continue to scan the area for Elsa. My eyes finally settle on her balled form in the corner. She is so motionless I wonder if she's hurt or even alive.

"May I take this bottle to her?"

"Be my guest, but don't try to be a hero, Doc." He rips into the ice bag and grabs a handful of ice to rub on his face and chest.

I walk over to Elsa and kneel down with my back to Overton. When I place my hand on her shoulder, she flinches. It takes a few seconds for Elsa to realize it's me. She looks in shock. Except where the heat has flushed her cheeks, her face is gray as chalk. I remove the cap from the bottle and wave it in front of her. She doesn't immediately take it.

"Take it, Elsa. Take a drink," I say. I hold onto the bottle as she cups her hand over mine and takes a swallow.

"Take another. I'm going to get some ice."

I walk back toward Overton. "Okay if I take a handful of ice back to her?"

"Yeah, go ahead," he says, watching me intently.

Kneeling in front of Elsa, I take hold of her opened hand and place some cubes in it. They slide onto the floor. I pick them up and fold her long fingers around them.

Leaning in closer to her, I whisper, "Look at me, Elsa."

She remains downcast. I lift her chin and see that her eyes are dazed. I take the ice from her and rub it against the back of her neck, causing her head to reflexively tilt upward. A large brown spider is crawling over her hair, attempting to bury itself in one the braided folds. I swat it to the floor and quickly crush it without her apparently noticing.

"Elsa, look at me," I whisper. Her pupils constrict enough for me to believe she's listening. "There will be someone coming back there."

I twitch my head in the direction of the roof's recess. "While I occupy Overton, you go over to that man. Do you understand?"

Elsa looks confused and distant. I'm not sure she is hearing me at all. Then ever so imperceptibly, she nods.

"What are you two doing back there? Getting touchy feely with each other?" Overton says, walking toward us.

I turn back to him. "She isn't doing well in this heat. I think she may have heat exhaustion."

"The water and ice will bring her around."

"I think she needs medical attention."

"You want to get a doctor up here to exam her? Maybe we could deliver a bed for her while we're at it."

"Maybe we could let her go. After all, you still have me."

"I feel better with having both of you near me."

He moves in between Elsa and me.

"Do me a favor, Doc. Move away from her, and let her breathe. If you want to help someone, help me. Put some of that ice on my neck, will you?"

"Okay," I say, walking back to the landing where the bag of ice is. Overton remains near Elsa, hovering over her, not wanting to leave her alone.

"Do you want some of this or not?" I ask, holding up a handful of ice. Overton slowly inches away from Elsa.

"It would be easier for me to put this on your neck if you sat down on the landing," I say.

As Overton returns to the stairwell, I can see the flattened shape of a trooper emerging out of the darkened recess. He is slowly creeping to where Elsa has positioned herself.

"It might be better if I could wrap my shirt around the ice and just hold it to your neck. Okay with you?"

"Strip down to your skivvies if you want, Doc." Overton takes a seat on the landing, facing the steps. "Don't think I can't get to you, Doc. I'm faster than you think. So, no funny stuff."

I unbutton my shirt and take it off. I am tempted to take off my pants as well given that the heat is overpowering. I pour half the ice in the shirt and pull the ends together forming an ice pack, and lay it against Overton's thick pockmarked neck. He gives off a moan of relief while slumping his head forward.

"So, you're the kind of guy who will give someone the shirt off his back, huh, Doc?"

"Yeah, I guess so."

I turn to see Elsa disappearing into the corner of the room. I assume that she is being led to safety and the other troopers are on their way to deal with Overton. There is something about the genuine sounds of relief he is making that hits one of my sympathetic nerves.

"Listen, Garner. I want you to give yourself up, peacefully," I say, rubbing his neck. "I don't want to see you get hurt."

"Get hurt? The heat starting to get to you, Doc? How can I get hurt?" he says, abruptly standing up and facing me. He pushes his fingers into my chest. "You don't look like you weigh more than a hundred and fifty pounds, little man. You think you can hurt..."

His voice trails off as he notices Elsa's absence.

"What the hell! Where did she go?"

I back up and push myself against the wall. Overton hears sounds of footsteps coming toward us.

"Why, you little bastard, Doc. You got the best of me, and here I thought you were being straight up."

"Stop where you are," a trooper shouts.

"You're not taking me alive," Overton shouts back. He clumsily scurries backwards, vanishing around the corner.

Two troopers rush ahead with their weapons drawn. Perhaps, Overton's words accusing me of being insincere combined with the suppressing heat has gotten to me.

"Stop! Wait!" I shout at the advancing troopers. "I'll get him."

I sprint in the direction where Overton disappeared.

"Get back here! Let us handle him!" a trooper shouts.

Too late. I'm not going to risk him getting shot. I don't go far before I see a shaft of light streaking the floor ahead of me. It is coming from an open door. I turn toward the light and follow it up a staircase that leads to one of the roof's twin towers. I carefully climb up the narrow staircase trying to avoid several broken steps and pigeon carcasses. The light becomes brighter the further up I go, as is the oppressive heat. I hear footsteps behind me and increase my pace. When I get near the top, I can see Overton. He has opened the tower's small window and has perched himself half in and half out of the window. He looks exhausted and is sweating profusely.

"Just stay where you are, Doc!" he shouts. He turns to look out the window. "What a view. So, this is what freedom looks like."

A breeze enters the window, carrying Overton's heavy body odor in my direction.

How am I going keep him from jumping? If I try grabbing him, he could easily pull me over with him.

"Okay, Doctor. We'll take it from here," says a trooper approaching me.

"No. Wait. He'll jump if you come any closer. We don't want him to do that. So, please, wait where you're at and give me a chance," I plead.

"Let them come, Doc. I'm not letting any of you get to me."

"You had enough of living this way?" I ask, stepping closer.

"You got it."

"You don't know any other way?"

"Any other way? What other way? The only way left for me is out there," he says, pointing out the window.

"That's what I was thinking as well."

"You want me to jump?"

"No, I want you to realize what's out there. What's outside yourself. This world that you've known isn't the only possibility for you. I think to a degree you already know that. I think you realize it each time you become awestruck with beauty and vulnerability...how it frees you and helps you transcend your dissatisfaction with how you're living. Except of course you're going about it the wrong way...in an aggressive and criminal way. But you don't have to. You have the capacity to appreciate and honor the delicate aspects of life without using force to subdue them. You have that capacity."

"And do what with it? If I let these cops take me, I won't see the light of day for the next twenty years."

"You'll need every hour of that time to get rid of your past. And once you do that you'll need more time to form a responsible attitude, and to develop a compassion for the softer, more fragile facets of this world. Don't get me wrong; I'm not saying it's going to be easy. It won't be. But you know what it's like to live a hard life and to not succumb. We could recommend that you receive treatment while in prison. There are some programs for restructuring and rehabilitating your behaviors that you could engage in. Not fun by any means. But it would be worth it. You could still have many years ahead of you where you could enjoy the subtleties of life."

"I've been in prison. There wasn't any rehabilitating or whatever you think there is."

"You may not realize it, but places like Kinzua State are shutting down...just too expensive to operate. People with mental problems are being discharged back into the community. Many are getting into trouble with the law and are being incarcerated. In fact, the numbers are staggering. Most states, including ours, are responding by providing more mental health treatments in jails and prisons."

"Yeah, you're talking about pill popping. I've seen how pills are being pushed, but none of these other treatments that you're talking about."

"Not every place has them yet. But many do. I'll recommend that you either go to where treatment programs are available or that they are brought to you."

"You talk like you can snap your fingers and make things happen, little man. I don't think you can."

"I believe I can get our hospital to recommend it."

"Even if you could, I don't think it would help. From what I have seen, once a psychopath, always a psychopath."

"Some, not all. And I think you're one of them who can change."

"I would like to know what you're smoking, Doc. Wouldn't you, boys?" Overton casts his question over my shoulder to the troopers.

"I'm basing my opinion on research findings, clinical theories, and on your history."

"On my history? You must have read someone else's chart. I ain't done anything right since I was an altar boy."

"Actually, you have done quite a few things right. You graduated from high school with honors. You were a reliable construction worker with a decent work ethic. From what I have read, you paid your bills and have no debt. And even though you engaged in criminal acts, you never were violent or brutal. And what's more, you were reported to have written personal letters of apologies to your victims. All examples that you have the capacity to know right from wrong, and to have a conscience."

"According to you, except for all the sinning, I'm a real saint."

"No saint. However, potentially a repentant sinner."

Overton turns to look at the crowd of onlookers who have gathered on the lawn and parking lot to see why a man is perched out the tower's window. I'm aware of how hot I am, and wish I had something to drink. I lower myself to the floor and wearily put my head between my knees. A walkie-talkie screeches and the sergeant's crackling voice breaks the silence.

"What's the status up there?"

"Our man is leaning out a window, and the psychologist is trying to talk him back in. Over," the trooper replies.

"Well, then, unblock this door down here so I can come up."

"Ten-four."

I watch the trooper descend the stairs. "Any chance you can bring back some water?" I say.

"We'll fetch what is down on the landing."

After watching both of them disappear, I turn my attention back to the window. But Overton isn't there.

"What the hell! No!"

I rush to the window sill and stretch out as far as I can to scan below, but there is no sign of him. I notice the crowd is still looking up at the tower and not on the ground. I can see Cora Ruth in the throng, shielding her eyes as she looks up at me in wonder.

He must not have jumped. Maybe he's scaling the outside wall.

A trooper squeezes next to me and peers below. "Did he jump?"

"No, I don't think so, but there's no of sign of him," I say.

Suddenly, something brown whizzes by my head. Then another flies by.

"What the hell!" I yell, ducking.

"We've got bats in the belfry, fellas."

Startled to hear Overton's voice, the trooper and I spin around in near unison and look up. There clinging to one of the roof beams is Overton. Somehow, he has managed to wedge his back and feet against the tower's narrow interior walls and shimmy his way up.

"Okay, Garner. What do you say? Ready to come back down and start the rehabilitation process?"

"Why not? I've gone as far as I can at this place."

Slowly, he inches his way down to where the trooper can grab a hold of him. The other officers join us, and soon Overton is well in hand.

"We got some medical staff down in the library to check you men out before we head back to the Forensic Unit," the sergeant says.

"I'll be right there. Just want to close this window," I say.

Before closing it, I look out and give a thumbs-up to the onlookers. Even from way up here I can hear them cheering.

∽

Regrets

Even though I'm not injured or showing any symptoms of heat exhaustion, the medical team at the library recommends that I go to the infirmary to rest and get hydrated. That's where Elsa was taken. Overton will be wheeled on a gurney back to the Forensic Unit and given medical attention there.

KSH's infirmary is situated in Manchester building. It is on the first floor and is comprised of two relatively small treatment rooms. Although I can easily walk, the nursing staff drives me to the front entrance and insists that I use a wheelchair to be taken to the infirmary, where I'll receive cold compresses and hydrating fluids. I'm too tired to argue with them, and within short order I'm wheeled into the same room where Elsa is lying on a bed receiving treatment. Although somber, she's alert and has her energy level restored.

"Hello, Elsa," I say, feeling somewhat self-conscious about my disheveled appearance.

"Hello, Dr. Masonheimer. Are you all right?"

"Just hot and tired. Other than that, not bad. What about you? How are you doing?"

"I'm doing better as well."

A nurse brings me a glass of water, two salt tablets, and a cold wet towel for my forehead. She then presses me to lie flat on a bed across from Elsa. Returning my attention to her, I say, "Good to hear you're feeling better. We both have been through quite an ordeal, haven't we?"

"Yes. I'm so sorry, Dr. Masonheimer. I never thought this would have happened. I really can't believe I could be so stupid...so naïve to think I could trust him at his word. And to have so many people be put in jeopardy, especially that state policeman whose arm was broken. I can't believe I did this."

Elsa slides her hands over her face.

"Listen, Elsa," I say, sitting up, holding the wet towel in place. "You didn't do any harm to anyone. Overton is the one who hurt the trooper and put you in harm's way. Not you. You're not responsible for any of that."

She peers through her fingers, staring at me in disbelief. "Do you mean that? Really?"

"Absolutely. I feel bad that the police and you were subjected to this incident. An incident that Overton engineered and will be held accountable for."

"You have to admit, I did use poor judgment."

"Do I wish you would have checked out your plans with me first before you went down to the dental office? Sure I do. But do I blame you for wanting to be helpful? No. Not at all. I think what you have found out is that some people will take advantage of our kindness. And in a way, I hope Overton will take advantage of what I will be doing for him."

"What do you mean?"

"Well, after you escaped, Overton fled to the north tower, opened a window, and was threatening to jump. I was able to convince him that we could get him help for his preying compulsions, so to speak, and that when he gets out of prison he would be in a position to lead a more normal life. He finally agreed and gave himself up. So now I have to follow through and fight for the treatment he will need. Which isn't going to be easy."

"Do you really think he can be helped? That he can change?"

"As hard as it may be to believe, yes I do. There are some habitual criminals that I don't have much hope for, but I do for him. Given what you have been through, that probably sounds crazy to you."

"Right now I don't have much hope for anyone, including me."

"What he put you through was pretty overwhelming."

"I can't ever remember feeling so powerless, so helpless. I never felt that way before. I always felt in control of every situation, no matter whom I was with. No one could push me around. I was in charge. When he was dragging me around, forcing me to submit to his control, the air went out of me. My self-confidence collapsed like a deflated balloon. I never felt so lifeless...so vulnerable."

"Getting the wind knocked out of you can do that."

"I didn't like it, and even now the thought of it makes me shiver."

"Well, you're safe now. If you don't want to talk about it anymore, that's okay. There'll be time later on to process the details and for us to learn from it."

"If it's okay with you, I would like to rest for a little bit."

"Sure. No problem. I was hoping to take a little nap myself."

We both lie back down. I unfold the towel and drape it across my face, surprised that I can still breathe through it. I generally don't like anything interfering with my breathing. It reminds me of when I had the wind knocked out of me a long time ago. To my surprise, I find myself drifting off. I must be tired.

The Fallout

Waking with a headache and a dry mouth, I find that I'm alone in the treatment room. Elsa is gone as are all the nurses. I run some tap water to wash my face and rinse my mouth. I look like hell in the mirror and probably worse in person. Glancing at the wall clock, I see it's almost three p.m. Shift change. I'm surprised no one has tried to reach me. I decide to head over to my office, but I discover that I'm pretty wobbly. Once outside the infirmary, I regain my balance but opt to avoid the sun and anyone else walking about by taking the elevator to the basement, then accessing the tunnel to Dix.

In the tunnel, the temperature is noticeably cooler, and my head starts to feel better. It dawns on me that I should talk with Aggie about what happened in the tower. I take the exit nearest to her office, and upon entering the first floor discover that the security staff has cordoned off the front entrance to Dix. As I get closer, I can see why. A throng of news reporters is clamoring to get an interview. Reaching Aggie's office, I find both the outer and inner door to be open, and inside, various administrative staff and state police are milling about. Phyllis and Elsa are seated in a corner of the room. Elsa looks very uncomfortable and is shielding herself from others by letting Phyllis field inquiries.

"Hey, here's the hero!" someone says, triggering a round of applause.

I lift my hands as if to deflect the recognition and try to catch Aggie's eye. She sees my distress and quickly asks that everyone leave her office, even the state police.

"Please, everyone, I need to speak alone with Dr. Masonheimer. Please. Thank you. Sergeant, would you and your men give me a moment with the doctor? Thank you."

After everyone else exists the office, I ask Phyllis and Elsa to stay behind. When the four of us are alone I voice my concerns.

"I know that there has to be a debriefing meeting, but we need to be sensitive to Elsa's well-being," I say, looking at Aggie, then at Phyllis. "The ordeal has been very traumatic, and both of us are trying to regain our bearings. I would be willing to meet with the police if needed, but if it could be postponed until tomorrow that would be better."

"Jerome, everything is chaotic right now. We have the governor's office, the press, and the police all demanding information. I wish you could take some time off, but I need you here to answer questions. Can you muster the resolve to be up for this inquisition?" Aggie asks.

"If that's what's needed, yes. But could Elsa at least be excused from all this? She's been through enough for one day."

"It's okay, Dr. Masonheimer. I can manage to answer their questions," Elsa says.

"The sergeant has already gotten your statement, hasn't he, my dear?" Aggie asks Elsa.

"Yes, he has, but I'm willing to answer more questions."

"Actually, I don't think you need to. I agree that you have been through enough for one day. Why don't you go with Dr. Bergist and get some rest."

"I think that is a good idea," Phyllis says. "But before she can truly rest, Elsa and I need to call her parents and her university supervisor."

"That would be very appropriate. All I ask, Elsa, is that if either your parents or your supervisor have any questions or concerns that they call me before contacting anyone else. And if there is anything, Elsa, that you personally need, I don't want you to hesitate to contact me as well," Aggie says, putting her hand on Elsa's shoulder. "I'm so sorry that you were dragged into this dreadful affair, my dear."

"Thank you, Dr. Daltry." Elsa replies.

After seeing Phyllis and Elsa to the door, Aggie returns her attention to the issue at hand.

"Well, Rome, are you ready for the next phase?"

"The debriefing?"

"The barbeque, Rome. Out of this investigatory grilling, someone is going to get served up as red meat. Do what you need to do to make sure it isn't you. I'll do everything I can as well. Hopefully, both of us get through this with our jobs intact."

"Sounds like this is going to be a long afternoon."

"Very, very long," Aggie says, buzzing her secretary on her intercom. "Essie, let the mob back in. And sharpen your pencil; I need you to take notes."

Compassion Is Needed

The grilling ended near midnight. I was wiped out when my head hit the pillow, but this morning I'm feeling and looking a whole lot better. A long hot shower and Despina's breakfast of French toast, homemade yogurt, and espresso has me feeling human again.

As I drive into the parking lot, my eyes zoom in on the north tower. Before yesterday, I barely noticed it. Now it looms ominously, forcing me to hold it in mind. From this distance, it doesn't look like a sparrow could fit through its window, let alone a two-hundred-fifty-pound man. I shake my head. I would be feeling a lot different today if he had decided to jump. *Got lucky with that one.*

Sitting in front of my computer, I dread checking my e-mails, but it's got to be done. As I feared, there are dozens of posts pertaining to the Overton incident. I open one message from Aggie that indicates she has received approval from the regional office for us to petition the courts for the treatment programs I promised

Overton. That's a relief. Now, all we need to do is send out a slew of correspondence to the judge's office and respective attorneys.

My last e-mail is an inquiry from a social worker wanting to know if I have any experience working with multiple personality disorder. Apparently, a woman with that problem is being considered for placement at KSH. I reply that I have limited experience but am considered the department's expert, for what that's worth. *Just what I need, more challenges.* I head out to make the rounds of seeing Phyllis, Aggie, and patients. After that, it's documentation, and more documentation.

After throwing away my empty pen, I glance at the clock. Three fifteen. Time for me to see Elsa before she heads home for the weekend. I knock on her office door.

"Come in," Elsa says softly.

"Hey, Elsa. Ready for me?"

"Yes, I am. Come on in. Or if you want, we could meet in your office."

"My office attracts too many problems. Here would be much better."

I take a chair in front of her desk. Elsa gets up and positions a chair across from me. She's dressed per usual in her black pantsuit, but her hair isn't braided or pulled back, and she's not wearing any make up. Her face is drawn, and her eyes are sad.

"So, how are you feeling today?" I ask.

"I'm much better today, but still out of sorts. Spending last night at Dr. Bergist's house helped me relax and to sleep better than I would have in my apartment. What's more, Dr. Bergist cooked a wonderful meal, which was a special treat. But today I'm tired and down again. All day I have been thinking about yesterday and what I could have done differently."

"To be expected. I have been replaying everything in my head as well. Did you get through to your parents and Dr. Daugherty?"

"Yes. They were all concerned and urged me to come home, even Dr. Daugherty. My mother said I should go to the hospital and have a formal evaluation, even though I told her I wasn't injured and that I had been checked out here."

"What did your father say?"

"He said I should call our attorney and pursue legal action."

"Against the hospital?"

"Against the hospital, Overton, and you."

"I see."

"My father has always tried to protect me, but I never would let him. And I won't this time either. I'm twenty-four years old and responsible for myself. And I'm especially responsible for placing myself in harm's way with Overton. You didn't put me there nor did anyone else. Actually, if I had been open with you, I'm sure you wouldn't have agreed for me to have been in that dental office with him. So I didn't give you a chance to protect me, either."

"Not wanting anyone to protect you. Do you think it's a pattern?"

"Admittedly, it is. I never liked being controlled or passively going along with anyone who supposedly knows better than I do. I've known it for some time. And before you jump to the conclusion that it's because I was mistreated or abused, I wasn't. No one assaulted me. From early on I was headstrong, which may be putting it mildly. That I wasn't mistreated is testimony to my parent's patience and love for me."

"That's quite an insight."

"Like I said, I've known it for some time. What's different now is that I'm willing to admit it to someone else."

"Even your parents?"

"Yes, I'm ready to do that. In fact, I will tell them that this evening when I go home. It's time for me to bring them into my world. And I think it's time for me to listen to what they have to say without overreacting."

"Bravo, Elsa. It seems something positive did come out of this mess after all."

"What about you, Dr. Masonheimer? Did anything good come out of it for you?"

"Fair question. I guess what immediately comes to mind is that I realize now that I appreciate not having to work alone. Without the support of others—Gunner, my supervisors, the police—I wouldn't have dealt very well with this crisis. I guess I should also include you in those that I appreciate."

"Me? How could you possibly appreciate me?"

"If it weren't for the background work you did on Overton, I would never have known that there was a soft side to him."

"If only I had paid more attention to his bad side, I could have avoided looking so dim-witted."

"Sounds like you have a case of the 'if-only's.'"

"I guess I do. So, how do I get rid of them?"

"What I have found helpful is to pay attention to what you have learned from all of it. Write it down if need be. Then walk away from it. It'll be behind you. And when you drift back there again, remind yourself what you learned so you can apply it to the here and now."

"If only I could. There I go again."

"Look, I realize it's not going to be easy to shake off what has happened. It'll take time and effort on your part."

"I wish I had listened to you before. But then that is just another 'if-only,' isn't it?"

"Yeah, I guess so. All I ask is that you take in what I'm saying, chew on it, and only swallow it if it seems right to you; spit it out if it doesn't. Trust the wise part of you to know what is true and healthy for you."

We both pause to reflect on what has been shared.

"Well, I guess I should go and let you be on your way," I say, rising. "If you should need anything, call me at home. You have my number, right?"

"Yes, I do, but I don't think I'll be bothering you. I'm going to be all right."

"I'm sure you will be, but please call if you need to. Believe me, you wouldn't be bothering me," I say, opening the door.

"Thanks, Dr. Masonheimer. See you on Monday," Elsa says, remaining in her chair. She forces a weak smile, attempting to reassure me that she's all right. She's not successful.

~∽

Summer Festival

It has been two weeks since the Overton incident. The negative publicity stirred up by the media has died down and the hospital is back to normal, so to speak. Elsa and I are working more cooperatively, and she is showing no signs of post-traumatic stress, which is a relief to all of us. Overton is back at the county jail and reportedly participating in programs. I still find myself thinking about him and our time in the tower, but oddly it is the virga event that marvels my mind. It was such a strange phenomenon. One that defies rational explanation. Of course for Sherm, it was and remains a confirmation of his delusional belief that the Chinese are attempting to assail America with technological trickery. It will be harder now than it ever was to pick away at this distorted perception of his.

At least Cora Ruth is less entrenched in her depression. Perhaps it was the storm shocking her senses, or the camaraderie she discovered in the Love Nest that jumpstarted her assent out of her melancholic abyss. I don't know. Then again it may have had something to do with Ophelia, Kim, and her being found by Luther in the greenhouse. I'm still not sure what actually transpired between them. Cora Ruth hasn't disclosed the details to me, and I haven't pressed her on the subject. What I do know is that Luther came forward and confessed to his supervisors that he was carrying a weapon when he apprehended the women. Why he was armed and why he even went to the greenhouse hasn't been made public. But it is known that Luther tendered his resignation in lieu of being criminally charged with possession of a firearm on hospital grounds. And as for the women, they were disciplined for trespassing by having their ground privileges suspended for one week. Oddly, none of them seemed to mind.

I suspect that the truth of that day will be revealed in due time. And I imagine that whatever occurred will be linked somehow to a meaningful interaction, which compelled all of them to take shelter in the Love Nest. This morning there will be another opportunity for patients to interact, albeit by design: The Summer Festival.

The Summer Festival is a fun event where patients, staff, and the community come together to eat, drink, and engage in recreational play. Leisure activities and organized outings are longstanding traditions at Kinzua State. Beginning in 1902, when weekly dances and fishing outings at the local creek were arranged for patients, to the 1960s when the Summer Festival began as an annual event, the hospital has provided periodic leisure gatherings to break the monotony of living in an institution.

This year the festival will be located on a grassy expanse of the campus near the ball field marked by colorful striped canvas canopies that have been erected to shelter the food servers and diners, in case of rain, or if the sun becomes too intense. Although yesterday a huge amount of rain fell and created puddles in low-lying areas, today looks like sunshine will prevail and make for a pleasant outing.

The festival will be open to all non-forensic patients assessed as not being acutely disturbed. Even the major-ity of closed ward patients are escorted outside to attend the festivities. It's also open to the public and former patients, which provides an opportunity to see how they are faring in the outside world. It will be interesting to see who shows up.

Nursing has asked for volunteers to help escort the closed ward patients to the festival. I said I would be willing to lend a hand, and was given instructions to show up at 10:45 a.m. on the Men's Closed Ward. As I enter the ward, I spot Delbert Schupp walking stiffly toward me. At one time the sight of Del's automaton appearance made me cringe and cower for cover. That changed when we had an unexpected encounter at a hospital dance several months ago. I discovered that old Del and I both jived to music.

Apparently, he is feeling differently as well. Approaching me, he offers a greeting by raising a rigid arm and directing his palm toward my face, all done in a mechanical fashion as if his elbow were a rusted hinge. A grimaced smile stretches across his elongated face.

"Hi Del," I say, mirroring with a hand flap.

"Howdy," he replies, leaving his hand frozen in the air.

"Ready to go to the Summer Festival?"

"Yup. I even brushed my teeth," he says, opening his mouth wide for me to inspect.

To my amazement, I see that he has recently received dental care. Although many of his teeth are still discolored and several new gaps exist, the overall appearance is much cleaner and healthier looking.

"Looking good, Del. Listen, I'm going to ask Mr. Worman who he wants me to escort, so stay put. I'll be right back." He remains by the door, his eyes fixed on the doorknob.

Approaching the nursing station, I can see that Jake is busily directing staff and patients. He appears flustered. I hang loose while waiting for the traffic around the office to thin out. Many of the patients are clinging to the mesh barrier separating the station from the main ward. They are entranced with their cigarettes being systematically transferred into a plastic carrier, which will be taken out to the gathering. Generally, patients seem oblivious to the actions of others, but when it comes to their cigarettes or snacks, they are as vigilant as sentries.

"All right, everyone, move back from the office. Go ahead, back up. Back up. Emil will be bringing your cigarettes with him. So, unless you want him to leave your smokes behind, I advise you to back up and calmly walk down to the end of the hallway," Jake instructs.

Haltingly, and suspiciously, the mass of gawkers backs away from the office.

As the patients disperse, I approach Jake, who is now cradling a phone to his ear. I wait until he is finished dialing.

"Just want to let you know I'm here to help escort," I say.

"Okay. Why don't you take Del, Sherm, Killer, and Dr. Burda with you," Jake says.

"Dr. Burda? He's a patient?"

"Why so surprised, Rome? Even doctors get sick."

"Dr. Burda is a real doctor?

"You got corn growing in your ears? I just told you who he was."

"Can't wait to meet him, Jake."

"Well, you won't have to wait long. There he is," Jake says, pointing to the black-suited little man coming out of the bathroom.

"Dr. Burda. Come over here please," Jake says.

With his Yankee baseball cap pulled down to his eyebrows, Dr. Burda approaches the nurse's station. He says nothing.

"This here is Dr. Masonheimer. He's a psychologist, but don't hold that against him," Jake cracks. "He'll be escorting you to the festival. So be nice to him, okay?"

Dr. Burda salutes from the bill of his cap, turns, and leans against the wall. Apparently, a man of few words.

"Wait here, I'll be right back," I say, heading in the direction of Daniel's room.

Along the way, I spot Sherm and give him a heads-up about meeting me at the nursing station. I find Daniel waiting in line to receive his noon meds an hour early. I guess Dr. Gobind has decided to slow him down before the party begins. As the queue moves along, I wonder how often this routine has been played out since medications became the standard method for treating serious mental illness. Adults waiting obediently in line to receive their prescribed salvation. A slow, solemn procession without any words being spoken. *Is there anything in everyday life that parallels this ritual?* The only image that comes to mind is holy communion. Receiving the host to transcend oneself and be in communion with God. Receiving the pill to transcend one's distorted self and restore sanity. Hmmm. An interesting analogy, but...I don't know. Maybe, I'm forcing a square peg into a round hole.

"Captain, you okay?" Daniel says, staring down at me.

"Huh? Oh, yeah, I'm fine. Just got lost in some thoughts, I guess."

"They got a pill for that," he says, pointing to the medication room.

"I imagine they do. But let's skip it and head outside. Some fresh air and sunshine will clear my head. How about you?"

"Every time I get outside of these stone walls my spirit is set free, Captain."

Daniel and I head to the nursing station where we find the enigmatic Dr. Burda still holding up the wall, and Sherm bartering with Jake over cigarettes. When the haggling ends, Sherm walks away with half a pack of Camels and a sour mood. Getting outside will be good for him, too.

After picking up Del, we exit Dix and are greeted by clear blue skies, sunshine, and a gentle breeze. It feels heavenly to me and apparently to Daniel as well. He leaps off the top step poised like Fred Astaire and begins dancing to music playing in his head. The party is already going on inside of him.

"Come on, Captain, let's dance," Daniel says, trying to grab my hand. I fend him off by taking cover behind Sherm. Daniel prances and twirls ahead undeterred by the rest of us killjoys.

Sherm pulls out a cigarette. "Got a light?" he asks.

I'm prepared and reach for my box of matches. But Dr. Burda flips out a shining new Zippo and lights Sherm's smoke.

"You smoke, Dr. Burda?" I ask.

"No," he replies.

"Then how do you account for the Zippo?"

"I like how it feels."

"So, you own a lighter and are allowed to carry it around?"

"My degree has its privileges."

"Mr. Worman knows about it then?"

"He personally keeps it safe when I don't have it."

Jake is taking a risk, letting this strange little man carry his own fire-starter. Clearly a violation of the hospital's safety code. Of course, Jake has a deferential reflex when it comes to doctors, apparently even those at the hospital for court-ordered treatment. As I walk next to Dr. Burda, while keeping an eye on Del and Daniel, who are rushing in the direction of the food tent, I ask a question.

"Are you a doctor of medicine, Dr. Burda?"

"Hard to believe, isn't it?" he answers.

"Not really. We've had doctors hospitalized before," I respond. "When did you arrive at the hospital?"

"About a month ago. Why?"

"I somehow failed to notice you on the new admission list. Usually, I know who is scheduled to be admitted. But in your case, I didn't."

"That's because I was a lateral transfer from Philadelphia State Hospital. An overnight delivery, so to speak."

"Philadelphia. Is that where you were practicing?"

"No. New Jersey."

Now I more confused. "You were practicing in New Jersey but were admitted to the state hospital in Philadelphia, then transferred up here. Sounds like something was going on that you needed to get away from," I say, feeling a twinge of alarm that I no longer can see Del and Daniel.

"A sticky wicket indeed." He offers nothing more.

Although I'm highly intrigued by this little doctor, I'm more immediately concerned about Daniel and Del. So, I instruct Sherm and Dr. Burda to keep walking toward the food tent while I double-time ahead. I find Del waiting in the food line, but I can't locate Daniel. I scan the recreational booths and picnic areas but to no avail. A steady stream of patients is now arriving from both the men's and women's wards, as well as from Manchester building, and it is starting to get crowded. I'm confident Daniel isn't going to run away, but I would feel better if I could find him. As I look around, I see that Sherm and Dr. Burda have reached the food line, which is now a good twenty feet long. Hot dogs, macaroni salad, and beans are a definite draw.

I wander over to a portable bandstand where staff members have just finished setting up some massive speakers. There in front of the DJ's turntable is Daniel standing next to Clarence Odell, an ex-patient who apparently has returned for today's event. I sidle next to them.

"Hey, Captain. Got any requests?" Daniel asks as the CDs are brought out and set on the table.

"As long as it's rock and roll, I'm good," I say. "What about you?"

"I want to hear some Jimi Hendrix or Rolling Stones. James Brown would be good, too," Daniel says.

As we watch, one of the staff members does a sound check and then puts on Springsteen's *Born In the USA*. The speakers are way too powerful for me, and I back up a few feet. But I'm still in earshot of Daniel and Clarence and overhear Clarence tell Daniel that he, Clarence, wrote *Born In the USA*.

"Get out," Daniel says.

"Yes, I did. I wrote quite a few of Springsteen's songs, and the Beatles, too. Remember *Back in the USSR?* I wrote that," Clarence says, dryly.

"I thought the Beatles wrote their own songs," Daniel says.

"They needed a lot of help. That's why they bought my songs."

"If you wrote and sold all these songs, why ain't you rich?"

"My agent stole my money. Used it on drugs."

"What about royalties?"

"Stolen by the IRS."

Daniel turns to look at me. He makes a circling motion with his index against the side of his head. I scrunch my face and lift my shoulders, then motion with my hand for him to come closer.

"What do you say we go over and get something to eat?" I ask him.

"Sounds good. That guy's short a few playing cards, isn't he?"

"Well, apparently, he's doing well enough to stay out of the hospital, and that's what counts." I say, leading Daniel toward the food tent. At the back of the line are Eliot and Paula. I introduce Daniel to them, and we exchange some light banter as we advance along.

"So, Daniel, have you been to one of these festivals before?' Paula asks.

"Yeah. This is my third one. I try to time my coming back in order to make the Summer Festival and the Christmas party," he says with a hungry eye on the hot dog grill.

"Sounds like you don't mind being at the hospital, Daniel," Paula replies.

"This bug farm ain't bad, miss. It's better than out there," Daniel says, motioning with his thumb in the air. "At least here I can be safe and don't need to watch my back all the time. Yeah, sure, there ain't no satellite TV, but just looking around is enough entertainment for me."

"I detect a strong stream of rambunctiousness permeating the air," Eliot announces.

"Sure you ain't smelling those hot dogs that they're grilling, Mister Eliot?" Daniel asks. "They smell awful good to me."

"No. No, it's definitely not a greasy or charred odor that is wafting about. More uproarious and high-spirited, I would say."

"Well, those sentiments seem very appropriate for today," I say, noticing that Sherm, Del, and Dr. Burda are at a picnic table next to Dr. Gobind and some other psychiatrists.

As we pass through the serving line, I shepherd Daniel to sit next to Dr. Gobind.

"Let's sit right over there," I say, nudging my head in the desired direction.

"Not with my shrink, Captain."

"You can have what's on my plate if you sit there," I offer.

Daniel eyeballs the food. "I guess she ain't that bad after all," he says.

"Hello, Dr. Gobind. Mind if we sit down?" I say, sitting without waiting for a response.

She looks aghast as Daniel sits across from her. "Jerome, why are you here?"

"It's the Summer Festival, remember?"

"I mean why are you at my table?"

"Thought we'd give you some company, and I can update you on Daniels's progress," I say, pushing my plate of food in his direction. Not waiting to give Gobind a chance to respond I continue.

"As you can see, Daniel is doing rather well. His appetite is good, and he isn't groggy any longer. His mood is well modulated, and for the most part he has reduced his intrusive behaviors."

As if on cue, Daniel wipes his mouth with a napkin, smiles briefly at Gobind, then resumes his attack on my plate of food.

"Perhaps you would want to verify what I am saying by talking with Daniel yourself, Dr. Gobind. I'll just pop over to the popcorn machine and get a bag. Be right back," I say, quickly taking my leave despite Gobind violently shaking her head at my suggestion.

Chuckling to myself, I head for the popcorn while scanning the crowd. There is a large contingent of clerical staff loudly talking at a nearby table. They appear to be happy to be gossiping and not chained to their computer monitors. Nearby there is a group of maintenance staff members who appear to be talking about motorcycles while scarfing down seconds of chow. There also are a good number of geriatric patients in attendance. Most are bedecked in a variety of straw hats, and many strapped securely in wheelchairs that are being pushed by nursing and recreational staff. As I grab a bag of popcorn and walk about, I spot Pepper and Hubie leaning against a tree feeding each other green and red cotton candy. They look happy.

"Rome!" Woody calls out. He's hurrying my way, appearing to be holding the revised petition I recently mailed back to him.

"Rome, you did a great job editing this petition." He waves the document above his head. "Somehow you managed to write it using elementary terms without sacrificing the content."

"Simple words from a simple mind, Woody," I reply.

"You're too modest, my friend. I think you might have a talent for converting the complex into pedestrian language. Anyway, now that this document is complete, why don't we start collecting signatures?"

"You mean right now?"

"Of course. Look around you. There are hundreds of potential petitioners just waiting for someone to put a pen in their hands."

"Well, maybe you're right. Except that I can't freely walk around right now. I have some patients that I need to keep within sight. But I'll sign the petition and give you my pen if you want to begin the collection process."

"Absolutely. I'd be delighted."

I affix my signature, give him my pen, and shake his hand. "Good luck, Woody. Hope you succeed in saving the greenhouse."

"Not only will we save the greenhouse, Rome, we will use the momentum to move on to the next project—demanding the end to the shameful practice of patients being handcuffed when they are brought to this hospital. After that, who knows? Maybe abolishing segregated patient and staff bathrooms, or putting a patient in an administrative position."

"You sound like the next Dorothea Dix, Woody."

"Lord knows we could use her, Rome."

And with that Woody is off, more energized than I have ever seen him.

I reorient myself to my charges. I see all of them—Del, Sherm, Dr. Burda, and Daniel—still seated at the picnic table eating away. Even Gobind is just where I left her. Maybe she's finding Daniel to be more palatable and less intrusive.

"Look who's here, Jerome."

I turn to see Amerika arm-in-arm with Hort. Not surprisingly, he is uniquely attired in black, with bibbed culottes over a black T-shirt, and a red kerchief protecting his dome.

"Hort! You S-O-B. You look great. How are you doing?" I ask, submitting my hand to his pincer grip.

"Good to see you too, Doc," Hort says, squeezing my paw even harder.

"How's life on the outside?" I ask, trying to withdraw my smarting hand in a dignified manner.

"Free but lonely," Hort says, putting his arm around Amerika's shoulder.

"That might change soon, honey," Amerika says. "There is a good chance I will be coming home in a week or so. At least that is what my doctor told me."

Hort kisses Amerika's cheek. "I'll empty the ash trays and stock the refrigerator."

"So, you have an apartment?" I ask.

"Yeah. A small one-bedroom. Even has an elevator. No pets, but they let you smoke inside."

"Sounds right for you and your Mrs."

"Life is good, Jerome," Amerika says, grabbing a hold of Hort. I temporarily lose sight of Hort as Amerika puts a full-body hug on him. He emerges somewhat wrinkled but smiling.

"Time for the egg toss!" the recreational aide, Zinnia Worman, announce through a bullhorn. "Team up with someone, and line up down here in front of me."

Amerika grabs Hort and drags him unwillingly to the event. I hang behind. As the participants line up across from one another, I am bowled over to see that Daniel has somehow convinced Gobind to pair up with him. This will be a sight I don't want to miss.

"Okay, the way this game is played is that one teammate tosses an egg to his or her partner to catch. If the egg breaks, that team is out of the game. If the egg doesn't break, both team members will take one giant step back, and the egg is tossed again. We keep stepping back and tossing the egg until only one team is left with an unbroken egg. Understood?" Zinnia says.

"When I blow my whistle, the eggs are tossed. Okay, here goes. Get ready. Get set." And with that, the whistle sounds off and eggs fill the air.

To my surprise, Gobind successfully catches Daniel's toss. No egg on her lovely saffron sari...yet. On the next toss, Daniel easily catches the soft lob that Gobind offers up. I await the inevitable as they take another step back. But to my surprise Gobind again deftly catches the descending egg. I'm impressed. She's pretty good at this. It appears that half the teams are out, including Hort and Amerika. As the next round begins, Daniel seems to be blinded by the sun. He is shielding his eyes with one hand when the egg is tossed his way. The throw from Gobind is a bit strong, and Daniel has to backpedal. He appears to have the egg in sight and prepares both hands for the reception, but he misjudges, and kerplop, the egg shatters on his head. Its runny contents mixed together with pieces of shell dribble down his forehead, finding his nose to be a perfect path off which to drip.

We all break up and laugh, including Daniel. He seems delighted with his egg facial.

Gobind attempts to disguise her laughter by covering her face with both hands. But it is clear that she's amused with her partner's fate. Protecting her pristine sari, she offers her condolences from a safe distance.

"Are you all right, Mr. Killebrew?"

"Sorry for letting you down, Dr. Gobind. Looks like I got egg on my face in that game. Want to try the balloon toss?" he asks, pointing to the next event being set up.

"No. No more for me. I will watch only," she replies.

Gobind's judgment proves sound as Daniel emerges soaking wet from the balloon toss event. Undeterred, he heads with recreation staff members to the baseball field for a quick game of softball. With Del, Sherm, and Dr. Burda in tow, I accompany Gobind to the bleachers near the field. We find front-row seats and await the first pitch. Taking seats behind us are Ophelia, Kendra, and Kim. They are apparently in good spirits, giggling and chatting freely. Across the field I spy, Cora Ruth, Lincoln, and Autumn walking in silence. Sauntering slowly in nature seems to satisfy their temperament. They appear to be at peace.

"Play ball!" Ron Peters, the appointed umpire, shouts.

And the players oblige, kind of. Even with a slow pitch, most hitters have trouble connecting the bat to the ball. The game becomes a test of patience for the bystanders. My attention drifts to the water puddle between the bleachers and home plate. A lone mallard duck is waddling toward the muddy water with the apparent intent of adopting it as his personal birdbath. An odd duck for sure. I nudge Gobind to check out the feathered critter splashing about.

"Looks like he is acting more like a pig in a mud hole rather than a duck in a pond," I say.

"I would say it is right at home at this hospital," she replies.

"Crush the ball, Killer!" someone yells as Daniel positions himself in the batter's box. He crouches down and coils his bat in anticipation of the pitch. With his game face on, Daniel unleashes a powerful swing, and like his namesake, cracks the ball deep into the outfield. I don't recognize the centerfielder but whoever he is, he's taking his good old time retrieving the ball. Hustling, Daniel easily reaches second base, and with a full head of steam runs for third. Without looking back, he rounds third base heading for home plate. Everyone is cheering him on. Even Gobind is standing in support. Then without reason or warning, Daniel careens off the base path and slides head first into the muddy puddle. As he belly surfs through the puddle, a stream of water shoots high in the air as does the startled mallard. In what seems like slow motion, I watch the dirty water cascade down, splattering everyone in the first two rows of the bleachers.

Temporarily stunned, no one makes a peep. Then a thunder of laughter erupts, particularly from the upper rows, which have escaped being soiled by the brown spray. The rest of us gradually join in the uproar, except for Gobind. She remains immobile staring down at her speckled sari in disbelief.

Daniel lumbers over to the bleachers shaking himself off like a dog.

"I always wanted to do that," he says, receiving a cross look from Gobind.

Picking a feather off her sari, I sheepishly remark, "I guess we still need to work on that rambunctiousness, huh?

Unexpectedly, a smile creeps across her face.

Made in the USA
Charleston, SC
30 April 2012